SURYA
RAMKUMAR

THE
SKY HAS
MOVED
AWAY

This edition was published by The Dreamwork Collective

The Dreamwork Collective LLC, Dubai, United Arab Emirates

thedreamworkcollective.com

Printed and bound in the United Arab Emirates

Cover and design: Nuno Moreira, NMDESIGN.ORG

Text © Surya Ramkumar

ISBN: 978-9948-782-29-2

Approved by National Media Council Dubai, United Arab Emirates

MC-02-01-5811513

This is a work of fiction. The names, characters, businesses, places, events, and incidents in this book are either the product of the author's imagination or used in a fictitious manner. Any resemblance to actual persons, living or dead, business establishments, institutions, locales, or events is purely coincidental.

SURYA RAMKUMAR

A NOVEL

THE SKY HAS MOVED AWAY

For

Nikita & Anika

May you inherit a world
where the sky has moved
closer to us again.

PROLOGUE

Every beginning carries within itself the seed of its ending, just as it is from endings that all beginnings are born. Beginnings and endings, particularly those that led him to the present moment, are on Martin's mind as he walks in through the gates of Ignatius Gymnasium in Amsterdam.

"Congratulations to the graduating class of 2023!" A banner announces the occasion.

It is a warm summer day. The sky is clear, leaves are as green as they would ever get in the year, and tulips bloom in all shades of red, yellow, orange, and pink.

"Van Oost," he gives his name to the usher, who looks it up in the parents' register.

"Oh, your son is giving the valedictorian speech," the usher says. "Congratulations! We've two seats reserved for you in the front, you'll see it when you get there."

The woman next to him squeezes his hand, smiling, as they walk through to the courtyard where the ceremony would be held. Martin's heart swells with pride, even as it aches like it hasn't in a very long while.

PART I

CHAPTER 1

The day was perfect. Ayomide Akande did not have many perfect days in his life, but when one presented itself, he believed in making full use of it.

Ayomide, or Ayo as he had been called ever since he could remember, was lying in a beautifully landscaped pool surrounded by tastefully groomed green foliage and bright red and white flowers. The pool was rectangular, modest in size, but at one end of the pool, steps had been cut out in concentric half circles, combining beauty with functionality in a perfectly symbiotic fashion.

It was the day after New Year's, 2009, and it was starting well for Ayo. After the wild party that he had hosted, he was relaxing with his friends.

They were in the back garden of Rose Villa, a large colonial-style villa on Bennett Road in Victoria Island, the posh residential district of Lagos that was home to the Big Boys—the multimillionaires of Nigeria—and the *oyibos*—the white expatriates who lived on fat expense accounts. Ayo was neither. He was the housekeeper of an empty home that was in transition between one *oyibo* and the next. With only a few months between two occupants, CBX Corp, the European oil company that owned the villa, had not bothered to disband the staff. That gave Ayo time to live it up as if he owned the house.

"Here's your beer, please." Ayo had not even noticed that the bottle in his hand was empty before Scrawny-boy offered him another one.

"You want me to open it myself, you monkey?" replied Ayo, lifting his head off the side of the pool just enough to see that the bottle had not been opened.

Scrawny-boy hastily pulled open the lid and handed the bottle over, nearly falling into the pool himself as he reached out to pass it to Ayo.

"You've a lot to learn, Scrawny. Now go get us all another bowl of chicken wings," Prince said, laughing at the young boy's clumsiness.

Prince was one of Ayo's oldest friends, in the loose definition of friendship in Lagos: mutually beneficial relationships cemented by wads of cash and nights of debauchery. Prince headed the team of Mobile Police, MoPo as they were popularly known, that was assigned to protect CBX Corp's interests in Lagos. But it was not the government salary that paid for his lavish lifestyle, complete with a constant coterie of cronies and concubines. From phishing scams to fake lotteries, Prince believed in trying his hand at every new con, many of which Ayo had played a significant part in, his position at Rose Villa allowing him not only a respectable cover but also access to the rich and the naive.

"Scrawny, these taste like stone. Go bring us new ones, and

this time you had better not screw it up," Ayo said, throwing the hardened wings at the young boy. Scrawny was the latest addition to Prince's cronies, the rules of apprenticeship changing very little, whether it was with fancy suits or cruel thugs.

Ayo eyed the women in the pool, some topless, some in skimpy bikinis, mildly attractive but all eager to please. He pointed to a voluptuous young girl at the other end of the pool and called out, "Rosie, how about you come give me my massage?"

"I am Candy. Rosie is there, over there. But my hands very good too, I give you massage."

"Candy Rosie whatever," Ayo muttered under his breath as he pulled himself out of the pool and walked toward the massage mats that Scrawny had laid out for them. He let himself fall into a massage-induced slumber.

The sound of a gunshot rudely woke him from his blissful sleep. He looked up just in time to see the falling victim of the playful shooting: an unfortunate pigeon that had wandered into the courtyard. The pigeon had been injured by Scrawny's attempts to catch him with a catapult and had not been able to fly away fast enough when one of the older men decided to end its life with a rifle.

The bark of the tree next to the pool was splattered with blood. A pattern of red—a concentrated blotch interrupted by a few feathers on either side, its odd symmetry beginning to be distorted by drops dribbling down through the crevices of the bark—was forming on the trunk.

"Oi! Do you have to do that? Let a man enjoy a massage in peace," Ayo shouted at the shooter. He settled back onto his massage mat.

But his sleep had been disturbed and memories best left forgotten had been stirred up. Even as Candy's fingers kneaded concentric circles on his shoulders, Ayo could not fall back to sleep.

He thought of Salim. The hapless security guard who had been the beginning of the end of his miseries. The first stepping-stone in his journey from the slums of Lagos to the world of con artists and easy money, and eventually to Rose Villa.

Six years ago, Ayo had been sitting in the back of a silver Toyota Prado, a car that had once seen good days but had been subjected to every imaginable abuse since then. Whip marks dented the sides of the car. At regular intervals, one of the passengers would thrust himself out of the window and unleash a long metallic whip, hitting hard on their car and any vehicle that dared to come too close. Each blow was a demonstration of strength, power, and recklessness, and it worked; even in the go-slows of Lagos, the Prado never stopped. There was a bullet hole near the back of the car, shot by someone who did not have the nerve to aim at one of the passengers or the ability to hit one of the tires he had probably targeted. It was left unrepaired, a reminder of the invincibility of the car's owner.

The car belonged to Petrol, Ayo's cousin, whose parents had felt gratitude for the newly discovered oil in their country. Petrol, though, decided that working as a laborer in an oil refinery was nothing to be grateful for. Being a moneylender to the poor and the easily abused was a much more lucrative vocation. At first glance, Petrol might have been mistaken for an unremarkable man—he was short in stature and had the kind of features that could let him disappear in a crowd if the situation warranted it—but the AK-47 that never left his shoulder and the numerous knife hilts visible from under his coat jacket made him formidable.

The car jerked to a stop in front of the gates of a large, whitewashed mansion with manicured lawns, much like Rose Villa. The driveway was empty, and all the doors and windows were closed tightly shut. The house seemed to be unoccupied. Petrol jumped out of the car and walked toward the lone security guard.

"Do you have the money, Salim?" The voice that boomed out did not seem to match the gaunt body from which it emanated.

Salim fell to his knees, touched Petrol's feet, and begged. "I tried everything. I don't have it today. I will give it to you tomorrow."

Ayo looked at the man's face and felt contempt at his helplessness and absolute stupidity. If he did not have the money to pay, why wasn't he in hiding? Did he really think he could inspire pity from a man who had built his career on a reputation for cruelty?

"If you don't have it today, how will you have it tomorrow?" Petrol wanted to be sure that it would be worth his while to make a trip back tomorrow. He was, after all, a reasonable man who did not want to hurt anyone if there was a possibility that he could get money otherwise.

Salim mumbled something inaudible.

The voice boomed again. "Speak up, you monkey! Or I will shoot you now."

"Trying" and "some way" were the only words Ayo could discern from Salim's desperate whimpers.

"Where are your masters? Those who live in this villa? Can't you ask them?"

"No, they just left for holiday, they won't be back for a month. I will definitely get the money then." Salim's voice seemed a little louder now.

"Month? One month? You think I am crazy to wait that long, after you haven't paid me back for so long? I want the money tomorrow. How will you get it?"

"I am trying. I will find a way." Salim's voice was barely audible again.

The next thing Ayo heard was a gunshot. Little droplets of blood landed on his face.

"What's up, Ayo? Never had blood on your face?" Petrol turned slightly toward Ayo, smirking as he noticed Ayo rubbing the blood off with his shirtsleeve.

Ayo straightened his back and hoped that his cousin would not notice the tremor in his voice as he said, "Of course I have."

Salim's body had slumped forward. Petrol had deftly moved aside just in time to prevent the body from touching any part of him or his clothes. He stared at Salim's body for a minute, as if contemplating how he could retrieve the cost of the bullet that had killed the man.

"Boys, move him out," he shouted to his helpers. Ayo and three others moved swiftly to Salim's body and pulled it into the back of the car. The three other men had climbed into the car, and Ayo was just about to get in, when Petrol called out, "Ayo, you don't get in. Come here."

Ayo could feel a lump in his throat. He tried to recall whether he had been lax in collecting money from Salim, but no, Salim was not even his account. And as far as he could remember, he had done nothing that could have angered his cousin. Still, he walked timidly toward the front door of the car.

Petrol regarded the boy carefully for a moment.

"You've been three years with me now, Ayo?"

Ayo nodded. He knew that most boys did not stay too long with his cousin. Either they left to manage another area of their own, taking over as local debt collectors, or Petrol fired them, usually after some brutal torture, the severity of which depended on how much money he had lost because of their incompetence.

"You take care of this," he said, pointing to the white mansion. "You squat, sell, and give me seventy percent. No less or I will chop your balls off. The rest should give you enough to start on your own."

Ayo was not sure whether this abrupt dismissal from his

cousin's service was a punishment or a reward. The shadow of tenderness that Ayo could have sworn passed over Petrol's face made him inclined to believe that it was the latter. Ayo had heard much about the easy money in 419 housing scams, but he had never managed one by himself before.

Named after the Nigerian penal code under which it was prosecuted, 419 scams covered a whole variety of schemes, some so complicated that they required years of planning. But the one that Petrol wanted him to execute was simple: Pose as the owner or as an agent of the rightful owner of the property and sell it to a gullible buyer before the owners came back and realized that their property has been bought and paid for by someone who would now lay claim to it.

"Make me proud. Do a good deal, do it quick, and don't go to jail," Petrol shouted as the Prado sped off. Ayo was left speechless.

Ayo closed the tall gates; he did not want the passersby to see the blood on the ground. The house looked cold and foreboding at the end of the driveway.

He remembered the loneliness that had engulfed him. It was just before dark when the sky was bathed in varying hues of red. The loud sirens of the MoPo as they escorted the rich and the famous to their gated homes reminded him that this was where the wealthy of Lagos had their homes. The street in front was busy with people getting back from work. But inside the tall walls protected by shards of broken beer bottles on their top and the formidable gate made of thick sturdy wrought iron, he was alone. The blood from Salim's head was still warm on the dark brown soil. He made sure the bolts of the gate were firmly done, as if willing the spirits to leave him alone.

Turning around, he could see the blood splatter on the tree trunk right behind where Salim had knelt before he was shot. Ayo stared at it, a dense crimson patch trickling down the fissures of the tree bark until it merged with the red earth below.

"Ayo! Ayo!" Ayo woke up out of his thoughts, this time to Candy shaking him. "You have a phone call."

Ayo dragged himself to the phone in the hallway. The caller was from Headquarters and the message was brief: "The new occupant of the house, Martin van Oost, is coming next week. Have the house ready."

Next week? Shouldn't he have received the news earlier?

The caller said it all happened in a rush, but in any case, Martin will likely spend most of his time in Port Harcourt, so he will be in Lagos only for a few days.

Ayo frowned. *One of those oyibos*, he thought, *who like to get their hands dirty.*

Ayo didn't look forward to frequent trips accompanying his boss out of the daily comforts of Lagos. He would need to find some comforts of his own in Port Harcourt too.

He looked over to the women in the pool, the booze, and his friends.

"When does he get here?" Ayo asked.

"Monday morning."

"Get the house ready." The instruction was repeated for clarity before the caller hung up.

"The bloody *oyibo* is coming after all," Ayo grumbled as he walked back to his buddies by the pool.

"Why? Why do they have to come? We take good care of the place, don't we? All your *oyibos*, they don't know how to enjoy. No women, no real alcohol." Prince was not too pleased that his indulgent days at the Rose Villa were about to end.

"And what do they really do? They just mess around, get paid lots of money to do it."

"Well, if the new one is anything like the old, he might spend some of that on us." Prince laughed. Indeed, they had made some good money through a variety of tricks, from unnecessary MoPo protection to commissions on bribes and, sometimes, even just made-up sob stories.

"I hear this one is quite a loner. No family coming with him, and no girlfriend. Might be someone for you girls to make some money off. You know my commission, don't you? Be good to me and we'll all be happy people." Ayo smiled, jumping into the pool next to one of the women and cupping his hands around her breasts.

"So I guess this is it, guys. Drink up all the beer and let's make today a day to remember."

Ayo was determined to make the most of the last night of fun. He would need the next days to call all the house staff back.

Shit, the cook, Ayo thought. He had fired the last one in a drunken fight he didn't care to remember. The last guy was really good too. *Ah damn!* He wished he had more time to get things in order. But three days is all he had to clean up the mess, get the house back in order, and make it ready in time for the new *oyibo*'s arrival. He would make sure that there would be no remnants of the revelry that happened on these grounds.

Cleaning up after a mess was not new for Ayo.

After that fateful evening of Salim's death, Ayo had to will himself to sleep in the guard's shack. But he had woken up the next morning, infused with a sense of enthusiasm and excitement. He saw the opportunity that fate and his cousin had presented to him and he immediately set to work. He went around the house, found a pail and a tap of running water, and cleaned up all traces of blood from in front of the tree. He then set about finding his friend, Kwasie, who he knew could teach him a thing or two about selling houses that were not his own.

Ayo was a fast learner. He promised to give Kwasie 50,000 naira in exchange for names of potential buyers and recommendations that would get him into the right circles. It took Ayo just ten days to find a gullible prospective buyer who believed that Ayo was the bona fide agent in charge of selling the property. It was a corporate buyer, under pressure from his superiors to find a property in Lagos at a reasonable price and as soon as he could. He paid Ayo the money and signed the deed papers, carefully inspecting the power of attorney that authorized Ayo to sell on behalf of the owners. The buyer could not have guessed that a week after owning the house, the rightful owners would come back, a lawsuit would follow, and there would be no trace whatsoever of Ayomide Akande.

CHAPTER 2

Martin van Oost looked out of the KL 587 from Amsterdam to Lagos as it descended through Nigerian airspace. The city below looked like a patchwork quilt. Colored roofs in orange, blue, and gray crowded together, held at the seams by roads that crisscrossed in no particular pattern. For as far as Martin's eyes could scan, this eclectic mix of houses, slums, and the occasional skyscraper went on and on. Lagos, he had recently read, was one of the fastest growing cities in the world and was already considered the powerhouse of the continent.

Martin leaned closer to the window. The tiny porthole didn't afford him a very good view, but he could feel the buzz of energy emanating from below. Even from the distance, he could sense the relentless motion, a primal push to expand, ruthlessly crushing constraints and breaking borders in an insatiable greed to grow.

"There are few places on earth more reminiscent of hell than Nigeria"—Martin tried to shut out Teun's final words after he had given Martin his latest assignment—"but I'm sure you'll survive, van Oost."

Teun Bergman was a senior vice president at CBX Corp,

one of the earliest foreign companies to explore oil in Nigeria. The first oil was discovered in 1956, rocketing the country from a poor African nation to one of the leading petrostates in the world economic order. All the companies who had worked to discover the oil wanted a substantial share of the profit pie. As did the governments who maintained order through fear and force rather than good governance. Alliances were formed, deals were finalized. And CBX Corp had made themselves and their shareholders an unimaginable fortune and secured a firm foothold in the country.

Teun was an influential member of the executive team, responsible for all overseas operations. Ever since Martin began working directly for him during his first assignment in Singapore, Teun had taken an active interest in Martin's career and been a mentor to the young man. From Singapore to Brunei to the Middle East, Martin had moved wherever he had been asked to, racking up airline miles and earning himself a solid reputation as a corporate leader in the making, astute, confident, and willing to do whatever it takes.

"You would join as the deputy country chair," Teun said, "reporting to Obiora."

Martin knew such a role didn't exist. He suspected Teun had created it just to place Martin right in the heat of the situation to ensure direct and unfiltered access, through Martin, to the goings-on on the ground.

"You would need to manage Obiora," Teun continued. "He's been heading up our Nigerian business for over three years and is well connected in local circles. But he is not a favorite of the environmentalists and has made a few gaffes recently. I need you to cover the situation."

Teun paused and looked him straight in the eye, as if trying to gauge Martin. How far had he come since his first innocent days nearly eight years ago when he first reported to duty in Singapore?

"Nigeria is important to us," Teun said. "A strategic assignment at this critical period is a vote of our confidence in your capabilities, Martin. I was pleased at how well you handled the last deal in Oman. This situation is of course many times more complicated, but it is also one of those that, if handled well, will make your career for good."

Or break it forever. Teun left that unsaid.

Teun had been assigned to Nigeria during the Ogoni uprising in the early 1990s, and it had been one of the defining chapters of his career. Martin had heard many stories about those times. The land around the oil fields belonged to the minority communities, including the Ogoni people, who had organized peaceful protests demanding fair financial compensation. The official company history documented that they had collaborated with the local authorities and settled the issues. No details were specified. Twenty years later, the situation was heating up again.

Martin was up for a challenge, and as far as opportunities went, he couldn't have asked for anything bigger. Nigeria topped the world in inequality. The local population claimed that the oil only made a small minority super rich while worsening the lives of the rest. They complained that the oil spills, pollution, and environmental damage made it impossible to continue their old ways of living. Violence had increased manifold. Farming and fishing had been rendered entirely unsustainable in many areas, and according to the protestors, even the simple pleasures of breathing clean air and enjoying a dark night sky devoid of light and air pollution had become luxuries for most Nigerians. People revolted, and as the years passed and the income gap widened, the protests turned nastier. And this time, it was not just from one minority community but across the region. CBX Corp did not consider social inequality their problem, or corruption by third parties their responsibility. But prolonged protests would hurt their reputation and their bottom line, and therefore they were keen to settle the issues before they grew any greater.

"I appreciate your confidence in me," Martin said, not blinking as he returned Teun's steady gaze. "Thank you, I won't let you down." Martin was a company man. He considered it his job to do what was required, and he was savvy enough to figure out what was required without Teun spelling it out.

"Good," said Teun. "You've a week to pack up and start the year in Nigeria. New year, new start. We've offices in Port Harcourt, Abuja, Lagos, and a few other places. Base yourself in Lagos. They'll ask you to stay in PH. Don't. Oh, and one more thing. Keep your eyes and ears open. All the time. Keep me posted. Regularly. You know how I hate to hear news too late."

"Yes, of course," said Martin, before wishing Teun a merry Christmas and heading out of the office.

As the cold winter air bit into Martin's face, he felt a chill down his spine and an unease in his belly that he chalked up to the uncertainty and excitement of a new assignment. Little could he have imagined how drastically the stint at Lagos would change his life and challenge everything he knew to be true.

Applause burst out among the passengers as the plane touched down in Lagos. The passengers got up all at once, even though the seat belt signs told them to stay put, the impatience of the city egging them on to break free from the confines of the metal bird and hurry on ahead.

The sun was sweltering hot, but the humidity bothered Martin more. He stepped off the plane onto the blistering tarmac of Murtala Mohammed Airport, sweat filling the inside of his socks. In the distance, illusions of water from sunshine creating mirages on the concrete and tar played tricks on his mind. The brightly colored clothes of his fellow passengers against the backdrop of the gray runway overwhelmed his tired eyes.

The welcome of the tropics, Martin thought, as he peeled off his sweater. The sweater, the shawl, and the thick coat he was carrying in his arms, essentials in the cold European winter he had just left behind, were burdens in this heat. He wished he had sandals on rather than shoes.

The glass doors of the airport felt like a welcome dream while he was walking toward it, but as he entered, new sensations engulfed him. The hallway that led from the gate was filled with shouting passengers, announcements of late flights and security warnings, a surprisingly large number of crying children, and many other sounds that mingled into one constant throbbing in Martin's head. The place was crowded. A portly old man stepped on Martin's toes and glared at him as if expecting an apology. The smell of cheap perfumes clashed violently against the stench of sweating bodies.

Martin was still trying to find his bearings when he noticed that many of his fellow passengers had started running. He looked around to make sure there was no imminent danger to his being, and then followed them at a brisker pace.

A short walk through the hallway brought him to an escalator that led down to the main hall. The notorious place where many a foreigner had lost money and, sometimes, even their bags and passports. Martin had heard about the various cons and was determined not to fall for any of them. He stepped onto the escalator just as he realized the folly of what he had done.

The door to the entrance hall was closed. As the escalator deposited more and more people, together with their bags and suitcases right in front of the door, which was less than a few meters from the escalator, they had no place to move to. They were getting jammed, like sardines packed into a very small tin.

"Move-oh! No space here!" A woman's loud shout came

from somewhere down below.

"No push, where you think I go?" called out someone else.

Martin held his breath and felt himself pushed into the crowd, most of them yelling and shouting. He held on tight to his carry-on bag and let his body just go with the flow, the pressure mounting as more and more people innocently walked onto the escalator.

"Open, open door!" the voices shouted while the guards looked calmly on.

Suddenly, just as he was beginning to think that he would be crushed to death, the pressure was released. He felt himself being pulled, as if caught in the aftermath of a dam that burst after being relentlessly pounded on by the water it held. A security guard had finally decided to open the door and release the flood of humans.

The crowd rushed toward the immigration counters and Martin joined them.

He was still drenched in sweat when after waiting in four consecutive queues and firmly denying bribes, he finally had his visa checked and the smiling face—the first he had seen since he checked in to the flight—said, "Welcome to Nigeria."

Martin saw a man dressed in a cheap but well-pressed suit rushing toward him. "Sir, you are Martin van Oost?"

"Yes, I am. And you must be…"

"Ayo. Ayomide. But you can call me Ayo," the man said, holding out his hand to take Martin's suitcase.

"Sure, thanks," said Martin, nodding. But the man's shifty eyes made Martin slightly uneasy.

Ayo deftly maneuvered through the crowd of harried passengers and dogged peddlers and led him to the road just under a bridge, all the while keeping up a loud and steady stream of conversation. Martin could barely hear the words, but he got the gist that Ayo was to be his 'man in Nigeria,' taking care of his house, his travels, his needs whatever they maybe, and clearing obstacles whenever they arose. Martin was tempted to ask what sort of obstacles they were expecting, but decided against it.

Ayo made a quick phone call before turning back to Martin. "Mohammed—our driver—will bring the car in a minute. We wait here. This is called the second bridge."

"Do we have to wait in the middle of the road? Can't he just bring it to the airport terminal?"

"See those men over there," Ayo said, lowering his voice. "They clamp your car when you come out of the terminal. You have to pay them a few thousand naira before you can get it out. Not worth the trouble."

Martin looked at the men in uniform, each armed with an AK-47. As if sensing his disbelief, one of them stopped a vehicle that was just coming out. The other one deftly clamped the car wheels. Martin could not hear what transpired, but after a while he saw the exchange of cash and the wheel clamp being lifted.

Ayo beamed, happy to have had a live demonstration of this danger that he cleverly averted for Martin. "Our car is here, *Oga*, let's go."

Martin took in the hustle and bustle of the streets as they drove out of the airport. A nation in motion, that's what came to his mind. Well, everything except the cars were in motion, because they had come to almost a standstill in the traffic. But the traffic jam provided a rich breeding ground for a flurry of activity. On either side of the highway were street markets selling everything from vegetables and meat to clothes and jewelry. Little boys went from car to car selling magazines and phone cards and water. One even offered Martin a pup, a little Labrador.

"See those motorcycles, sir. *Okadas*," Ayo said, pointing to the bikes that whizzed past the traffic, making space between lanes where there was none. "They're dangerous. Don't ever get on one. A few years ago, the *oga* before you, he tried one and got a head injury."

"Who are they? Why would I get on one?"

"They're for hire, sir. And faster than cars too. But they drive like maniacs."

"I'll keep that in mind."

"I'm born here, I know everything here, sir," Ayo continued. "And I've been with people from your country and company for many years too. You can ask me anything."

"Please don't call me sir. You can call me Martin."

"We call you *Oga*," chipped in Mohammed, breaking his silence. "*Oga* is what we call our boss."

As the three of them danced the delicate dance of finding

the right balance between employee and employer, master and servant, local and foreigner, each judging the other, mainland Lagos passed by and they were soon in Victoria Island. Traffic had cleared, and the buildings looked better kept.

It took them another hour or so to get to Rose Villa. This was the first assignment where Martin had been given a house to stay. Lagos boasted some of the most expensive real estate in the world. "More expensive than even Los Angeles," Ayo had proudly claimed during their drive. Hotels were no exception. CBX Corp found it cheaper to lease out houses and maintain house staff rather than put up their staff in serviced apartments or hotel rooms.

Rose Villa was a beautiful mansion, with a long drive that led up to the house. Rose shrubbery lined each side of the driveway, even though flowers were few and far between. While Mohammed and Ayo carried his luggage into the house, Martin stood back and admired the colonial architecture. Inside, a beautifully decorated living area led off to another reception room and dining area and eventually the kitchen.

"You like the place, *Oga?*" Ayo asked, obviously proud of how he had kept up the house. "There are three bedrooms upstairs too. Some of the people before you had families here." Ayo pointed to the stairs that led off from the hallway.

Martin was surprised to see five men lined up in a straight line.

"Hello," he said, unsure of who they were.

"Let me introduce the house staff to you. This is Raphael, the gardener, he also cleans the house. Chinua and Ben, the guards outside. Eugene, he's the cook, he's new here. And you have obviously met Mohammed before."

Martin shook hands with each of them, trying to remember their names. He had not expected that they would need so many people to take care of one house, but then the house was well kept, he had to admit.

"Go back to your jobs, *Oga* needs to rest now." Ayo dismissed them with a quick gesture of his hand.

Ayo led him upstairs and left him at the door of the master bedroom. Martin walked into the room, barely looked around, walked straight to the bed in the middle of the room, and let himself fall onto the large luxurious bed.

CHAPTER 3

Ansara could hear her mother's shrill voice calling her from her neighbor's house. "Ansara, Ansara, are you there?"

Ansara had just put the rice and the water into the boiling pot. She had got some meat from the market and still needed to clean it, cut it, and put it in. It was only on rare occasions that they had all the ingredients necessary to make jollof rice, and she did not want to be interrupted while she was in the middle of cooking it.

"Ansara, come over here. It's important." Ansara knew that the calls would not subside until she responded. Reluctantly, she put out the fire she had just started and left her kitchen for the neighbor's. It was almost like stepping into another room in the same house, the two houses were so close. Ansara couldn't help but sometimes wonder, why, when there was so much wasteland in their country, did people still live in such cramped houses and in close proximity to each other.

In Mrs. Jideofor's kitchen, Ansara found her mother and Mrs. Jideofor engrossed in deep conversation.

"It's very rare to find such a man." Ansara's mother was adding more force to her remark with an exaggerated nod of her head.

"Yes, Chidera is lucky, very lucky." Mrs. Jideofor smiled happily and looked over at Chidera with contentment. Chidera, her youngest daughter and the only one remaining in her family to be married, seemed overwhelmed by all the attention. She tried to move herself farther into the corner of the kitchen, where she was attending to the lunch being cooked. Ansara could discern the slight whiff of the *garri* coming from the pot.

"Ah, there you are," said Ansara's mother, noticing her at the doorway. "Did you hear the news? There is a good man who has come from far to marry Chidera. He's from the north but lives in Lagos. And they say he has a very good job there. Works for a white man in a big house, and he takes care of the whole house."

"Not just work in the house. He is the boss of the house. All the other staff have to do as he says," Chidera's mother added.

Ansara walked over to Chidera and hugged her crouching body. "Chidera, I'm so happy. Good things always happen to good people. You're a lucky girl, Chidera. Now, tell me, have you seen him yet? Is he handsome, like a king from the north?"

Ansara's light-hearted teasing made the timid, shy girl blush. Smiling, she replied, "No, I didn't see him. But he's coming next week. Madu says he's handsome."

"He's a friend of Madu?" Ansara asked, keeping any suspicion she felt out of her voice.

"Yes, a cousin, I think," said Chidera, "but on the other

side, not related to us."

Ansara hoped for Chidera's sake that the man would be kind to her. Madu, in Ansara's opinion, was not to be trusted, but then it would be entirely out of place for her to voice her concerns. Madu was the local loafer, someone more interested in the pleasures of life than anything else. But he was also Mrs. Jideofor's cousin, so whatever his other shortcomings might be, Ansara liked to think that he would do the right thing by Chidera. Besides, Chidera seemed genuinely excited, and Ansara felt happy for her.

"That's good," said Ansara. "You're lucky. God bless you, Chidera." She squeezed the young woman's hand in affection then walked over to the cot where her mother and Mrs. Jideofor were seated. "It's very good news. Chidera will be very happy. She'll have a good life in the city. When is the wine-carrying ceremony?"

"We haven't planned anything yet. Madu just told us about him yesterday. He's a cousin on Madu's mother's side and visiting Port Harcourt on some important business. Madu says he would be just right for Chidera. Madu has already told him about Chidera. It seems he's very interested. If all goes well, I hope we can have it in a few weeks, as soon as he can come here again." Mrs. Jideofor could hardly contain the excitement in her voice.

"God bless." Ansara smiled at Mrs. Jideofor. "I better go and finish the cooking now. But I'll come in later, to help you with the preparations."

Ansara hurried back to her own kitchen. She could still hear Mrs. Jideofor's voice telling her mother about all the preparations they would need to do to hold the wine-carrying ceremony in a few months. Ansara smiled. She was glad Chidera seemed so happy at the marriage proposal.

In the dog-eat-dog world of Port Harcourt, Mrs. Jideofor was one of her mother's oldest friends and the most trusted. The two families had shared happiness and misfortune together and stood by each other in times of need. Happiness, in their lives, came by so rarely that it was better to share in each other's joy than to harbor neighborly jealousy.

Ansara opened the lid of the pot of rice. The rice had not boiled yet; it would probably be another good twenty minutes before it was done. She continued peering down into the pot. It was almost as if the pot enclosed a landscape of its own. A microcosm of milky white hills and troughs that kept jumping up and down, as if an impatient puppeteer were pulling their strings violently and with no decipherable pattern. Change, rapid unpredictable change, that was the only constant in their motions. Rather like her own life, she thought wryly.

Ansara's own wedding was meant to have taken place five years ago. Her mother had been so happy that she was getting married; somehow, she had thought Ansara would never get married. Every time Ansara brought a new book home or told her something new that she had learned at school, her mother was afraid that she would learn some of the modern ideas that plague women in cities and not want to get married. Or worse, expect so much from a man that she would never find one that lived up to her expectations.

Only Emeka, her brother, was not happy. Emeka and Ansara had always been close, with just over a year separating their births. Emeka thought that Ikenna was not good enough for his Ansa.

"Emeka, he is a good man. You just need to give him a chance." Ansara remembered pleading with him a few weeks before her wine-carrying ceremony.

Emeka's approval was important to her, and she just wished he would be open to the possibility that Ikenna could make her happy.

"He may be good, Ansa, but he's not good enough for you. He likes you because you're beautiful. Maybe he can read a few books, sing a few poems, but you need a man, a man who can protect you, take care of you, fight for you. You deserve more, Ansa."

"He makes me happy, Emeka. He's always there for me. He never looks at another woman. And he wants to marry me. You should be happy for me, brother."

"Is that all you want? That he doesn't look at another woman? Who is there to look at, Ansa? Look at yourself, Ansa, and tell me honestly, how many girls here are more beautiful than you? He would be an idiot to look at someone else. You're still young, why the hurry? Give me some time, I'll find you a better man myself. As your brother, let me find you a man."

"I have my man. I don't want anyone else." Ansara was stubborn.

Emeka had stormed out of the house.

Ansara wished now that she had given more thought to Emeka's concerns.

Ansara stirred the rice that was slowly getting redder in color. She hurriedly finished cutting the meat and moved over to the stove, determined to make a good jollof rice on the one day she could afford to buy meat. She then added all the usual ingredients to the rice: tomatoes, onions, and ground meat. And unlike traditional Igbo recipes, she threw in a good measure of cayenne pepper. She took a small dollop of rice from the pot, blew at it for a while, and trickled a few drops onto her tongue. It tasted good. Femi would definitely love it.

Where was Femi?

She hadn't seen him for a while. Ansara gave the rice a last stir, put out the fire, and stepped out to look for her son.

Femi ran to her as soon as he saw her. The happy excited face of her son lifted her spirits. He had inherited Ansara's wild frizzy hair and her sharp eyes. Add to that his eager, boyish grin and it was difficult to look at him and think of him as anything other than a healthy boy. It was hard to believe that he had not yet managed to utter a single word in the four years of his life.

Ansara asked him to come in to eat, but he seemed to have other plans for her. He tugged at her, urgency evident in his pull.

"Femi, what is it? Did the cat give birth to the kittens already?"

Femi shook his head and pulled her again. "Ok, Ok, I'm coming, pumpkin." She laughed at the boy's enthusiasm and impatience.

Soon, she got close enough to the house to see what Femi was pointing at: a little shack that he had built. To call it a shack might really be an exaggeration, because it was more like two planks of rusting tin that had been slanted onto the walls, to double as a roof as well as two sides of a wall. The house walls were the third side, and the fourth open side acted as the door and was protected by a ragged old cloth. Ansara had no idea where he managed to get all the materials to build this. From inside the house crawled out Inni, Mrs. Jideofor's fourth grandson. The two boys were so proud of their new "home" that Ansara could not help smiling at their ingenuity and simple pride.

"It's very nice, boys. You've done a very nice job. Can I come in?"

Femi looked rather worried at her suggestion. It was clearly a house for children and there was no way a grown up could fit in.

Inni seemed to have thought of a solution for that. "No, No! This is only for children. When we get bigger, we'll build a big house, and then you can come in."

"Ok, I'll wait for that." Ansara smiled, ran her fingers over her son's hair, and kissed him on the forehead. Femi protested when she asked him to come in. He wanted to stay out for a bit longer, play in the house he had built. Inni brought in an old radio and turned on the music. Loud. They both started dancing, with Inni singing along with the radio.

Ansara let Femi stay on outside, asking him to come home in a bit, whenever he felt hungry. It was not every day that Ansara had seen him so happy. She caressed the top of his head again, his bristly hair brushing against the rough inside of her overworked hands, and headed back inside.

The day they decided on Femi's name was one of the happiest days in Ansara's life. She could not have foreseen at that time how unfortunate their choice of name would turn out to be.

There was joy and laughter in the house. Emeka, her brother, was still around. Ansara was nursing the baby. They had so far just referred to him as "the little one." Ansara rejected every name that was suggested to her, and she hadn't been able to come up with one herself.

"How about Ozioma?" her mother suggested. "This boy has brought so much good news to the family, we can call him Ozioma."

"Ozioma? No, it doesn't sound nice." She couldn't remember which of her two brothers had turned down the name.

"Kachiside?" her elder brother suggested.

"As the God's will? No, my son is going to be a great man, whatever be his destiny." Ansara turned down that name too.

"How about Onyinyechukwu?" someone, it must have been her sister-in-law, asked. Onyinyechukwu means a gift

41

from God, and the atheist in Emeka had strongly protested.

Ikechukwu, Chiziterem, Tochukwu…the names considered had been many and varied. And the reasons for rejecting had been just as diverse. She remembered it had gone on for some time, almost like a game.

After a while, Emeka with his ever-restless spirit had gotten bored and turned on the radio. It must have been the song "Beng beng" that Ansara adored, she couldn't be sure now. But the music of Femi Kuti had filled the room. And before she knew it, everyone in the room, including her little nieces and nephew, had started dancing to the rhythm of his music. When the music ended and they all sat down, they realized that the little boy of two months was also trying very hard to gyrate to the music, shaking himself on the bed he was lying on.

"You should call him Femi. He'll be a great singer when he grows up," Emeka suggested.

"Femi oh," his little cousins joined in calling him Femi.

And the name just stuck. In the happiness of the moment, in the joy of togetherness, in the beauty of music, Ansara had imagined her son singing to crowds and keeping them enthralled. And so it was that her newborn son had been named Femi. Femi Okafor.

It was not until almost three years later that they realized Femi could not speak. Ansara refused to think of the irony of naming a child who cannot speak after a famous singer, and thankfully, no one had pointed it out to her. The name had stayed, and by now, she could not imagine another name for her son. She had taken him to the doctors she could afford. But she was told that he needed more specialized treatment that was beyond her means. She would need to save up for many more years or get a much better job. In her moments of despair, she felt that the name still gave her hope, as if by just calling him Femi, he would one day find his voice and that it may be even as beautiful and powerful as that of her favorite singer.

CHAPTER 4

Martin barely had time to settle into Lagos before he left for Port Harcourt. As the city closest to the Niger Delta, home to Nigeria's massive oil resources, Port Harcourt had the most valuable assets the company owned. It was also the hotbed of the current unrest. A workers' meeting was taking place that evening. It might have been a regular affair except that activists were expected to gatecrash the meeting. The local team had asked for support from Headquarters. Martin was the answer.

By the time Martin walked into the building, it was 5 p.m. The journey had been longer and more arduous than he had expected. He felt as if he was ready to end the working day, not start it. Sweat streamed down his face, the sun still blazing in its full equatorial glory. But by the time the meeting ended, night would have fallen, and the city would be lit with hundreds of oil flares. The crowds inside would want to know when the company would stop burning the gas that was the byproduct of oil extraction. Or when they would clean up the oil spills that were killing the fish. Or the countless other issues he knew they would bring up.

Never answer the question, Martin reminded himself as he walked into the building. If there was one thing he had learned from all the corporate spokesperson training he had attended over the years, it was to evade well.

Eyes on the prize, van Oost. Just do your job and get out.

His job that evening was to convince the people gathered there, who had decided that their lives were being exploited by global corporations and their local leaders, that he was going to make a difference. That things would change for the better. That all they needed to do was to stop the protests, put their heads down, get back to work.

It's not what you do, it's not what you say, it's always about how you make them feel. He had been trained well, and now it was time to use it all.

Regardless of what he intended to convince them of that evening, the overall objective of Martin's assignment was simple enough: Don't change what already works. Preserve the status quo. The protests were threatening the way things were, so make them stop and return things to how they had always been. How Martin got that done—how swiftly and with as little noise as possible—would determine the trajectory and velocity of Martin's career.

Martin was determined to make the most of this opportunity, to cement his reputation as a loyal and competent businessman who could be relied upon under even the most trying circumstances. That meant he had to keep his mind focused on what mattered to the company, and firmly away from any wider consequences and concerns. *End-product focused.* That was one of Teun's earliest lessons to him way back when they were both stationed in Asia. After all, the eyes cannot see what the mind doesn't know.

"Welcome, *Oga*, welcome. We're waiting for you, sir." A stocky young man came out to greet him.

"Martin," he replied. "How late am I?"

"More than an hour. But it's no problem. Traffic in Nigeria is always bad. Blessing kicked off the meeting."

Martin frowned. Blessing was the head of the workers' union. He wished he had been there to listen to her kick off the meeting.

The man said, "Not to worry, you'll meet her after."

"And you must be…" Martin asked.

"David. The manager of this refinery," he said, straightening up a little. "We spoke on the phone."

"Right, yes. Nice to meet you in person finally." He'd had a few calls with David in the last few days, trying to get a lay of the land, the hot topics that were likely to come up. Martin pointed to a sheaf of papers in David's hand. "What you got there, David?"

"Employee grievances. Blessing wanted to give this to you. If you got here earlier. Now you got no time to read."

"It's fine, I'll take it. David, are there any"—Martin hesitated, looking him up and down—"troublemakers in there?"

"No sir, they're ok, but there's one man, sir, Udo, he's loud, leader, troublemaker."

"Which one is he?" Martin asked.

"Front row, sir. Red shirt."

"Hmm..." Martin gulped down half the bottle of water that David handed him.

He handed the bottle and his bag to David, looked over at the crowd, and tried to size up the situation. Martin could feel adrenaline rise in his body.

A tall man with curly blond hair and blue eyes, Martin could have stepped out of any of CBX Corp's corporate brochures. He was an attractive man. In his late thirties, with chiseled features and an athletic body, he wielded charisma, the kind you need to be born with but which is honed to perfection with deliberate determination. Dressed in a slightly rumpled striped suit, he had a carefully cultivated casual carelessness about him, a sincerity that he could turn on and off as the situation demanded.

He took a deep breath as he stepped onto the podium.

The crowd was brutal.

As soon as David introduced Martin and got off the stadium, the audience came at him, with Udo leading the charge, question after question, accusation after accusation. Relentless, their pain pouring out in sharp words and angry complaints. The art of listening without being affected by the words was one of Martin's skills. *Be Teflon, never let it stick*, he reminded himself.

The next hour passed by in a blur.

Oil spills. Air pollution from the flares. Inadequate compensation for the workers. Lack of development in the region. Fishing and agriculture affected by the oil.

The environmental concerns were real, but Martin was not going to concern himself with the specifics. If he did, he would get trapped in trying to address them. Generalities were his haven in a situation like this, and he knew it. He let them speak on, head bowed and acknowledging the concerns as best he could.

There were a few questions on the running of the operations that he hadn't expected, but he deftly sidestepped them too.

"There were five accidents in just the last month due to safety regulations. What will the company do to stop them?"

"How will the injured workers be compensated?"

Martin let his gaze linger on Udo before looking back at the room and speaking in a calm voice. "Thank you for waiting for me, and for raising your concerns. I'm here to help." He knew that the only defense to such a crowd was acknowledgment. Never in words that could be quoted, but in body language and postures. Martin could look at an entire crowd in one gaze, and then home in and make every individual feel as if they were the only one that mattered. Whether it was a natural talent or an acquired skill, he didn't know. It didn't matter which, so long as it got the results he wanted. His words spewed out the corporate responses while his eyes and body reflected their pain. The dissonance between the actions and the words, subtle as it was, always did the trick.

"You are not the first one to say you will help. No one does anything," someone shouted from the back of the room. The crowd murmured agreement in a low rumble. "Yes, why should we think you are different?" came another voice from the right.

Martin nodded, he bowed his head again, he let the crowds shout out for a while. The empathy and concern on his face seemed genuine. When he spoke, he met their eyes. "We've been in the Niger Delta for decades," he said, "and we're fully committed to the region. To you." His words didn't show any hint of irony or doubt when he said, "I feel your pain." When he said, "I'll do everything in my power to make sure we do the right thing," he believed his own words.

Martin waved a sheaf of papers in the air. "I've carefully gone through all your grievances, and we have plans to help you. Each one of you."

The crowds started to quiet down, little by little. The shouts became rumbles, the rumbles reduced to murmurs, and eventually they listened. He pacified them with long and hollow words that made up for their lack of substance in sonorous and convincing delivery. Or perhaps the crowd was tired. It had been a long day, a long wait, and this was not the first time they were airing their grievances. And they just wanted a respite. Hope, even if it was temporary.

Martin spied David at the back of the room. His feet shuffling, his hands crossed, he didn't seem like he believed a word of what Martin was saying. But David was a company man, and Martin knew he could be trusted.

Martin stepped off the podium right into the crowd. A collective gasp could have escaped from them, but silence prevailed. They were not expecting him to get into their midst.

Martin shook Udo's hand and said, "I'll be in touch." He looked straight at Udo, who seemed unsure for the first time that evening. And then Udo said, "We've been waiting so long." As if he believed, for the first time, that there would be answers, and it was just a question of pace. His voice had lost some of the earlier vitriol.

"Yes," responded Martin, 'far too long." He then walked through the crowd, which parted to let him through. With a deftness that would have put a politician to shame, Martin navigated through the people, stopping to hear a few questions, the answer always a variation of the same, "we will do the right thing," never quite defining what the right thing was.

He seemed unhurried, but in half a minute, he was out of the room and in the car, where the driver was waiting. Ayo, who had accompanied Martin from Lagos, jumped into the front seat beside the driver.

"*Oga*, that was very good," said Ayo. "You handled that very well."

Martin nodded.

"The man, Udo, I can help handle—"

"It's ok," said Martin, cutting him off. "We're good here, Ayo." Martin was still trying to figure out Ayo, who seemed to alternate between ostentatious servitude and utter disregard when he thought he could get away with it.

David joined them, jumping into the seat beside Martin, just before the car sped out of the gates.

"Well done, David," said Martin, "that was a good meeting."

David seemed confused. Had he actually done anything? Wasn't it Martin who had done most of the talking?

Martin continued. "We need to act fast on these protests."

"Sure, yes," said David. "I've a plan on how to address some of the most critical issues. That's what I wanted to—"

"Hold on," said Martin. "First things first. You need to send a strong message, before you start solving any of the issues. You know what I mean?"

David hesitated.

"Fire a few, David," said Martin, his tone brisk.

"What do you mean?"

Strike the shepherds, and the sheep will scatter. A simple principle, really, but it had always surprised Martin how few people followed it.

"Ok, here's what you do," said Martin. "Make a list of names of the ones who give the most trouble, but add a few more names, and I want you to let them go."

"But that would affect operations," said David, "and what would be the reason, in any case? I cannot possibly fire people for protesting."

"David, let's back up here a bit," said Martin, his tone still entirely unchanged. "We're not firing because of the protests. Of course not. Perhaps we need some time to assess the safety of the refinery before we can operate at full capacity. That starts with the number of workers."

"Decreasing headcount?" asked David. "That's for HR—"

"This is not an official firing, David," said Martin. "Let go of, say, five to ten percent. That won't make a difference to daily operations."

"So, we run at ninety percent capacity?"

Martin didn't answer, but his glance made it clear that that was a ridiculous assumption on David's part.

"Can't you cut some from other parts of the org? Maybe the field workers?"

"No, not at this point," said Martin. "Well, your refinery seems to work with many people on the streets already. I'm sure you can make it work with them not officially on your payroll."

"But that makes no sense," protested David, "especially if safety is your concern."

"David." Martin stopped him. He could see Ayo listening to the conversation, his head slightly tilted. "David, we need to send a strong message. Whoever was making the most noise at the meeting—I trust your team has a good idea of who they are—let them go. Except Udo," Martin added. "That would make it too obvious."

"Yes, I understand." David sounded dejected.

Maybe Martin had overestimated him. "Make sure the communications team sends me everything for approval before it goes out," he said. "It's important that this feels like it has nothing to do with them voicing their concerns. Or at least it should not be obvious enough for them to make that connection directly."

"Yes."

"I'll head back to Lagos soon, David. Just put this in motion, and if there is any fallout, I'll be back as soon as you need me."

"Blessing will want to meet with you."

"Yes, I know. Arrange for her to meet us in Lagos. Better there than on her home turf."

David started to say something but decided against it.

"Look man," said Martin. "I don't want to make this difficult for you. Let's keep it simple. I have three things I intend to do here—approved all the way from Teun Bergman himself—and you are going to help me do it."

"Yes, of course," answered David.

"Make the protests stop. Pay as little compensation as possible. Admit no guilt, because you know, we are not guilty of anything. This is business, and there are no rules we have broken."

"And firing workers?" asked David.

"…is the fastest way to quell protests," said Martin. *Strike the shepherds and the sheep will scatter.* It was human nature, Martin had observed, and it worked all over the world, regardless of culture or context. Every protest has a passionate few. The rest are followers, and usually smart people who would choose their daily livelihood if there was any perceived risk to it.

"But it will lead to even more problems, Martin," said David. "In fact, I've made a detailed list of what we can do to solve the real problems."

"I don't disagree. And I will look at the list soon. But for now, take strong, clear action. This is not the one thing that will make it all stop. But it is the first step. I'm here because this has gone on for too long and has grown too big."

David was beginning to protest, but the car was pulling up at the hotel where they would part ways.

"In the end, David, we're here for the long haul. The winners are not those with the loudest voice, the biggest talent, or even the deepest pockets. The winner is the last one standing. Remember that," Martin said, reaching over to David, patting him on the shoulder, "and I hope you know how to be the last man standing."

"Martin, you don't understand. Losing a job at CBX Corp…for many of our workers, that's not just a job, it's a livelihood, an entire family's—"

Martin got out of the car, came toward David on the other side, smiled at him broadly.

"Trust me, this is for the good of everyone, in the long run." He took David's hands in a firm grip. "I do understand."

He waved David and Ayo off, agreeing on a time to meet the next morning.

As he headed into the hotel lobby, Martin thought to himself, *I do understand. More than you will ever know.*

Martin must have been eleven years old when he first heard about the company. His father had applied for a job in one of their upstream facilities. A job at CBX Corp would have meant a significant jump in his father's salary and in the standard of living of the five-member family that was crammed into a tiny house in Rijswijk, a suburb just outside of the Hague. For a few weeks, the family was hopeful, and everyone was excited about the potential new job. With the naiveté of children, they had not considered the possibility that the company could choose someone other than their father.

The day his father got the letter was still vivid in Martin's mind. As soon as they saw the postman arrive, they stopped everything they were doing and gathered around the table. The entire family waited expectantly as his father opened the letter. He took a minute to read it, shrugged his shoulders, and said, "Oh well, they don't think I'm suitable for the job."

Probably seeing their woeful faces, his father had laughed and hugged his wife and kids and said that the job was not that good anyway, and he would have had to travel too much, and that he would get a much better job. And they had gone back to living in their tiny house and being conscientious about every cent spent.

Getting around in a chauffeur-driven car, walking into a five-star hotel, Martin mulled over David's last words of protest: *Martin, you don't understand...* Having traveled miles upon miles to get to the position of power where Martin decided who got into or stayed on in CBX Corp or not, not the other way round, it felt ridiculous that someone would presume he didn't understand what he was doing. It almost felt flattering, a testimony to the distance he had covered.

CHAPTER 5

It was a day of excitement in Ansara's neighborhood. In the small, close-knit community, a visit from a future groom was a cause for celebration. "He is handsome, black, and strong. And not old at all, Chidera, not old at all," Madu kept saying, and Mrs. Jideofor passed on sweet treats to the neighbors who had come to join in.

"Ah, there you are!" Her mother was just coming over from Mrs. Jideofor's, still beaming at Chidera's good fortune. "You left too soon. Are you ok?"

"I'm fine, Mama. I just didn't..." Ansara hesitated. "We can talk about it after Chidera's big day."

"You're not going to get away with your face like that over there," her mother said. "Tell me what happened."

"I lost my job," she replied. Her mother seemed as shocked as she had been when she got the news. "I don't really know why, but many of us were fired. Udo thinks it is about forty or fifty of us who lost our jobs."

"Udo? Is it because of all the protests?"

"No, I didn't go to any of them," said Ansara.

"What happened then?"

"Nothing, Mama. I did my work as always. I don't know

why. The protest this week was big, was not just the workers. They say activists had come in too. But I wasn't—"

"Was he there?" her mother asked. "Emeka?"

Ansara looked away.

"Ansa?"

"No, Mama," she replied, "he wasn't there."

"He'll come home. Soon," her mother said. "I know it."

Emeka, her brother, had joined the activists after their father died during his shift at work. *"It was not his fault!"* She could still hear Emeka's loud voice in her head, shouting at the refinery management. But his vocal protests had not done any of them any good. Safety measures were lax at many oil companies in Niger Delta, but CBX Corp insisted that her father's death on the job was his own fault. Nothing the company could have done anything about.

Emeka had started off trying to get fair compensation and justice for their father's death, but there were no witnesses, at least none who would testify, and it was closed as a case of a worker falling from a height due to personal negligence. Emeka wouldn't let the case go. His frustration found its outlet in the broader issues of their region, from corruption to pollution to exploitation. He was young, articulate, and passionate, so it was only a matter of time before the activists recruited them into their fold.

More than a year ago, the local authorities started cracking down hard on activists, and one day, Emeka disappeared, presumably for his own safety. Ansara and her mother used to get occasional notes from him at first, but eventually they trickled to a stop. Every time her mother heard about some activist presence at any event, she always found new hope that Emeka would come home.

But he hadn't. And it had been up to her and her mother, with their meager and uncertain jobs, to keep the household going.

"What do we do now, Ansa?" asked her mother, sitting down on the cot. Ansara sat next to her mother, holding her close.

Ayomide Akande finally arrived late in the afternoon, along with Madu, in a dusty black car whose noise they could hear from half a kilometer away. Children from the streets were running after the car, curious to see a car in their neighborhood. The car stopped outside their door and out stepped Ayomide.

Ansara watched the pompous entry from behind the curtain of the main room. He certainly did not look like the handsome black prince Madu had kept describing. The first image that came to Ansara's mind was that of a slimy slug. Ayo was a short, stout man, who was covered in sweat, which made his jet-black face shine in the sun. His eyes darted occasionally from side to side, like someone who had slithered away just in time to not get caught in yet another con act. Despite the heat, he was wearing a Western pantsuit that was obviously not suited for the equatorial climate.

He had barely sat down in the main chair in the room

when he asked, "Where is the woman?"

"He's in a hurry. He needs to get back to Lagos later today," Madu explained.

Chidera came into the room. She felt uncomfortable at being looked up and down as if she was on exhibition. But Ayomide seemed pleased.

"Hello, Chidera, how are you?" he asked her in English. Ansara felt just a little bit of annoyance at his affectation. He must have known that this poor uneducated girl would not know English. He smiled and repeated the greeting in Igbo. "It is no matter you don't speak English. In Lagos, my boss, he is English. We have to speak English the whole day."

After observing the prospective groom from afar and listening to his tales for a while, Ansara and her mother left the house and went back into their own. A few hours later, they could still hear Ayomide's loud voice telling them about his luxurious life in Lagos. He seemed to have forgotten all about the hurry that he was in when he first arrived. Then there was a lull in his voice for some time, and Ansara imagined that after lunch, the family had let him rest. After all, siesta was in vogue among the rich and the aspiring rich.

It was almost night when Ansara heard a knock on their front door. She was surprised to see Ayomide and Madu at the door.

"I hear you just lost a job. And you speak English," Ayomide stated. The man obviously did not believe in introductions, or maybe just did not consider them worthy of such niceties. "And I hear you cook very well."

"I suppose," Ansara answered, not quite sure where all this was leading. "Yes."

The conversation about her job loss and cooking skills had come up in passing while they were at Mrs. Jideofor's earlier. She wasn't even sure if Ayo had been listening then, but clearly Mrs. Jideofor must have put in a good word to try and get her a new job.

"Who is it?" Ansara's mother came in from the kitchen. "Oh, Ayomide, how nice to have you here. Please come in." She cleared the clothes that Ansara had folded and arranged on the cot, with one big sweep of her hand. Ansara looked in dismay at her work gone to waste.

"Yes, yes. I was on my way back to Lagos. I heard your daughter wants a job. My boss in Lagos—a white man—he wants a cook for the house. A good one. He's not happy with all the fellows I bring so far. It's very good salary, good job. Your daughter, she speaks English, doesn't she?"

Not waiting for answer, Ayomide turned to Ansara and said, "Hello, how are you?" Perhaps it had dawned on him that speaking to her in English was a better option to confirm that she spoke English than asking either of them.

"I'm fine, Ayomide. Thank you. But I was not looking for a job in Lagos. But here in Port Harcourt. I hear you have business here too."

"What? You must be stupid to turn down such an

opportunity in Lagos! I've so many people who want this job, it's a job with good money and not so hard work. You just have to cook and some clean, and for just one boss. Not family. But I just want to give job to neighbor of my future wife." He then repeated everything in Igbo to her mother, probably realizing that it would be easier to convince her than Ansara.

Ansara's mother looked at her expectantly. They needed the money. Good, steady jobs were hard to come by, and most of the jobs Ansara would get involved hard labor in the hot sun for very meager pay. Ayomide's offer seemed too good to be true.

"Salaries in Lagos are much better than here," reiterated Ayomide.

"I can take care of Femi. Don't worry about him," said Ansara's mother. She knew that the main thing holding Ansara back was her reluctance to leave her son.

"No, I'll take Femi with me, if I go," Ansara said.

"Can she take her son with her, Ayomide?" her mother asked.

"Son? She has a son? No, of course not. This is for white boss. They don't let you have your family with you. This is work, not family."

"Yes, of course, we understand. Femi can stay here with me. He'll also have other boys to play with here. She's a very good cook, Ayomide. Very very good. You'll be happy you give her this job."

Ansara was silent. It had been several years since she

worked in a household, and she was desperate to support her mother. Her mother, who was fast approaching her sixtieth birthday, still worked very hard to support her family but was getting more and more ill. But on the other hand, leaving Port Harcourt, her family and, most importantly, her son behind, was not an easy decision.

"Look, I'll come back in two weeks for the wine-carrying ceremony. You decide by then. If you want the job, you come with me to Lagos then, ok?" Ayomide hesitated for a moment, and then continued in a lower voice, "I do this for my future wife's family, you know. But I've many cooks I know who all want the job. But I give it to you if you want it. The standard rate in Lagos is that you give me thirty percent of your salary. But even with that, you'll get much higher pay than you can dream of getting in your low jobs here."

Ansara was once more taken aback by Ayomide. She had always considered Chidera as her own sister, part of the family, and the man marrying her would have been family to her. But this man obviously meant business.

"Two weeks, she'll be ready, Ayomide. We see you then. Thank you very much for your generosity. Have a safe trip to Lagos," her mother replied in her stead.

Without even a customary goodbye, Ayomide turned and walked out of the house. Madu grinned at them briefly and followed him like a faithful puppy. A little while later, Ansara heard the whir of the car and the Jideofor family wishing him a safe journey.

A marriage had been sealed, a job offer had been made, and a commission rate had been settled. It was all in a day's work for Ayomide, Ansara thought as she went back to folding the clothes on the cot again.

CHAPTER 6

It was a little after 7 p.m. when Blessing, along with another representative from the workers' union, arrived at Rose Villa. David was already at the house, making sure that the setting was just right for the dinner Martin had invited the three of them to. Ayo was barking last-minute orders to the cook to make sure the food was in order, when the bell rang.

"Blessing, how lovely to see you again." Martin welcomed her warmly into the house, along with her deputy, who introduced himself as Winston. It was Martin's idea to have the initial conversation in Lagos, in a setting that was less corporate than a sterile meeting room, and he hoped that they would start off on a good note, regardless of the inevitable adversarial nature of the relationships between employer–employee representatives. Blessing Adewale, Martin had found out from his network in Europe, was born in Nigeria but raised and educated in the finest universities in London, until she decided to relocate back to her home country. Definitely with a hefty pay cut, his friend who helped with the due diligence had told him, especially if she's helping labor unions now. But she had always been something of an idealist, the friend had remarked. Martin hoped that with her affluence and knowledge of what he called "how the world really works," they might find common ground.

But it was not to be.

Right after the serving of *Isi Ewu*—a goat head soup that Martin had been told earlier was a Nigerian delicacy—and before they could really dig into the grilled tilapia that looked fiery with its red marinade and side of tomatoes, Blessing brought up the recent firings.

"You mean the head count reduction we had to implement?" asked David.

"Whatever you want to call it, David," said Blessing, "more than fifty people lost their livelihood overnight, and without a reason." Blessing looked straight at Martin when she said, "Except perhaps that we have a new boss in town."

Martin hadn't expected it to go bad so fast.

He took a moment to swallow the food in his mouth, cursing the choice of spicy dishes, and said, "Blessing, that was not our intention. Our hope, just as I'm sure is yours, is to make sure that we give employment and a decent livelihood to as many employees as we can. But you heard the grievances they brought in, about the safety, about getting the operations on track—"

"It's not about the safety, more about—" started David, stopping as he caught Martin's glare.

"As I was saying," continued Martin, "we need to just review the operations in its entirety and make sure we can keep everyone safe."

"Ah, you're saying this is about safety," Blessing asked, "and nothing to do with the increased unrest among the employees?"

She stopped short of asking outright if the employees who were fired were the ones who had spoken up or were somehow involved with the protests. David had done a good job of randomizing the names of those who got fired, and adding several who were not directly connected to the protests. Whatever Blessing said would have come across as a baseless accusation. It was smart of Martin to blame the reduction in head count on safety concerns and their need to assess conditions before running at full capacity. Not untrue, but not the real reason either.

The conversation ebbed and flowed in intensity and antagonism, Martin navigating and distracting, sometimes by serving a dish, or giving another helping of wine, or introducing another topic. By the time a dessert platter of Puff-Puff was served, occasional laughter and levity had found their way to the dining table.

After dinner, the guests found themselves in an informal setting in the library, where unpacked boxes still lay piled up in front of empty shelves.

"That's a lot of boxes, Martin," commented Blessing.

"Yes, books. I've many of them. I don't have much else to lug around, but these I like to carry with me to all my long postings around the world," said Martin. "Gives a sense of home, you know?"

Blessing swirled the wine in her glass, trying to take him in. "I'll be straight with you," she said. "I would like to work with you to find some middle ground."

Martin was quiet. This was progress.

"But you've got to meet me halfway," she said.

"What do you mean?"

"You made an impression at the last meeting at the refinery," she said. "For the first time, I think they all believe the company will do some good for them."

"I'm glad that—" started Martin.

"But I don't buy it." Blessing was blunt. "I know you had not even glanced at the reports I gave to David before the meeting." She glanced toward David and Winston in the center of the room. "You couldn't have. And then the firings. It's not difficult to guess how the names were picked."

Martin didn't answer.

"All I'm saying is, you seem to have convinced some of us that you'll do the right thing," she said. "And maybe you will. Question though, Martin, is, what is the right thing?"

"What's best for the company, and the employees." Martin was earnest, and he meant it. "And, of course, your country too, Blessing."

"In that order?" asked Blessing. "It's not that simple, Martin. And a lot will hinge on you. All I ask of you is, look at the full picture. I've faith that you and the company will be entirely above board, within the law"—she paused, looking around—"but please consider, is it enough? Does it mean really that it is the right thing?"

"Blessing, what do you mean?" said Martin. CBX Corp

had a stellar compliance record, and a legal team that insisted they stayed within the rules, never straying onto the wrong side of the law.

Blessing hesitated for a bit. "Martin, following the rules after you write the rules yourself isn't really doing the right thing, is it?"

Martin thought of the leagues of lobbyists CBX Corp employed to influence the laws before they were formulated, allowing the company preferential regulations and tax regimes, among other perks. It was the way business was done, and so long as they convinced the government and authorities, as far as Martin was concerned, the company was well in the clear.

"It pains me to say this," Blessing continued, "but our government, our administration, and even our police—those who are supposed to protect the people—you know as well as I do that they protect themselves first. And companies like yours give them legitimacy and resources. You turn a blind eye to their atrocities, and in turn, they turn a blind eye to yours."

Martin protested. He was not here to solve the social and political problems of Nigeria, and he didn't see how Blessing could expect him to. CBX Corp was a profit-making corporation, answerable to its shareholders, working well within the rules of the land, admittedly some that the oil companies themselves had helped craft. But accusing his company of being in cahoots with the government and local authorities, especially of being complicit in their corruption and cruelty, was an accusation Martin was not willing to accept.

"Just keep your eyes and your mind open, Martin," said Blessing. She was not about to let him off the hook easily about the recent firings. "I don't expect much from CBX Corp, but let's at least acknowledge what really goes on here."

The conversation continued for a while longer, the four of them each with their own personal agendas, fears, hope, and insecurities, caught in a situation fraught on many dimensions—historical, cultural, social—yet hoping that, ultimately, their own humanity would help them find commonalities more than differences. Whether they would succeed, that evening was not going to provide final answers.

Martin thanked Blessing and Winston later that night, bidding them goodbye.

"Sorry," started David, "did I misspeak? We've the operations under—"

"It's ok, David. I know you run a good plant," said Martin. "Don't worry about it." He bid David goodbye too, pacifying him that things were alright and thanking him for making the trip over to Lagos.

Martin headed upstairs into his library. He grabbed a book from one of the boxes, replaced his wine with beer, and sank into his armchair.

Martin was no stranger to getting fired, for being punished for the strength of one's convictions.

His last job, nearly nine years ago, before he started at CBX Corp, was at a warehouse in one of the Netherlands' many cheese factories. A position that his best friend, Jaap, got for him after he had been unemployed for several months.

"Hey, Martin, you better get a move on things, man! The supervisor is going to be here any moment." Martin could hear Jaap's holler from across the boxes earlier that day, ringing loud in his ears even after all these years.

Martin and Jaap were packers. Their job was simple: Jaap would inspect the wrapping of the cheese that came out on his side of the conveyor belt, and if he did not take it out as a defective piece, it moved onto Martin's side. Martin would then put the cheeses into a box and fold in the flaps of the lid before it moved on to the labelers, who were next in line. The only thing that made one day different from another was the topic of the conversation he would have with Jaap. But after many months on the job, Martin was beginning to notice a repetitive pattern even in that.

Martin eyed the slow motion of the cheese boxes along the belt and surveyed the men and women performing their various tasks on the warehouse floor. There were those who seemed happy and relaxed, their arms performing the action in an effortless motion while their minds focused on the conversation with their colleagues. Some of them had worked there for years and had more daily conversations with their coworkers than they had with their own families or friends. Then there were others who seemed grumpy and listless, mechanically doing what was required of them while secretly counting the hours until the end of their shift when they could get out of the windowless hall. Martin even noticed an unlucky few who, despite putting in their best work, seemed to struggle to finish the task at hand, as the next item on the conveyor belt made its way to their station before they had a chance to send the previous one off.

The strong smell of cheese in the dingy warehouse was giving Martin a headache, but his eyes gleamed in excitement. "Jaap, don't you see? Don't you see how suboptimal this plant is?"

"Oh, man! Don't start. I know what comes after. One of your far-fetched ideas." Jaap looked around to check whether the supervisor was within hearing distance before continuing. "You know how the sup is going to react. Why don't you just give up, man, and get on with your job like the rest of us?"

"Well, I can't give up. I have to tell him. I have to tell him till he understands the potential in my ideas. Listen to this—" Martin's enthusiasm was making his voice go up.

Jaap cut into his sentence. "I've heard enough of your ideas. This factory is not functioning efficiently, it can produce double the things in half the time, we don't need so many people…blah blah blah. Here's news for you, brother. All those brilliant ideas of yours, all they do is get you in trouble. The sup hates it, he hates you, and if you stick with this for long, he's going to fire you. End of story."

Martin was just about to reply when the supervisor walked into the room.

"Van Oost, what's happening here? How many times have

I told you not to waste your time talking?"

"*Baas!* The work is all going fine. I was just about to tell Jaap how we can significantly increase the output by rearranging a few of the belts."

The supervisor's eyes bore into Martin. "Van Oost, come into my office when you are done for the day."

Jaap waited until the supervisor was out of earshot. "Oh, man, you're done for! He's going to fire you."

"No, he's not. He's finally going to see how good my ideas are!"

It turned out that Jaap was right. At the end of his shift, the supervisor categorically fired Martin for meddling where his input was not required.

Martin had walked out of the factory, dejected but determined.

CHAPTER 7

"Ansa, have you given any thought to Ayomide's offer?" Ansara's mother asked. It had been over a week since Ayomide's visit and she had just a few more days to decide whether to take up the job in Lagos.

"I'm still thinking about it. It seems like a good job, but I just wish I didn't have to go so far away from you and Femi," Ansara said as she straightened her t-shirt and tightened the wrapper she had just changed into.

"You're wearing your nice clothes. Where're you off to?" her mother asked.

"Down to the library. Maybe they need someone to clean the place or rearrange the books or something. If there's any job, I'm sure Ngozi will help."

"They don't pay much, Ansa."

"I know, Mama. But it'll leave me enough time to do another job, and I don't have to go all the way to Lagos."

Deep down in her heart, she knew that a temporary job in the local library did not compare with that of a household cook for an *oyibo*. Ayomide's offer was not one she could reasonably reject; it was not every day that she was offered a job in Lagos. She would finally be able to help more with the household expenses, and possibly even afford to have the treatment for Femi that she had always wanted. Even so, she had spent the last week trying to find a job in Port Harcourt. She was not ready to make the decision just yet.

Ansara's mother sighed. "I guess you're right. At least Ngozi will not fire you just like that."

Ngozi was one of her father's old friends. Both shared a love of learning. They had met each other in an adult literacy program and helped each other through years of learning to read and write, and then decades of literary appreciation. After Ngozi retired from his job, he had managed to open a local library, which had been one of Ansara's favorite haunts ever since her father took her there when she was merely four.

It was still one of the places where Ansara felt safe, almost like a second home. The library always made her dream about what her life would have turned out to be if her father hadn't died. He had always insisted on Ansara's education— an anomaly in their social groups—and despite any financial challenges he might have had, he made sure she went to school without fail and got any books and help she needed. When his friends pointed out that it was stupid to lavish the money on a daughter, he would retort that she was smarter than both her brothers combined. Ansara would blush and pretend not to have heard it, but she worked extra hard every time she heard him say it.

Ansara was surprised to see a flurry of activity as she approached the library. Able-bodied men were taking out the books and placing them in bundles held together with brown string. A few of them were loading the bundles into an old, dilapidated van parked outside.

"Ngozi, how are you? Did you finally manage to get a new place?" Ansara asked as she walked toward the old man who stood crouching outside, watching the men at their job.

She looked around the old building. As much as she would hate to see her local haunt move, she knew that it was much needed. It was a small, nondescript building badly in need of repair. It consisted of a few adjacent rooms, filled with books that seemed as old and tattered as the building that housed them.

"Ah, Ansa…I wish, I wish, my child." Ngozi came out to greet her and led her in. "How are you? You haven't come around here for long time now, all ok? How's Kisi, and little Femi?"

"All well. You must come visit sometime. I'm sure Mama would like that. What's going on here?" she asked, looking around. The inside of the library was damp and dark, as always, where it was often difficult to read the titles of the books in the rooms. Ngozi tried to light candles whenever there were more than a few people. But more often than not, there were not enough candles and prospective readers would bring stacks of books out into the sunlight where they could read the titles and the back covers. During the monsoons, Ngozi encouraged the readers to keep the books for longer periods because two of the rooms would be flooded with water leaking from the roof and the shelf space would be effectively halved.

A forlorn look came over Ngozi's eyes. "We're closing down. The books are going to an NGO, which will redistribute them to other libraries in the country."

"Closing down? Why? What happened?"

"Well, I'm too old to run this place anymore. I couldn't find anyone to take it on. There's not much money to be made here. I don't know, Ansa, I kept it open as long as I could, but now it's time." Ngozi coughed violently, shrinking his shriveled body even further.

"I'm so sorry to hear that. There will be no more books for the children around here. I don't think I would have managed to read at all if it wasn't for this library," she said, fingering the dusty books on the shelves.

"Come on in, I may have something for you." Ansara followed as the old man shuffled inside. Ngozi walked to one of the shelves and carefully pulled out a handful of books and gave them to her. "Keep them. No one is going to miss them, and they will find better use with you."

Ansara looked at the bundle of books—Rumi, Soyinka, Gibran, Bronte—a random assortment of poetry collections from various writers. "Thank you so much, Ngozi. Are you sure this won't be any trouble?"

"Of course not, of course not. I know how much you like poetry. Just like your father," he said, wistfully looking into the distance. "There're not many people these days who even know these writers."

"Thank you," she said, hugging him. "Can I help you with the move? It looks like you still have a lot to do?"

"If you're not in a rush, yes, I wouldn't mind a bit of company," he said. "It's painful to pack all this, and you know, watch them take it all away. With no care what is in it. All these words, worth so little."

"Of course, I'll stay and help. Just tell me what to do."

Ngozi pointed her to some shelves where he wanted her help to sort and stack into different boxes for the different libraries and excused himself to go out and get them some tea.

She gave herself time to take it all in one last time before diving into the packing. It was sad that her much-loved library was closing, and more selfishly, she realized that one more of her local job searches had ended in vain. She was running out of reasons to not take up Ayomide's offer for the job in Lagos.

When she got back from the library, her house was empty. Ansara still had an hour or so before she had to start cooking lunch. Just enough to indulge in some reading before getting to the household chores. She sat on the floor by the window, with the books Ngozi had given her spread out around her, and picked them up one by one, browsing, reading through her favorite poems and losing herself in the beauty and magic of the great poets' words.

But soon her reading was interrupted by shouts from the

boys next door. Inni and Femi had been joined by some of the neighborhood kids and they were chatting animatedly with Inni. She looked out of the window and saw Femi standing just outside the circle, still smiling and happy but decidedly out of the conversation that the boys were having.

Ansara put down her book and sighed. She thought longingly of a time when Femi might be able to speak. On some days, she would wake up from her sleep thinking that her son had called her. Believing that she had heard the word "Mama" that she so longed to hear. But then she would open her eyes and realize it was just a dream. Those days, she felt it was a sign; it was a sign that there would be a way, there would be some way to get his voice back.

Ansara got up from her seat by the window, stacked up her books, and went out toward the children. By then, Femi was nowhere to be seen. She knew he must have crawled inside his new shack, his "home," sitting by himself while the other boys were noisily involved in their games.

She walked toward him, shading her eyes from the strong rays of the sun. As she peeped inside the shack, getting down on all fours, the walls too narrow to comfortably fit her adult body, she saw her son, sitting still, his head on his knees. Little tears had formed around his eyes, and she knew, even as she knew that he would never tell her about it, that the other kids must have made fun of him. She resolved that although she may not be able to change the past, she could definitely shape her future. If there was any chance that she could get Femi his voice, she needed to make the money for his treatments, and if taking up a job in Lagos was the way to get that, that is exactly what she would do. She hugged him, wiped away his tears, and brought him back into their home, feeling a ray of hope about what the future could hold for them.

CHAPTER 8

When Martin saw Ansara, she reminded him of an animal, a caged panther, graceful and elegant but who had yet to lose the wild look in her eyes.

"She cooks all European food, French, Italian, Mexican, and even German food," Ayo was saying.

Ordinarily, Martin would have chuckled at Ayo's enthusiastic and ignorant overselling. He would have considered proficiency in German cooking a definite blemish on anyone's culinary résumé. But then he did not quite believe everything that Ayo said either. The last cook Ayo had brought in came with, apparently, recommendations from the best Thai restaurant in town but could not tell the difference between a *tom yum* and a *khao soi* soup.

Today, he was barely registering Ayo's droning voice. It took him a while to connect the dots and realize that the woman standing in front of him was to be his cook. The food in the house had been abysmal of late, and the breakfast he was eating was no exception. He had gotten used to the erratic quality and didn't bother to intervene in Ayo's decisions, but the woman Ayo was introducing to him looked nothing like domestic help.

Probably in her twenties, Ansara was the epitome of feminine grace. She had the most flawless complexion he had ever seen, almost glowing in the morning sun that came in through the window. The gentle, soft features of her face contrasted with the cascade of stubbornly rebellious thick black hair that seemed to hate the restraints it was under. Her long lashes softened her gaze as she looked up at Martin as if expecting him to say something. But he was too distracted to take his eyes off her, or to listen to what Ayo was asking him.

The familiar shrill ring of his Blackberry brought his attention back to reality and succeeded in shutting Ayo up. "I'll think about it," Martin hastily told Ayo while reaching to answer his phone.

There had been an insurgency at Port Harcourt, and they needed him there right away. Martin hated being interrupted in the middle of his breakfast, but leaving immediately was the only way he would make it to the airport in time.

It was a typical Lagos day, and it seemed to Martin that the entire city was driving out to the airport, the roads clogged right from the start. The air conditioning, on full power, did little to relieve the drudgery of the journey. The bridge connecting Victoria Island to the mainland was entirely gridlocked.

A distinct smell of roasted peanuts found its way into the car. Martin looked up and was startled to find a pair of eyes peering at him, the puckered nose almost touching the glass of his window. The little boy, who must have been barely ten years old, was gesturing toward the small cones of peanuts in his hand.

Mohammed, Martin's driver, rolled down his window. "Hey, you boy, go away, we don't want no peanuts."

The boy was interested only in Martin and stuck his hand through Mohammed's window toward the back.

"Sir, best peanuts in Lagos for cheapest prices. Just roasted."

Martin could see the image of a wealthy Nigerian party in the tattered tabloid that was used to make the paper cone. The boy's hands had burn scars, the kind that could only be made by leaving a hot metal rod on flesh until it melted. His fingernails were caked with dirt, and his shirt had more holes than cloth.

"Sir, please sir, you like these peanuts, I promise." The boy continued his sales pitch even as his eyes darted to the side, scouring the surrounding cars for potential buyers.

"How much?" Martin asked.

Mohammed turned around as if a bee had stung the back of his neck. "*Oga*, don't buy this. We can buy roasted peanuts at the supermarket. This was fried at the roadside."

"Sir, fried at the roadside but very clean. Please try some." The boy was about to open one of the cones.

"Don't open them. I'll take two." Martin handed the boy the ten naira he asked for.

Mohammed was still muttering something under his breath as Martin offered him some peanuts and said, "Mohammed, I'm not going to die from eating some peanuts. Besides, the boy needs the money more than the supermarket tycoons."

Mohammed nodded, thanking him for the peanuts. "*Oga,* I'm going to get out for a while. Looks like we will be stuck in this go-slow for some time."

Martin popped a handful of peanuts into his mouth, glad to have some solitude in the confines of his car. He had to spit out the few grains of sand that had inadvertently found their way into the cone, but the crunchy taste, Martin thought, was unlike what he had tasted from most supermarkets.

Martin studied the scene around him. There must have been at least a few hundred cars on the bridge, with about six or seven in parallel on a four-car lane, parked as if they had been struck motionless by a magician's wand right in the middle of their attempts to get ahead of each other. The drivers had switched off their engines and some had even got out of their vehicles. The car owners were in the back seats, most of them on their mobile phones, with windows firmly shut against the dust and grime of the Lagos roads, and the tinted shades perched on their noses offering some protection from the sweltering sun. The little boy who sold Martin the peanuts was not having much luck in getting any of them to notice him, let alone open the windows.

It would probably be another hour before they would get to the other end of the bridge. The Femi Kuti music playing on the car radio offered a modicum of relief. Martin's mind drifted off into a Femi Kuti concert. He could see the beautiful cook Ayo had introduced him to dancing in rhythm to the slow music. She had let her hair down. Thick black curls swayed wildly in tune with the slow motions of her graceful body. She was dressed in a plain white t-shirt and blue jeans, as he had seen her that morning, but not even the blandness of those clothes could take the sensuality away from her perfectly carved female body. While gyrating with the crowds, yet clearly standing out from them, her eyes seemed to stare straight at him, unapologetically dark and intense. Mysterious, they seemed to him, like the depths of a moonless night, enchanting and brimming with undisclosed mysteries.

Martin shook himself out of his daydream, shocked at himself for being so blatantly enamored. He knew well that the realm of his thoughts was the only one not bound by social constraints.

He must tell Ayo not to hire her, he told himself firmly. He could not have someone around the house whom he obviously found very attractive. There was something about Ansara that made Martin determined that she would not be just one of his conquests. He was sure hers would not be the name he would struggle to remember as he remembered a passionate night in Lagos. And the best way to let it not happen was to not have her around in the first place.

Martin called Ayo.

"Ayo, the cook you brought in today, what's her name? I think we shouldn't hire her. She doesn't seem experienced enough."

"Her name is Ansara. But *Oga*, I've tried her cooking. She's excellent. And she can cook European food much better than all our cooks before."

"You said she used to work in a refinery or something, so how can she have experience in cooking European food?"

"She has worked with foreign families before. She comes with high recommendations. I'm sure she will be much better than other cooks. Very hard, very hard to find good cook."

"Ayo, I'm getting another call, and I need to go. But just ask our current cook to stay on while you look for a new person. I don't think this woman—Ansara?—is the right one for us. Bye. I see you later."

Ansara. He let the name linger in his mind for just a moment more, before answering the waiting call.

It was close to 10 p.m. by the time Martin got back home. As was his usual routine, he came in, dropped his laptop bag on the sofa, and headed to the kitchen to pour himself a drink. He was taken aback to see Ansara sitting on a stool by the kitchen counter.

"What are you doing here?" Martin probably sounded harsher than he had intended. Ansara seemed as startled to see him as he had been to see her. "Didn't Ayo talk to you?" he continued.

"Good evening, *Oga*! How was your day today?" Ayo's booming voice came from behind Martin before Ansara could answer.

"Ayo, what's going on?" Today was not a day that Martin had patience for Ayo's antics. He looked straight at Ayo.

Ayo's slick black hair was combed back, revealing a broad forehead. But the rest of his face was small, and a rather large nose and mouth seemed to crowd into a small area, as if unhappy to have given up so much room for the forehead, which was surely a waste of space.

Ayo's obvious deference to authority and conspicuous attempts to make life in Nigeria comfortable for Martin annoyed him, mainly because Ayo always managed to eventually find a way to do what he liked around the house.

"She really needs the job," Ayo pleaded. Martin was not willing to believe that a woman's plight had even remotely moved him.

Martin walked back to the living room, a cup of coffee in his hand, and grabbed his laptop. Work still waited for him. "Ayo, are you getting money from her for this?"

"No, *Oga*, of course not. Why you say that?" Ayo's hurt look, overtly exaggerated, was far from convincing. "Actually," he continued to mumble, "I already fired the old cook. He was stupid, idiot fellow, and had fight with me. So I ask him to go. And we have no one to cook, and I was so sure you like her, sir, why don't we try for few days?"

Martin was beginning to notice that the rotating roster of cooks had more to do with their incompatibility with Ayo, or whatever it is he wanted from them, rather than actual cooking skills. It had been a long day and Martin's patience was wearing thin. Anger was finding its foothold on him, uninvited.

"Ayo, I was very clear when I called you this morning,

wasn't I? I asked you specifically not to hire her. Can you tell me why you disregarded what I explicitly asked you to do?"

"*Oga*, I'm really sorry." Ayo seemed to have sensed that Martin was more annoyed than usual. "I really did not have a choice. But the old cook, he was very bad person and I had to let him go. And we need someone to cook for us."

After a day of mediation with shouting Nigerians, who Martin had decided had to be the loudest people on earth, he disliked any confrontation at home. He usually let Ayo have his way, rarely letting on that he noticed Ayo's noncompliance with his expressed preferences. But today, he was in no mood to let Ayo off that easily.

Martin found himself raising his voice. "Well, I don't care. I want to know why you deliberately ignored what I said and hired her."

Ayo hesitated, perhaps surprised by Martin's unusual outburst on banal household matters and unsure of what would make him calm down.

"Ayo, I know you well enough to know that there is a reason. There must be a reason why you hired her, and I want to know what it is."

Martin stood up, sighed, and went back to the kitchen to get a beer; a coffee was not what he needed right now. Also, he needed some time to clear his head. He did not like to shout at his house staff.

He had not quite thought about running into Ansara there.

"Sir, can I please speak to you?" Martin was struck by

the poise of her voice. Though slightly accented, it had a sophistication and propriety that hinted at an education beyond that of a typical household cook.

Martin hesitated, feeling slightly embarrassed that she had overheard his conversation with Ayo. "Yes."

"I really need this job and I promise I will do a good job," she said. "Some years ago, I worked for a long time with an English family. I know many good recipes from that time. And I learn quickly. I can change my cooking to whatever you like. I even know how to make a Dutch *stamppot*."

He could not help being intrigued. After all these years abroad, Martin had no craving for his country's unimaginative cuisine, but he was impressed that she knew enough about Dutch food to mention *stamppot*.

He tried to come up with a plausible excuse. "Ansara, is it? Ansara, I was really looking for a more professional cook, someone who is more experienced." His eyes wandered to her hair; the image of her dancing, her curls wild and free, that had come to his mind in the car ride resurfaced.

"Sir." She was calling him. "As I was saying, would you give me a chance, please? I really need this job. I've a boy, my son, he can't speak, and his treatment needs money. This job will really help me save up for it. Could you please at least try my food for a few days and then decide? I promise the food will be good."

Martin could not tell whether he was being conned by both his housekeeper and the new cook, but there was something so genuine about her that he just could not bring himself to believe that she would team up with someone like Ayo for a con job.

The last thing he wanted, Martin thought, was to be a person who denies a boy the chance to his voice, just because he did not trust his libido.

Ayo had followed him to the kitchen and seemed delighted that he was wavering. Martin ignored Ayo's smug expression. He was feeling too tired to continue their confrontation. He addressed Ansara. "You can stay for a few days, and we'll try out your cooking."

Martin did not wait for a response as he walked out of the kitchen with his beer.

PART II

CHAPTER 9

"To melt and be like a running brook

That sings its melody to the night.

To know the pain of too much tenderness.

To be wounded by your own understanding of love"

The words just would not leave Martin's head. He kept repeating them in an attempt to remember the words that came after. Earworms were a particular nuisance when they happened in the middle of a working day.

After he got home that evening, the words were still firmly stuck in his head, even as the subsequent lines remained elusive. He dropped his bag on the sofa and went to the bookshelf. The book had to be there, his copy of the *Selected Poems of Kahlil Gibran*. It had been a graduation gift from one of his professors, and he liked to read it every once in a while, to flip open a random page and read a few verses.

He looked at the boxes in his library-come-office in dismay. He had been meaning to unpack them, but work had kept him busy since the day he landed. He knew finding one thin volume of poetry among the dozens of boxes of books would not be an easy task, but he was still going to try, if only just to get the tune to progress in his head. He started unpacking the first box.

"Shall I get you your coffee, sir?" Ansara's voice nearly startled him.

"Yes, please," Martin said, his head still in the boxes. He could really get used to the fresh pot of coffee brewing by the time he got back from work every evening. The quality of food had seen a marked improvement ever since Ansara arrived, and she could indeed whip up a variety of cuisines with finesse. Since many household matters were now well taken care of, Ayo also didn't need to get in Martin's hair as often, an arrangement that both Martin and Ayo appreciated greatly.

Ansara was just about to leave the room, when Martin repeated the poem loudly to himself.

"To melt and be like a running brook
That sings its melody to the night.
To know the pain of too much tenderness.
To be wounded by your own understanding of love."

He heard a voice behind him.
"And to bleed willingly and joyfully.
To wake at dawn with a winged heart
And give thanks for another day of loving."

Martin wasn't sure he had heard right. He turned around as if a ghost had appeared behind him. "Yes! Yes!!" he shouted in his excitement. "I've been searching for those lines the entire afternoon."

It took him a moment to realize that his cook, who he had

assumed was uneducated and unread, had just helped him remember the lines from an old Arab poet.

"You read Gibran?" As soon as the words were out of his mouth, Martin wished that the incredulity he felt hadn't been so obvious in the tone of his voice.

"When I can, yes. I like poetry," Ansara said, smiling. "Is that what you were looking for in the boxes?"

"Yes, it's somewhere in here, I'm sure," he said, "but at least now those lines are not going to mock me, just out of reach."

"Let me get you your coffee," she said, leaving the room.

Like a dam that had been broken, the rest of the poem came to him in a rush. He took a piece of paper and wrote it down, deciding that would be easier than finding the book.

By the time Ansara came back with this coffee, he had gotten nearly the full poem down, reciting it as he was writing.

"To rest at the noon hour and meditate love's ecstasy;

To return home at eventide with gratitude;

And then to sleep with a prayer—"

He had just the last lines to go when she came in and put the coffee on his desk.

"Thank you," he said, frowning. His flow was broken. He groaned. He couldn't believe the last two lines were going to now trouble him. He looked at the boxes in dismay; it would take a lot of effort to find that one specific book.

Ansara, leaning over his writing as he set down the coffee, helped him out.

"For the beloved in your heart

And a song of praise upon your lips."

"Thank you! Again," he said, hastily writing the last two lines down and holding up the paper.

He still couldn't believe that his cook knew poetry, and that she could remember and recite it with such ease. She was about to leave the room, when he said, "Hold on a sec."

He came over from behind his desk and settled onto the sofa.

"Your coffee, sir," she said, moving his coffee over.

"Oh, please don't call me sir. I hate it." Martin took the cup of coffee from her hand.

"Sorry, I'll call you *Oga* then, if that's ok."

"No, don't. Call me Martin." He leaned toward her and whispered, "I hate it when the guys call me *Oga*. But hey, sometimes you've to give in, right?"

Ansara smiled nervously. But Martin was feeling exceptionally jovial. What he wanted now, and what had been lacking in his life in Nigeria, was a little less servitude and a lot more companionship.

"Tell me, Ansara, how did you come across Kahlil Gibran? I must say, I'm very intrigued."

"Oh, we had a library near our house. I went there when I was a child, and later I used to work there after school. Mainly cleaning the place. But I loved it. I could read all the books I wanted. And they let me sometimes take the books home too." She paused and continued. "And my father, he loved poetry."

"Wow, a fellow poetry enthusiast, right in the house! This must be my lucky day." Martin drew in a large sip of his coffee.

"I wouldn't say that, sir. I mean, Martin," she said. "We only had a few books, usually donated by families who moved out of Nigeria, and one of the books happened to be Gibran."

"Hmm," he said, sipping his coffee and wondering how he had not noticed her eloquence before.

"Well, and if you've only a few books, you read them again and again," explained Ansara.

"Ah yes, and not keep them unread in boxes, I suppose," he said, looking around.

"Oh, I didn't mean…"

"No, don't worry, I was just kidding," he said. "Sit down, please. You don't need to keep standing while we're talking."

Ansara hesitated. Martin moved over on the sofa, giving her ample space at the other end. "Come on, I need an audience as I recite this one. It's been bothering me the whole day, and finally…"

She sat down, on the edge first.

"Love has no other desire but to fulfil
itself.

But if you love and must needs have
desires, let these be your desires."

But then she seemed to settle in, smiling as if Martin's voice transported her back to a past that was happy, or a future that could have been.

"To melt and be like a running brook
that sings its melody to the night.

To know the pain of too much tenderness.

To be wounded by your own under-
standing of love;
  And to bleed willingly and joyfully.
  To wake at dawn with a winged heart
and give thanks for another day of loving;
  To rest at the noon hour and meditate
love's ecstasy;
  To return home at eventide with grati-
tude;
  And then to sleep with a prayer for the
beloved in your heart and a song of praise
upon your lips."

Martin beamed as he finished the last line with a flourish. With the comfort of a poem that had been read many times over, and the small pleasure of finally conquering something that had been elusive, despite dancing just at the tip of his tongue, a slow literary torture had ended.

"There, we have it," Martin said.

"Thank you," said Ansara, "for letting me listen. It was a lovely reading." She got up to leave.

"Hold on, I want to hear more about this library of yours," said Martin. He looked at her as she brushed back a strand of hair that had managed to break away from the tightly pulled lock. She hesitated, seeming to not know what to make of this unusual familiarity from an employer.

Despite himself, Martin could feel the familiar excitement

of attraction. He wanted to know how a well-read woman ended up working as a cook. He wanted to know when she had started reading poetry and which poets she liked. He wanted to know more about her, about anything related to her. Most of all, he wanted to hear her voice again and somehow not let her go back to the kitchen so quickly.

"It's ok, Ansara. I don't believe in hierarchies or stupid social conventions," he said. "We're just two people with a common interest. There's no harm in having a conversation, is there?"

"I suppose not." She glanced nervously at the door.

"Now tell me about this wonderful library."

"It was wonderful for me, but I bet if you saw it, you would think it was just a run-down old dump of tattered books people had thrown away or donated. But we did have the most eclectic collection, which no sane person would have put together on his own."

"That sounds awesome. You know, when I was a child, I used to go down to the library, close my eyes, and pick out a random book from the just returned books pile. And I would read whatever it was that I got. Looks like in your library, I could have just done that with any shelf."

Ansara laughed. "Yes, indeed. You could have."

She relaxed a little, leaning back.

When Martin went to bed that night, he couldn't remember how long they sat there, sharing long-forgotten stories, each laugh shared and each mutual interest discovered chipping away a little bit at the social barriers that separated them. He couldn't stop replaying the evening in his head: the conversation exciting in its unexpected ease, the camaraderie comforting in its simple warmth, and the curiosity fueled by the undertones of restrained attraction.

CHAPTER 10

It was the spring equinox in the northern hemisphere. The day when the earth was tilted neither away from nor toward the sun. When light and dark shared roughly equal parts of a day. A fleeting moment when inequality didn't seem like an inevitable reality.

Ansara stood in the library at Rose Villa, surveying the room. More than a month had passed since she arrived in Lagos. Over the days, Ansara and Martin formed a routine of sharing a conversation with coffee every evening. By the time Martin returned from work, most of the house staff would have left, their tasks for the day completed. Ayo and Ansara were the only ones who spent the night in the rooms adjacent to the house, their roles requiring them to be around the house even at night and early in the morning. Ayo, in his routine of dinner and drinks with his friends at the end of a day, was never around in the evenings, choosing to come home well past the time everyone else would have gone to bed.

Ansara noticed that Martin liked to take his coffee in the library (though, with the books still unpacked, it was more an office room with boxes) soon after he got home. She made sure there was a fresh pot ready for him. And lately, she also noticed that he was home on time most evenings, not staying late at work as often as he used to.

Though she still missed her mother and Femi very much, the days in Rose Villa were beginning to fall into a routine, and she had started looking forward to the evening coffee that she shared with Martin. In the beginning, she had found it a little odd that her employer wanted to talk to her, but Martin had a way of putting her at ease so utterly and completely that she often forgot that he was the employer and she the employee. He would ask her about her life and listen intently, leaning in as she answered, as if he couldn't bear to miss even a single word. He would share details about his life and work, and she felt that he listened to her opinions, often seeming surprised at her responses but always interested in what she had to say.

Ansara looked around. This room could look so much better, she thought. The empty shelves, the half-opened boxes, books strewn randomly around the room. She wanted to open them all up, look through his collection of books, and shelve them… Was she allowed to? Wasn't it her job? Was it? Would he be mad if she opened the boxes?

She couldn't imagine him mad at anything. Over the days, she had started a seeing a side of him which she felt sure he didn't share with everyone.

Just the other evening, she recalled fondly, he had asked her about her family.

"We were a big family," she had replied. "When I was a

child. Papa, Mama, and then the three of us—my two older brothers and me. Every evening, Papa would come back from work, and we would gather around him. The room was so small that if you sat close to the wall, there was a good chance you would get squeezed when someone else moved."

"That sounds lovely." His words were genuine and encouraging. He wanted to know more.

"Papa would tell us stories. Every night, he would have a new story. Papa, he read a lot. He learned to read late, and he always said he wanted to make up for lost time."

"Now I know where your love of books comes from," Martin had said.

"All he ever wanted was for us children to go to school, to read and learn. The neighbors all thought he was crazy to send his daughter to school when we barely had money to eat, but my father was adamant. He made sure I studied, and since I liked to read more than my brothers, he even took me to the libraries and bookshops with him."

"What about your mother, what was she like?" he had asked.

"Mama…is Mama. Love is all she knows. She loved us to bits. Like all mothers, I suppose," she said quietly as her eyes felt a prickle, thinking of Femi and her mother back home. She redirected the question back to him, not sure she would be able to keep the tears from her eyes if she talked more about her own family. "What about you, what was your mother like, and your family?"

"Fountain of love, I suppose. Like all mothers, as you

said. But also sad."

"Sad?" she had asked.

"Yes, she was often in a dark place, especially during the winters, which can be quite gloomy where I come from. They were hard on her. I didn't know what it was then, and medication and treatments were not as common then as they are now. I don't think my brothers realized... We're three, I'm the oldest." Martin had a faraway look, the last rays of the sunset highlighting his face as he turned to the window. Ansara had felt an urge to reach over and comfort him, but she stopped herself.

He must have been around twelve, he said, when her illness was at its darkest. They didn't call it an illness then, but she would withdraw, away from her children, away from life, or grow erratic, almost unrecognizable in her behavior. He described that winter, cold and biting, when thick snow blanketed the ground, when he first learned to recognize the signs. He learned, at the first indication, to take his brothers out of the house. They would head to the dunes with whatever food Martin could pack from the house. And they would stay out for hours, sometimes, hungry, often tired. He wouldn't let them return home until he knew the hours had passed, and that she would be calm again by the time they got back. His brothers complained sometimes, but he was certain that seeing their mother in that state of despair would be worse. And with his father at work, it was his job to spare his brothers that agony, and even more important, to protect their mother, during those awful hours, from the eyes of her younger sons.

Ansara had seen a glint of tears shining at the corner of his eyes when he spoke of that period in his life, but he had stood up, presumably to get a book, or to look away out of the window.

In such moments, it was hard for her to reconcile this image of Martin with the role she would have liked to peg him onto: her employer, the boss of the company that had claimed much from her life, an *oyibo*, and so many other ways that his life was different from her own life. Yet, sitting in that library, sharing details of their days, of their childhoods, she felt a connection with him that was hard to deny, and perhaps, at some level, she didn't want to deny.

He had wanted to hear more about her happy memories, and so he had turned the conversation gently back to her, and Ansara had recounted her memories of evenings with her family.

As her family huddled in their small room, Ansara's mother would finish her work in the kitchen and join the children listening to their father with his tales. Her mother would sing songs, folk songs, mostly, and some days they made so much noise the neighbors would look in through the windows and doors and eventually try to join them. At which point the group had to spill over outdoors, pull Papa's cot into the front yard, and the stories and songs would continue into the night, the sky and the stars looking down on all the joy and love.

She retold the jokes, the stories, and sang a few lines from their songs, and he had listened intently, smiling, nodding, lapping it all up with such a joy as if he could imagine himself there, with her, in the warm embrace of her family.

She smiled as she remembered how she and Martin had alternated telling their stories, finding an easy rhythm between sharing and listening, time always passing faster into the night than she would have liked.

As she looked around the room, she wanted to make it cozier. It was their space, and she could picture it so perfectly in her mind, the books on the shelves, the boxes cleared away, a lamp moved toward the corner. She felt confident that he would not be mad at her, least of all for unpacking the books. He talked so often about the books he had read, and she had seen him search the boxes so haphazardly and so often; the random books strewn all over were a good indication of that. Her curiosity got the better of her, in any case. She wanted to know all about him, especially the books he lugged around the world.

It took nearly three hours to unpack them all. She could have probably finished them a little earlier, but she was so fascinated by his collection—so many books, and so many topics that she found herself pausing to read a page or two, fingering the spines of some classics, gazing at the interesting book covers and titles—that she didn't hear Martin walking into the room.

"Ow," she said. "Oh…" she said as she dropped the book she was holding, a hardcover edition of the *Lord of the Rings*, on her foot.

Martin had walked into the room, startling her.

"I'm so sorry," she started, bending down to pick up the book.

"Oh wow!" said Martin as he looked around the books on the shelves. "Did you really——" He stopped when he saw blood on her foot. "Oh, that seemed to have landed pretty hard. Let me get you something for it."

He turned and left the room.

Ansara's leg smarted in pain; it was a sharp cut. It was still bleeding, not a lot but enough to darken the edge of the book. She hastily put the book back and hobbled toward the tissue box to clean up the drops.

"Oh sit, sit, don't walk." Martin helped her onto the sofa, despite her protests.

"Please, don't, it's just a small cut."

"Yes, and I would not want you staining the carpet, miss," he said, kneeling beside her, a wad of tissues in his hand sopping up the blood that was still coming from the wound. "Oh my! That book does seem to have done some damage," he said, looking at the offending tome.

"It's the power of the ring," she couldn't help but remark.

"Ah, my precious," Martin retorted, "can you now please sit still while I bandage this up?"

Ansara sat still, unsure of what else to do, but when his hands grazed her ankle, the white of the tissues turning red as he pressed them gently against her skin, she held her breath. She was glad he didn't look up, or she was sure he would notice the blush, even against her dark skin. His fingers felt warm to the touch, and she could smell his cologne, faint at the end of the day but still distinctly there, and she felt a tingle down her spine.

She tried to jerk her foot away, unsure what to make of this sudden sensation that she had not felt for a very long time.

"Hold on, hold on," said Martin, "I'm not done yet."

"I feel fine. It's just a small cut."

"Well, surprisingly, it's not. Who knew books could cut so deep?" He stood and picked up the book. "But I guess this is a big one."

She tried to stand up, but he gently pushed her back down. "Sit down for a bit, you don't look so well."

She tried to breathe as normally as she could, hoping he wouldn't notice anything amiss. If he did, he didn't show it, his face as nonchalant as always.

Thankfully, he just smiled at her as he left the room again, saying, "You'll be fine. But let me get our coffee today. Don't move till I'm back."

She sat on the edge of the sofa, her hand reaching down to the bandage he had just wrapped around her right foot. She looked at the book on the desk nearby; she must have caught the sharp corner of the fat hardcover. It still hurt, but the bleeding had stopped, and she was sure that it wasn't as big a deal as Martin had made it out to be. His care and concern, though, seemed genuine.

She chided herself for thinking about Martin as anything

more than an employer. A kind and humane one, but an employer nevertheless.

She sighed. It was hard for her to deny that she had come to look forward to and enjoy their evening chats as much as he seemed to. Unless she was completely wrong with her instincts, she knew that Martin's actions were not just passing kindness toward an employee, but whether it was just camaraderie to get rid of the loneliness of staying in a foreign country all by himself or something more, she couldn't be sure. Or rather, she didn't dare to be sure.

He was back soon, handing her the coffee as if it was the most natural thing in the world to do.

"I'm so sorry. I hope you don't mind that I unpacked the books. I didn't know—"

"Are you kidding me? Finally, I can read what I want to. Thank you for putting them, and me, out of our misery. These books deserved to be freed from the boxes," said Martin. "Well, maybe not this one," he said, wagging his finger at the thick *Lord of the Rings* that had fallen on her foot.

She laughed, he laughed louder. And they settled into another evening of conversation, and she pushed any doubts she had, at least temporarily, far from her mind.

CHAPTER 11

It was Saturday. It irked Ayo that he was still at Rose Villa. Even though he sometimes preferred to stay in the servants' quarters of the villa rather than go back to his one-room apartment on weekends, it felt different when he had been asked to stay. Martin had asked him to get the garden cleared up for spring. Somehow, the *oyibos* never got it into their heads, down here close to the equator, that the end of winter was just an arbitrary day in the calendar, and any day to clean the garden was as good as any other.

Ayo believed that Raphael should do it all, but Martin thought he would need help. Two extra men had been hired for the day to help Raphael with the heavy lifting, and Ayo had to supervise them.

He was in the shade of the large mango tree, shouting orders at the men who were removing the topsoil. Sweat kept reappearing on every part of his body, even as he wiped it off with his towel. His white singlet was muddied with specks of dirt flying from the workers' pickaxes. This was definitely not his idea of a weekend. He would need to ask Martin for an additional day off.

The gate opened. He saw Ben speaking with a frail old

woman dressed in tattered clothes. It annoyed Ayo that beggars felt entitled to walk into people's houses and ask for food. It annoyed Ayo even more when Martin indulged them. He never seemed to understand that the only way to get rid of them was to deny them food, consistently. Ayo knew that some of the neighbors even unleashed their dogs on people who came asking for food.

Ben shouted to Ayo, "Ayo, she's here to see you. Your cousin, she says. Shall I let her in?"

Ayo peered into the sunlight, holding up his hand to shade his eyes. He could not quite make out who it was. He had severed all familial ties quite some time ago, and he could not think of anyone who would come looking for him. He was just about to ask Ben to turn her away when she cried out.

"Ayo, it's Mgbeke. Petrol's wife." Her voice was hoarse, as if her throat had been squeezed dry from lack of water or from hours of crying.

Ayo's heart skipped a beat. *Petrol.* He had not heard of him or from him since leaving him at a house in Victoria Island, to clear off the blood of a murder from the grounds and to sell a property illegally. But he was eternally grateful for the one good deed anyone had ever done to him.

He waved to Ben to let her in.

"Mama, it's good to see you." He had met Mgbeke a few times before; she was probably close in age to his own mother. "Come in."

Ayo led her through the open courtyard to his room in the servants' quarters and brought her some water to drink. He let her sit on the cot, while he sat at the other end.

She finished the water in the glass in one long gulp, set the glass down, and started to sob uncontrollably.

"Petrol is in hospital... They shot... They stole all his money. He will die if..." She was struggling to get the words out. After a while, Ayo could fathom that one of Petrol's many enemies had shot him and had somehow managed to get hold of all their savings. And now that the formidable Petrol was incapacitated, none of his old friends wanted to have anything to do with him, mostly because they were scared of the man who had taken over Petrol's stronghold in the area. Petrol would die if Mgbeke could not get enough money to pay for the treatments at the hospital.

Ayo watched as she sobbed helplessly. As grateful as he might feel toward Petrol for the opportunities that he had given him, parting with money was not something Ayo was willing to do. If there was anything that annoyed Ayo more than unnecessary kindness, it was begging for that unnecessary kindness. Nothing had come to him because he begged for it, and he could never understand why so many people around him expected kindness as if it were a birthright.

"I'll see what I can do. Money is tight around here. Even though I work in this nice place, I don't have much of my own."

"Ayo, I've no one else to turn to. Please. You've to help us. Petrol always thought of you as his own son."

"Yes, yes, I'll do whatever I can."

"Thank you. Thank you, Ayo. I am so grateful. I'll come by in a few days, the hospital won't keep him much longer if I don't pay." Mgbeke hugged Ayo.

"Give my best to Petrol," Ayo said warmly. *The woman is naïve*, he thought. *She really thinks I would hand over money just like that.*

He stood up abruptly. "I've to get back to work now."

Mgbeke wiped her eyes, thanked Ayo again, and walked toward the door. Just as she was about to leave, she turned around and said, "Ayo. You should visit your mother. She could really use your help."

"My mother? Why would I visit her? It's not that she ever needs my help. Or really cares." Even as he said it, Ayo knew it was not entirely true. His mother may not have been the most affectionate, but somewhere at the back of his mind, he had always thought that she cared about him. Never quite sure whether it was just a product of his wishful imagination or a subconscious acceptance of a masked reality, he had decided that it was just a delusion.

"Oh, didn't you know? Since she lost her leg, she lost her home too. And now she lives in the streets."

"She lost her leg?"

"Yes, no one knows how. Your mother… You know her, she isn't exactly the kind to confide in others."

Ayo grunted impatiently.

"They say she got an infection and when she couldn't get it

treated, she chopped off her leg herself." She looked at Ayo's face and seemed to decide that it was best to spare him the details. "I should go. But she'll be happy if you visit her, I'm sure."

Ayo walked her out to the gate. He watched her walk slowly along the crowded road, then he turned back and motioned to Ben, who came running. "Ben, if you see that woman here again, don't let her in. Just tell her I'm not around."

Ben looked surprised. "Oh, I thought she was your family."

"No, she's not. Just another blood-sucking leech who wants money. She'll come back, but remember to not let her in."

Ayo walked back along the driveway. He could see the workers taking a break under the shade. Without supervision, he knew they would laze off and just drag the work on to another day. But he was too preoccupied with his own thoughts to stop and shout at them. He went back to his room and lay on the cot.

Ayo could not remember his father. From the stories he had heard from his mother, his father left them when Ayo was just a little toddler. He had gone to live with another woman, and according to his mother, that was a good thing, for he was nothing but a good-for-nothing alcoholic. Ayo did not need to have met his father to imagine him; half the men in the shantytown he lived in fit that description.

But his mother, Ayo smiled grimly, was an altogether different story. It would have been difficult to find another quite like her in that shantytown, or probably in the whole of Lagos. A large woman, Ayo's mother had an imposing presence. She had a voice as loud as the church bells, and when she wanted to make herself heard, there was nothing anyone could do about it. There was little she cared about, or so it seemed to Ayo in those days. She left for work in the morning, doing hard labor in the bus depot close to where they lived. She worked with the men, doing as much or sometimes even more than them, because it paid more than a woman laborer's wages.

Ayo had been ashamed of her when he was a boy, for all the boys used to tease him that his mother was a man. He hated her for doing man's work; he hated her for her callous ways and for walking and talking like a man, instead of being a woman in the family. But looking back, he felt a hint of gratefulness; even in that shanty colony, he was more or less safe. No one really wanted to attack or rob their house, and she did put food on the table at least every other day.

Chopped off her own leg... The words kept coming back to Ayo. Whatever would possess someone to do something like that? Even for someone like his mother, that seemed a little extreme.

He left his room and went back outside. He hurled some abuse at the workers. He didn't care whether they were working or lazing around; shouting at them would only make them work faster. And for now, all he wanted to do was to get out of there and find something to distract him.

As he looked toward the gate, he cursed Mgbeke for opening the gate to a past which he had firmly closed shut when he left his shantytown sixteen years ago. He had not gone back even once.

Chopped off her own leg.
Lost her home.
Not well.

In a few hours, Ayo would get out of Rose Villa and start his weekend. He would head out for the night and visit bar after bar with Prince and his other friends, and their coterie of cronies and women. The alcohol would numb his thoughts for a bit, but not for long. He would drink more and then some more, all in a vain attempt to keep away the images from the past that haunted him.

CHAPTER 12

It was nearly the end of June. Rains had been sparse that month as per the weather predictions, but different from traditional climate patterns. Martin came home earlier than usual, happy to have a longer evening with Ansara. It had fast become his favorite part of the day.

As was often the case in their conversations, they talked about books, and Ansara mentioned Ngozi and her local library, and he said, "Let's go there." It had been a good day at work, and Martin was in a jovial mood. He thought he could make Ansara's day too by visiting her favorite place that she talked about often.

"Where?" Ansara asked.

"To your library?"

Ansara looked surprised.

"It'll be fun. I'd love to see this eclectic place you always talk about," said Martin, "and I can ask Mohammed to drive us. It's still early."

"To Port Harcourt, you want to drive there?"

"Port Harcourt? Isn't the library in Lagos?"

Ansara seemed confused and didn't reply.

"I thought it'd make you happy, but if you don't want to,

that's ok," said Martin.

"You really thought I was from Lagos?" she asked, her words slower and softer than usual.

"I guess, I…" He didn't really have a good answer. Why had he assumed she was from Lagos? He realized he had just not given it much thought.

"Doesn't matter, I appreciate the gesture," said Ansara. "The library no longer exists. But if it was there, and if we could have driven there, it would have made me happy."

Martin was silent. Sipping the coffee slowly, feeling the warmth of the cup in his palms, he thought back over the last few months when he thought he had gotten to know Ansara. From his initial surprise at her interest in poetry, she had continued to impress him with her quiet and sensible wisdom. Of course, he found her beautiful and attractive in a way he had never felt before, but it wasn't just that.

He had often come back home frustrated over something or other at work, and she would listen, and with a few words, dissipate his tension and calm him down. And he enjoyed hearing about her life; as poor as it may have been, her stories were full of joy and familial love. How had he missed this important detail, which seemed to bother her so much? Had he never bothered to ask more about her, taking perhaps her companionship for granted?

"Are you ok, Martin?" asked Ansara. "You seemed very happy when you came in, and now…"

"No, no," he replied hurriedly. "All good. Yes, happy."

Ansara had a way about her, a generosity in conversation, a knack for listening, that put Martin at ease. That made him look forward to their chats, where perhaps he talked more than he listened.

Before he knew it, he was sharing with her about his workday: how the protests had finally slowed down, how everyone had doubted his initial decision on the need to fire people, how they had insisted it would slow production, but then, now, finally, it had all turned out exactly as he had predicted. Production was fine, protesters had disappeared, and people were back to work. He had just received a congratulatory email from Teun Bergman, the chief himself.

"Fired?" asked Ansara, her voice quivering. "You fired people to stop the protests?"

"Well, not—" Martin stopped mid-sentence. Ansara had an expression on her face that he had never seen before. A mix of shock, sadness and...anger? He couldn't quite tell. "What is it, Ansara? Did I say something wrong?"

Ansara took a deep breath. "Wrong?" Her voice had a slight tremor as she asked him, "How can you ask me that? I lost my job...because of you. You made the decision to fire me. And I'm here, working, far from my family, making you food and coffee, and talking to you, and all the while..."

It was Martin's turn to look shocked. He didn't quite know how to respond.

"No, it's not wrong. You're not wrong," said Ansara,

beginning to leave the room, "I'm wrong. I don't know what I was thinking. How didn't I see it?"

"Ansara, I didn't fire you," said Martin. "How could I have… Wait. I honestly didn't know." But she had left the room before he could complete the sentence.

Martin tried to go after her into the kitchen, but she wasn't there. He came back to the library, stunned that Ansara was one of the people who had been fired from the refinery. How did someone from there end up in Lagos as a cook in his household? He remembered the day Ayo had brought her in; perhaps he had met her in Port Harcourt. He might have even mentioned she worked at the refinery, but Martin had been too distracted to notice.

He tried to see the situation through Ansara's eyes, but that was painful. Seeing it through her eyes would mean seeing it through the eyes of every single one of the men and women who had lost their jobs because of his one decision. A decision that had earned him accolades just that evening.

Erika Smith arrived in Lagos on a Tuesday.

Martin could hear voices from inside his house when he got back from work. Multiple voices. Seemed like the television was on. *Strange*, Martin thought. *Ansara never watches TV at this time and Ayo is not in either.* He turned the key in his lock and entered his house silently, as if almost expecting someone to spring upon him.

"Erika! Is it really you?"

A tall blonde woman was languishing on his sofa, her legs stretched out, one hand on the remote control and the other dipped into a bag of potato chips. A half-empty bottle of beer sat on the floor by the sofa.

"Finally, you're home!" Erika stood up, pulled him close, kissed him thrice on his cheeks, pulled away, and looked at him. "You look good, van Oost! And still working too hard, I see."

"What a surprise! What're you doing here?"

"Oh, I was just in the 'hood. Can't a girl drop by an old friend's place?"

"In the 'hood? You live a thousand miles away."

"Not anymore. As of last month, I live nowhere. The world is my home, and my 'hood is wherever I am at the moment." She spread out her arms and twirled around. "For this week, it's here, good ol' filthy, dangerous Lagos."

"What does that even mean?"

"It means, my dear inquisitor, that I've quit the corporate rat race and am traveling the world. I spent the first two weeks in the south of Africa, last week in the Niger Delta, a week here in Lagos, and then I'm off again. Most likely Nigeria for the next few weeks at least, depending."

"Depending?" Martin laughed. Erika had always been one of the impulsive kinds, the type who would take a year off on a whim, travel the world with no concrete plans.

At almost six feet, with thick golden hair that flowed freely to her shoulders and twinkling eyes that always seemed like they were up to some mischief, Erika was blessed with an assured self-confidence that either captivated or threatened most people. When she spoke, she fixed her gaze firmly on the focus of her attention, no matter who he or she was, making them slightly disconcerted but definitely elated. And just when they least expected it, she would break into an easy beautiful smile so full of life that the listener felt completely at ease. There seemed to be no one and nothing that could rock her world. She was to be envied and she knew it.

"I was thinking we go out tonight. What do you say, sailor?" she asked.

Martin had just about managed to shake off all the many invitations to parties that seemed to come his way because of his job. Lagos had a vibrant nightlife, but it interested him far less than it would have a few years ago. And he had come to enjoy his quieter evenings at home. But an occasional night out, he still enjoyed. Besides, Erika would not let him be if she did not get to check out the clubs and bars. He hesitated just a moment before replying, "Well, yes, sure. Why not? Let me change out of this and have a shower. I'll get you some real food, maybe?" he said.

"Oh, don't bother. I already met your cook. We chatted. I'll ask her if I need anything. For now, I'm good." She lifted the bag of potato chips toward Martin and slid back onto the sofa. "Hurry back though. We've a lot to catch up."

Martin took one last look at her and headed to his room, baffled by his unexpected visitor.

They headed out to Bacchus, one of the fanciest clubs in Lagos. It was frequented by the well-heeled and it boasted adequate security measures—a necessary criterion to ensure safety in the dark nights of the city. A live band was belting out the latest chart-toppers. Dim lights and smoke made the room look smaller and cozier than it was.

"Martin, aren't you going to dance?" Erika tried to pull him off his bar stool, swaying her hips in tandem with the fast music.

"No, I'm fine here. It's too loud out there."

He looked at the crowded dance floor, packed with men and women, young and old, all eager to forget their day's troubles in a dancing frenzy. They danced, oblivious to their surroundings, gyrating together in tune to the music, like a giant snake writhing to digest the ample prey it had just devoured. It was hard to tell if they lacked dancing skills, or if the blame lay with the alcohol they had consumed. Martin was not about to be pulled into the middle of it, not even by someone as persuasive as Erika.

"I'll sit here with you then." Erika pulled a bar stool next to his and ordered a gin and tonic. "Wow, man! You've changed a lot since the last time we met, and that was less than a year ago, wasn't it?"

"Just because I'm not dancing?"

"Yes, that, and because there aren't like twenty women around you here."

Martin smiled as he sipped on his beer.

"Let's get out. It's stuffy in here." Erika pulled on his arm again, and this time, he complied.

The fresh air outside the club was a welcome relief. The latest models of sports cars lined the parking lots just outside. Men in suits stood chatting with women whose clothes left little to the imagination. Two bouncers stood guarding the doors, like gargoyles at the entrance to a church.

Martin and Erika sat on the curb, just a bit away from the main door.

"A cigarette?" she offered.

"No, thanks. I quit."

Martin watched as Erika lit up, surprised that he did not feel even the slightest longing, either for the smoke or for the woman beside him. There had been a time when he was addicted to both, but that felt like a lifetime ago.

It was more than five years since his relationship with Erika ended. Erika had been livid the day they broke up. It was his birthday. He remembered not showing up for the party even though he knew she had gone to extraordinary lengths to plan a special evening for him. There was something urgent at work, he had told her, but they both knew that was just an excuse. Erika had accused him of being cold and callous. He had left her alone with their friends the entire evening, knowing well the social and emotional hurt it would cause her. She had packed her bags, slowly, expecting him to stop her leaving, but he had just watched her, neither disagreeing with her accusations nor trying to salvage their relationship.

"Aren't you going to ask me why I quit my job?" Erika asked now, turning her head slightly away from him to blow smoke into the night air. "I know you want to say something. Call me crazy, perhaps?"

"No, I don't think you're crazy. It's just very you. I think more people should be like that. Take their chances and figure out what they want in life."

"Hmm…that's not the response I expected. The ever-planned, super-ambitious Martin seems to be relaxing a bit." Erika playfully jabbed a finger into his side and continued. "So, have you figured out what you want?"

"What makes you think I hadn't already?"

Erika raised her eyebrows. "I know you like others to think you've it all figured out. But come on, van Oost, I know you better than most."

Martin smiled. "I'm working on it. We'll get there, slowly, eventually."

"You know what they say: A single man in possession of a good fortune must be in want of a wife."

"Really? Who says that?"

"Oh, it's a universally acknowledged truth." Erika leaned back on her arms, looking at the stars in the sky.

"*Pride and Prejudice*, huh? That's what you got for me?"

"Well, what's true is true." Erika smiled. Her blue eyes sparkled, the revolving lights from the glitzy sign above the club's entrance making them shimmer like stars in the sky.

"You look beautiful tonight," Martin said.

"I know." Her eyes lingered on him for a moment. "But I'm not the one you're looking for, am I?"

"No." Martin shook his head. "But we were good together, weren't we?"

"Good while it lasted," said Erika. "You're a good man, van Oost. You'll find her, the perfect woman, just for you."

Martin wondered if he had ever loved Erika. They had been together for a few years, meeting for the first time on their first day at CBX Corp. Erika was the only woman in their cohort, and Martin considered whether it might have been a sense of competitiveness that made him chase her, the sweet victory over his peers.

They had naturally navigated to each other at first because they were both good looking and stood apart in a world of corporate clones. The outsider status that they both shared— Erika because she was the rare woman in a male-dominated industry, and Martin because he had entered the corridors of power and money without family wealth or connections —had kept them close. They had had a good relationship for a while, but Erika wanted more out of the relationship than he had been willing to give.

Being hired on his own merits, rather than because of his background, should have made him more proud, more secure, but oddly it made him feel out of place at CBX Corp, and deeply insecure. As if they would realize their mistake sooner rather than later.

"Do you remember why we broke up, Martin?" Erika asked him.

"Because I didn't show up for my party," he said, his tone more playful than flippant.

"You were never there, Martin," she said. "At first, I thought you were running away from something. You never liked to talk about your past, and then when I got to know you a little better, I thought you were running toward something. A goal, an ambition. But it wasn't that either. You were just running. Running as if you were too afraid to stop."

Martin didn't reply. Even after he had stopped loving her, though he wasn't sure it was love in the first place, he had admired her. For sure, as a peer and a colleague, but more importantly as someone whose strength of convictions he could never manage to muster for himself. Erika had been alone and scared, just like he had been, but the difference with her, he thought, was that she was not afraid to own the difference. Martin had to admit that there were times in their relationship when that boldness had alarmed him.

Over time, as they continued to work together, they had become friends, prioritizing a platonic relationship over the acrimony of the breakup. Martin couldn't quite remember how and when that had happened. He had felt consumed by guilt; he knew she deserved better than how he had treated her. It took him a while, but he persisted with his apologies. He didn't want a romantic relationship with her, but if he was honest with himself, she was one of the few people that he actually liked at an otherwise lonely workplace. Salvaging their friendship had been his atonement, and he was grateful that she had been willing to give him another chance.

"I hope that one day you see that you're a wonderful human being, just as you are, Martin," she said, "and stop trying to be somebody else."

"It's getting better," said Martin truthfully. He looked around them. The night was warm and humid. Empty bottles and beer cans littered the ground, the lights were more garish than glamorous, the bouncers at the gate were alert as if trouble was the norm not the exception. It was Lagos, no mistaking that, a city in a country that most people would rather get out of than travel in. Yet, Martin, after travelling all over the world, had for the first time felt the urge to stay in one place. In a life that had become one blur of whirring motion, for once, he didn't want to move on.

Since Erika, he'd had many one-night stands and short flings in many cities, the constant travel a good excuse for not committing to anything longer or more meaningful. But the truth was that he had not felt an intensity of passion until…

Martin sighed, remembering his fight with Ansara the previous day. He hadn't had a chance to speak with her privately since then, and now with Erika around, it would need to wait.

"Oh, what's with the long sigh?" Erika stubbed out her cigarette on the concrete curb and said, "Come on, let's go back in."

Martin let her walk in front, leading the way back to the smoky club.

The next few days passed by with late nights and long chats. And work, as usual. Even though Martin would have liked to talk to Ansara, it was hard to find a moment alone with her.

When Martin woke up on Friday, later than usual, Erika was at breakfast, dressed and packed. He smiled. Considering they had gone to bed less than four hours before, it was no mean feat to look fresh and poised the next day.

"Good morning, sleepyhead. Did you sleep well?"

"Yes, I did, thanks. You're leaving?"

"Yeah. Mohammad, your driver, he hooked me up with some trips to a shrine and then a whole itinerary of places to visit in Lagos. You want to come with?"

"No, all I need is loads of coffee and to get to work. My head hurts."

"It's Friday, take the day off. Join me." said Erika. "Here, there's still some coffee left. Oh, wait, sorry, it's empty."

Martin rose to go to the kitchen for coffee at the same time Ansara walked in with a fresh pot.

"Thank you!" he said as he walked over to take the pot from her hands, their eyes locking for a brief moment. Their interactions had been awkward the last few days, what with Erika around the house and their usual rhythms disrupted. Their last evening chat over coffee had been on Monday, and that had taken an unexpected turn that still bothered Martin.

Martin wanted to say something, but his head was still buzzing and no words came out.

"Can I get you anything else?" Ansara asked both Erika and Martin.

"No, no," Martin replied, "we can get it ourselves."

"Well," Erika said after Ansara left the room, "I could have had another round of croissants."

"Oh! I'll go get them. Wait, there are still croissants here."

"Oh, sit down, van Oost," said Erika. "I was just…I knew it! Clearly, now everything makes sense."

"Whatever do you mean?"

"Whatever do I mean? Martin, you're gonna play coy? With me?"

Martin stared at her, wishing he'd had a chance to finish his coffee before being pulled into the conversation he knew was coming.

"There's clearly something going on here, man," said Erika, glancing over at the kitchen door, "and I have to say, she's quite a looker!"

Martin felt hot all over, and an incredible urge to tell Erika to shut up. That she had got it all wrong. Erika leaned over. "You really like her. This is not a—"

"Erika, I don't know. I don't know, okay?" he said. "It's all very complicated."

Erika grinned. "Good for you, man!" She stuffed a mini croissant into her mouth, leaving Martin to wonder how someone so slender managed to eat so much. He stared at her. If there was a tinge of jealousy in her tone, she was quick at hiding it.

"Anyway, it's really not what you think. Nothing's happened. I swear," he said.

"I believe you, sure. I'm happy for you. Really. Very happy." Erika then shrugged. "Just don't screw it up."

Martin wanted to believe that he had changed, that he was mature enough to find room in his life not just for his ambitions but for someone else. But so far, he was not sure he was doing any better with Ansara than he had with Erika.

"I won't screw it up," replied Martin. "Well, I hope I won't. But it's not that simple."

"Well, Martin, here's something else I know—figured out recently, I suppose. Life is really not that complicated, it's just us humans who like to make it so."

Martin pulled a face at her.

"No, really, I mean it. I think she's gorgeous, and seems very…how do I put this…refined? Anyway, what I mean to say is, I like her. If you like her, dude, do something about it," said Erika, finishing off her croissant with a flourish.

Martin was grateful. He had been on edge the last few days, Erika's arrival not just keeping him away from Ansara but dredging up reminders of his old patterns. He hated to admit it, but Erika was one of the few people in the world who had managed to see beneath his façade, and it felt good to have her acknowledge and accept his feelings for Ansara, which he had been reluctant to articulate even to himself.

"And with that wisdom imparted, it's time for me to leave," said Erika, getting up.

"Where're you off to?" asked Martin.

"A trip to the shrine first, like I said, and then I want to go see the Slave Market in Badagry."

"Badagry? That's far, outside of Lagos, and not really safe, is it?" said Martin. "It's known for its rowdy Area Boys, one of the worst areas. Hold on, let me ask Ayo to go with you. It's good to have a local with you, and if you need to wiggle your way out of situations in Nigeria, there's no one like Ayo."

"The dude at the front?"

"No, that's Mohammed. Let me check if Ayo's in yet."

"Can't you come?" she asked.

"No, I wish. I'm already booked to Port Harcourt on an evening flight," he said. "Ayo is too, but I'll ask him to accompany you instead."

Even as Erika protested, Martin insisted. "Sit down. Eat more. I'm sure you'd like that." It was her turn to pull a face at him, their running joke that she could out-eat him on any day or meal.

She, nevertheless, decided to take up Martin's offer to send her with a local chaperone.

"Ayo's on his way here, another ten minutes or so, he says. Make it twenty maybe," said Martin, coming back to the table. "Trust me, you do not want to face the Area Boys of Lagos on your own."

"Thanks, Martin," said Erika, "but really, you needn't worry. Badagry is one of the safer plans in my itinerary."

"What else have you got planned?" asked Martin, his

concern unmistakable.

"Oh, don't look so worried," said Erika, "I'll be fine."

"No, really, Erika, where all are you off to? At least, tell me your plans here in Nigeria."

"After Lagos, I head off to Epebu. I'm meeting a professor there, a fisheries expert, I'm told. He's agreed to show me around the rivers and streams of Niger Delta. And then an old friend, who now works for Amnesty International there, has agreed to let me join him for a week or so. That's all I've planned for now, van Oost, one step at a time."

"You're walking into danger," said Martin. "Straight up. You realize that, don't you?"

Erika nodded. "When we joined the company, Martin, remember that was, what, eight years ago? Feels ages since then. Do you remember how they made it sound like we were so fortunate? Jobs that would set us up for life, careers that would be the envy of our friends, yada yada. I don't know. Now looking back, it all looks so…how do I put it? Farcical?"

Martin was silent.

"I mean, I don't want to judge. You're still going strong. Who am I to judge? I've had my share of profiting from the job and the oil industry, not just the years I worked, but my family's wealth too. But then, something changes within you. The job changes you, you know. It was good for a while, I even enjoyed it, but that doesn't mean I've to continue forever, do I? That I've to keep my eyes shut to what we really do?"

"So your sabbatical now, this is not a…"

"A year of partying and lying around on beaches?" laughed Erika. "No."

Martin looked at her with more than a hint of admiration. Erika was the only heir to an old wealthy family in the south of Holland, and it would have been easy for her to choose a life of leisure, free of all concerns. But then, he thought, she never was one to choose the easy path.

"What are you staring at, van Oost?"

"Just thinking," said Martin, "that you've a way of choosing the hard route."

"Ha, that one," she said. "I've heard that before."

They were silent for a bit.

Ayo was taking longer than he said, but that was not unusual.

"You know, Martin, I don't remember my mother," said Erika.

Martin nodded. It was public knowledge, given how famous Erika's family was, how her mother had left her father for another man when Erika was very young. Erika didn't talk about it much, but during the time they'd been together, Martin had come to see up close how deeply it had affected her. Her father had not remarried and had provided for her every material need, but he was never around, and she was raised by hired help and extended family.

"I used to, I'm told, call my nannies Mama," said Erika, a faraway look on her face. "My father hated it. Plus, it was always a rotating cast of helpers, constantly changing. Until one day, one of them, I don't remember who, took me out to the dunes. I remember lying down there on the flat lands, among the shrubs, staring at the sky, and she told me that Earth was my mother. She—Earth—was always there, always looking out for me, always with me, the ground under my feet, the sky above my head, all of it. Giving me all the comfort and love I need." Erika paused before continuing. "And I believed it. I felt so happy. I had a mother, and she had not left me. She was always with me."

Martin didn't know what to say. He reached out to take her hand, but she brushed it aside.

"And now, my friend," Erika said, coming back to her bubbling energetic self, "my mother is sick. We—you, me, the company, humans, all of us—have asked so much of her. And she is sick. Dying. And if I don't take care of her, if we don't stop the plunder and start protecting, preserving nature, who will? Huh?"

"It's admirable, Erika," said Martin, "I'll give you that."

"Not admirable, Martin. Necessary. Critical."

"So what's all this travel to do with it?"

"Research," she said. "My father has agreed to fund a nonprofit if I come back with a plan I can convince him of. I think in his old age he's going a little soft. In any case, if he doesn't, I'll have access to my own funds when I turn thirty soon. I hope to do some good."

"For your mother."

"Yes, for my mother—" She paused and corrected herself. "Our mother."

Before Martin could respond, Ayo walked in, "So so sorry.

Go-slow. Traffic, roads were so busy."

Ayo picked up her bags, and Erika was ready to leave.

"You've changed, Erika," said Martin, wishing her safe travels, insisting that she call him at the slightest hint of trouble. "I'm so proud of you," he added.

"You can too, van Oost. Change, that is. I've always liked you, but I think I'll like the new you even more," she said with a twinkle in her eye and a nod toward the kitchen.

After seeing off Erika with Ayo, Martin came back to the breakfast table. He couldn't shake off what Erika had observed about him and Ansara. And her exhortation to not screw it up. He was afraid that perhaps he already had.

Ansara was nowhere to be seen, and he was left alone to finish his breakfast. Even when he took his plate and cup to the kitchen, she wasn't there. He wanted to see her before he left for work, but it was getting late.

As he walked out of the house, an idea came to him. One that he thought would be the perfect way to show her that he cared about her. And to admit, at least to himself, that she had started to mean more to him than he had let himself believe.

CHAPTER 13

Ansara stepped into Martin's bedroom. The room was vast; it could probably fit five double beds and still have space to spare. Yet it contained just one king-size bed, a desk and a chair, and two chests of drawers, all lined against the walls as if afraid to break the monotony of space after empty space. A tall rectangular mirror on the wall at the far end of the room seemed to collude with the greed of the never-ending space, making the room look even bigger than it really was.

She looked around. Things were strewn all over the floor. Martin was a messy man. Discarded clothing; books opened and turned upside down to mark the last unread page; a laptop charger plugged in on one end to a socket on the wall, its other end trailing to the middle of the room almost like a snake that had had its head chopped off; and a mouse carelessly abandoned next to the charger. The cluttered floor almost seemed to be a desperate attempt to fill the empty space.

It was Raphael's job to clean the house, but he did little more than sweeping and mopping, never tidying up the tabletops or rearranging anything. Ansara had thought a few times about bringing it up with him, but he always seemed to be overworked, what with the gardening and the ad-hoc jobs Ayo found for him.

Besides, it didn't take her much time to cook, and she was happy to have something else to do with her time.

Ansara walked methodically from one end of the room to the other, carrying the laundry bin in her hand and putting the crumpled clothes into it. Then she tore off a page from last week's newspaper which was still on the desk, deftly shred it into small pieces, and dumped the rest of the paper into the trash can. She zigzagged across the room, closing the books after inserting strips of paper into the right places to mark the last-read page, and returned them all to a neat pile on the desk. She pulled the charger from the socket, folded it up along with the mouse into one tidy lump of wires, and left it by the wall.

Ansara picked up the t-shirt lying next to the bed. She hesitated for a moment, overcome with a desire to take a whiff of the faint odor that seemed to still linger on it. She had always been curious about Martin's cologne whenever he came close to her, although never close enough to quite figure out what it was, except the one time he bandaged her bleeding foot, but she had been too nervous then. He always kept a gentlemanly distance, painfully polite and kind.

Except perhaps one evening, while they were having coffee and chatting, he had moved closer to her, almost imperceptibly. Perhaps instinctively. She had noticed and moved away, unsure of what it meant. He had gone on with the conversation as if nothing had happened.

She sat down on the edge of the bed with the t-shirt still in her hand. She sighed. The week had been a difficult one.

She had missed her evenings with Martin. With Erika in town, he had been out most days, and their last conversation on Monday had rattled her.

Of course she knew that Martin had a senior role at the refinery. The same refinery where her father had died, and which, through their denial of responsibility for the death, had made an activist out of her dear brother. But she had never quite put Martin as responsible for any of it. After all, he had moved to Nigeria just a few months back, and he had seemed so kind and generous and…

How stupid she was! Seeing him that week with Erika had bothered her in a way that she didn't want to fully acknowledge. Erika was tall, blonde, and an *oyibo*. She was beautiful too, exactly the kind of woman Martin would want to be with. Had she really gone and started thinking of Martin as anything other than an employer who barely noticed her? He didn't even know she was from Port Harcourt, or that she had worked at his company's refinery! Granted, she had never talked about it directly with him, but she just assumed he would know. And now, it seemed that he had been the direct cause of her losing her job.

How could she reconcile that with the person she thought she had come to know in their evenings together? The one who listened to her, asked her opinions, saw her in a way that no one had for a very long time. The one who made her lie awake at night, wondering—

She shook herself out of her thoughts. *Stop, stop your fantasies, have you not learned already the price of such feelings?* she asked herself. *You've a job to do and you had better get on with it.* She stood up purposefully and deposited the t-shirt in the laundry bin. She finished up the rest of the cleaning and closed the door behind her, just as she heard the phone ringing downstairs from the hallway.

She ran downstairs, getting to the phone just in time to pick it up by the last ring.

"Hello," she said.

"Are you ok? You sound out of breath." Martin's voice was concerned.

She was a little shaken to respond.

"Ansara?"

"Yes, sorry, I was just upstairs," she said. "Is everything alright?" Martin rarely called the house during the workday. And the concern in his voice seemed genuine.

"Yes, everything is alright," said Martin. "In fact, more than alright."

She sensed the hesitation in his voice. It struck her that this was the first time she had ever heard his voice over the phone.

"I've a surprise for you," he said, "if you want it, I mean."

"Surprise?"

"Yes," he said. "I got you tickets. To Port Harcourt. For the weekend. You can go see your family."

Ansara didn't know what to say. She wasn't sure she heard him right.

"Ansara, you there? I mean, only if you want to go, of course."

"Yes, y-yes, but," she stammered, "isn't it expensive? And I've work here. Can I go just for the weekend?"

However troubling her feelings about Martin were, the job was important for her. She didn't want to jeopardize it, and she could only imagine Ayo's reaction if he found out.

"Listen, I'm heading there this weekend and you can join me. There are always two tickets booked. Ayo is gone with Erika, so he can't come with me. You fly to Port Harcourt this weekend, spend the weekend there, and take the first flight back on Monday morning. What do you think?"

Ansara was speechless.

"I've got to get back to work," she heard Martin saying, "but the flight is at eight p.m. I'll come by the house around four, can you be ready by then?"

"Yes, of course," she said.

"Sorry for the late notice," he apologized. "I should have thought of it before."

"No, of course not," she said and then added, "thank you."

Martin hung up, but she held on to the phone for a minute, the surprise still sinking in.

Then, she looked around, made sure no one was around, and whooped for joy.

The airport at Lagos was unlike anything she had imagined it would be. Perhaps she was naive in thinking that anything in her country would be free of chaos, but she had imagined clean hallways and men in smart uniforms, just like airports she had seen on television. Instead, what she saw was a colossal mess, with people clamoring at the check-in gates, some trying to bribe the officials to expedite their own check-in while others were arguing about the luggage weight limits allowed, and several others were waiting for their turn, insisting on giving a step-by-step account of their misery, loudly, to listeners at the other end of their mobile phones.

She followed Martin as he confidently strode through the crowds. It surprised her that he knew exactly where to go, when she couldn't find any signboards giving directions. It surprised her even more when, at the end of their long walk, they reached their check-in counter and were waved in ahead of everyone else.

"The perks of taking this flight many times a week," Martin explained as he handed both their tickets to the clerk behind the desk. It was almost as if he wanted to assure her that he did not receive special treatment just because he was an *oyibo*.

Ansara nodded. The clerk at the desk looked her up and down, but he did not say anything. He handed them their boarding passes before they started on the next long walk through the airport. The many security checks, the bribes she saw being handed over, the shouting and the rudeness... She realized that the airport was nothing more than a concentrated microcosm of the life outside it. But she felt as if she were in a secure bubble. Martin traveled with an ease that opened doors and cleared queues, and it was almost as if she was floating through with him, unaffected by the chaos around them.

The lounge was a welcome reprieve, a quiet oasis. They settled down after getting food from the buffet. "Please eat up," said Martin when he saw her eyeing the variety of foods he'd put on the plates. "It seems the flight is delayed. We have some time to kill."

"What time will we get there?" she asked, a little concerned.

"It'll be late, but don't worry, I'm sure my car can drop you at your house."

Ansara hesitated, not knowing quite how to put it. "Martin, you don't understand our, my, way of life. I can't just drive in a fancy car up to my house, without warning."

"Oh, it certainly won't be a fancy car, just my regular driver." Martin laughed nervously. He seemed unsure of himself, awkward in a way she had never seen him before.

"I'm sorry," he said after a while. "Ansara, I didn't know. I never intended to have you lose your employment. And I certainly didn't know when—"

"That's not the point, Martin," she replied. "Whether you knew it was me or not, fact remains you fired people, and you thought it was a good thing." She paused, collecting her thoughts. "It was, for you, just something to get favor from your bosses, to… Well, it doesn't matter why you do it. Fact remains that you do it, and that we lose not just our jobs, our lives, our—" She stopped. She didn't want to lose her composure. He was her employer, she had reminded herself many times over the last few days.

Martin was silent first, as if waiting to hear her out. After a while, his voice quieter than she had ever heard before, he said, "Ansara, no matter what I say, it's not going to make this any better. But I want you to know, I'm truly sorry."

Ansara didn't respond.

"I was new," Martin continued. "It was my first weeks here. It's true that I had no clue then, but over the last months, everything you've been telling me about life in Nigeria, about what matters to you, about what you think about the international companies and our work here, I've been listening. Trust me. I'm trying to change things. For the better. See things for what they are. I still regret firing the people after that first—"

"It's not just the firings," said Ansara. "It's just very complicated. My family has worked with CBX Corp for a very long time. My father, he lost his life while on the job. And then, my brother—" Ansara stopped again, unable to continue.

"I'm sorry, I truly am," said Martin.

Ansara looked at him, at this man who had been so good to her and was still good to her. Buying her the ticket for her trip home, she knew, was an act of generosity he didn't need to have made. And it meant the world to her. His words of apology sounded so genuine, yet he stood for everything she abhorred. The company had taken away her father, and her brother. And they had done it without remorse or even acknowledgment. But it also had provided for much in her life: her education, her home, the basic necessities. Without the company, their livelihood would be even more precarious than it already was. There was fire and water in her eyes when she said, "If only the company would treat us like humans, but instead…"

Martin reached out to wipe the tears from her eyes, but she pushed him off.

Ansara was suddenly tired. Their worlds felt so far apart that any attempt to bring them closer seemed to have a long-foregone conclusion: not meant to be. She needed to get away from him. She walked off quickly, searching for a restroom or anywhere away from the public eye.

She held strong until she reached a cubicle and closed the door behind her. And then she sat on the seat and cried. Cried for the affection she felt for Martin that she couldn't fathom, and that she was sure he felt too. Cried for her father who had passed away, for her brother who gave his life fighting for justice. Cried for her son who she could only help by living apart from him. She cried too for the injustice of a world where the man she had feelings for was also the one who had a role in her world falling apart, but perhaps was also the one who, for the first time in a very long time, had seen her for not just who she was, but who she could be.

CHAPTER 14

All Clouds and No Rain: Oil, Nigeria, Earth, Humanity, and more.

Posted on 22nd June, 2009, Monday. By Erika Smit.

Promise. *What a beautiful word. One that conjures up images of noble intentions and their fulfillment. Of honor.*

Today, I met with Chief Promise. It was clear that he no longer believed in the meaning of his own name. Chief Promise is the leader of Otuegwe, a Niger Delta village with large, high-quality oil fields. He takes us to a swamp. We hold our phones and bags above our heads as we wade through it.

Ah, the smell! Imagine the stench of garages, forecourts, rotting vegetation, decaying carcasses all rolled into one...I nearly drop my belongings so I can cover my nose. But if you lived here, could you hold your breath the whole day?

"This is where we fished and farmed," says Chief Promise. I look at the wasteland around me. "We lost our nets, huts, and fishing pots. And our forests. Our oil powers your lights and cars, but look! We're left to rot so the world can live in comfort."

The promise of their land has been taken away. Stolen. I look down at my hands, white and fair against the background of black oil spills. I see them tainted by the promises we didn't keep.

Together. *Am I the enemy, I wonder? Truth is, we all are.*

But this is not an enmity between me and them, you and us. Is it?

After we climb out of the swamp, I put my ear to the ground. I hear her weeping. The earth that weeps under the ground in Nigeria, and the earth under your feet wherever you are reading this, that is the same Earth.

We are not just humans, you and I. We are humanity. An interconnected, interdependent web. What starts here in the delta, or any one place, will spread. It will only be a matter of time before the devastation I see here, the stench of death that permeates the air, will be all around us.

It will be gradual, a slow unraveling, one that we can speed up or slow down. Not alone. Not by being on opposing sides of blame and benefit, but by being on the same side. Together.

Hope. *In six months, our world leaders will meet in Copenhagen. Many are calling it HopenHagen, the 15th meeting of the United Nations Climate Change Conference, COP15. It is our time to start making decisions that will stop the spills, stop the greed, turn back time. A chance to right our wrongs.*

It is our 15th try. How many more tries do we have before it is too late?

It rains usually in June, but this year, rainfall has been erratic, at best. The earth is dry when it should be wet. And where it should be dry, it is crying.

So am I. Literally.

My eyes are watering, my nose is stuffed, and I've had a headache since the morning, and I know this will spread. Soon, you will feel it too. This malaise, this malady of our mother, is coming. Slowly. Surely. Steadily. I do not want to imagine this for everyone on Earth. I cannot.

Do I dare to hope? I must. Because the alternative is unimaginable.

Martin read it again.

Erika had started a new blog. Chronicling her travels, she said, when she emailed him the link. The post was from last week, before she came to Lagos, but it was the first time he'd had a chance to read it. He tried to call her, but her phone was out of range. He pictured the dead phone, along with her other belongings, on her head as she waded through oil-filled swamps.

Martin picked up a book to read instead, but his eyes kept glazing over the words.

"The ones who remain in power for long," Teun Bergman had once told them, "are the ones who remain ignorant of their own power. By their own choice. We are not powerful," he had gone on to tell the cohort of young talent during their induction week, "we are mere actors in a grand system. Players in a game the rules of which we didn't write."

The delusion of powerlessness couched as the humility of insignificance. That was what had helped Teun get to and stay on the top rungs of one of the richest companies in the world. After all, acknowledging one's power is the essential first step to accepting responsibility for its subsequent consequences.

It had been erudite advice, the gist of which would dawn on the new recruits only much later.

It had been easy for Martin to follow Teun's advice. There was no world in which Martin could conceive of himself as powerful. Of course, he saw the trappings of wealth, privilege, and power all around him, yet in the deepest recesses of his mind, he still was the boy in class whose mother was sick, whose father was overworked, and who needed to be careful not to tear or ruin his clothes so his brothers could reuse them. And all he had ever wanted, he tried to tell himself, was to pull himself out of that life into a happier one.

Happy memories were far and few between for Martin, yet the ones he had, he cherished.

Around the time he turned thirteen, Martin's father started taking him fishing, a privilege that Martin, as the oldest son in the family, did not have to share with the two younger boys. Telling tall tales of adventure, passion, and riches was part of the tradition, and his father knew them in plenty.

But after a while, as the boat sailed out to the peaceful waters of the Ij, beyond the hustle and bustle of the canals, father and son would fall silent. Martin sometimes wondered, in all his boyish innocence, why those adventures—sharks jumping onto the boat or pirates in the distance or even just beautiful damsels in neighboring boats who waved at them— which his ancestors seemed to have enjoyed in plenty, never happened to him. But on most days, he was content just to spend some quiet time alone with his father, when his father was not busy with the routine of family chores or the clatter of his brothers or the care for their mother. The silence between them was like a gentle fire in an old cave, offering comfort in its warmth and familiarity while forging and strengthening a deep bond that only a father and son can share.

It was on such days that Martin would often notice his father stare wistfully at the horizon. It was not so much the words he said, it was more the ones that he did not, that spoke to Martin about dreams dreamt and dreams abandoned. Martin never quite knew what it was that his father had really dreamt about. But he was sure that a man of such suppressed intellect and unbound gusto could not have dreamt only of whatever it was that he had now.

His father's favorite stories were about the seas far beyond, recounting how generations of Dutch sailors had traveled to distant and unknown lands and brought back unimaginable wealth and about how they bravely fought off terrible dangers and won the hearts of beautiful maidens. Life beyond the Ij was a life to dream about, a life where freedom and adventure waited and where fortune favored the brave.

From as long ago as he could remember, Martin knew that he would not settle for a life where he was not happy with what he had. And he knew he would not be happy with anything mediocre. He was sure that if he was sitting on a boat with his son and talking to him about adventures beyond the Ij, it would be adventures that he had experienced himself. If he talked about unimaginable wealth amassed, it would be about fortune that he could lay claim to. If there was a beautiful maiden in the stories, it would be the mother of the boy he shared his boat with. Freedom. Adventure. Fame. Wealth. Passion. Martin had wanted all that and more. He was a young boy whose heart was set on the farthest horizons.

Ansara popped into his mind. Well, she had never left his mind since their flight, but he kept pushing her out of his immediate thoughts so he could get on with his day. The memories, when they rushed in, tore at his heart in a way he had never felt before.

Martin had tried to apologize to her while they were in the lounge, but she had rushed out. He hadn't wanted to push her, hadn't known how to broach the topic further. But stuck in adjacent airline seats, she had shown him, slowly, quietly, with pain in every word, her view of the world. A world they shared but experienced entirely differently.

"Martin," she said, "you've been very kind to me. But sometimes, sometimes, you just don't seem to understand what life here is really like. What the company does to us, to our country, the lives of ordinary people, like me, my family."

"I'm trying, Ansara," he said, his voice soft.

"Do you know, my son, he hasn't seen a night when the sky is dark, when the oil flares don't light up the night sky? The air we breathe, my mother says, is so different from what it was before they found oil. Our rivers don't have fish, they have oil instead. There are no jobs except if you work for the oil company, and there, you need to do as you are told…until"— her voice wavered—"you die."

Martin was silent. Was he to blame for the decisions, for the choices of a corporate maChiderary of which he felt no more than a cog? But if not him, then who?

"My father, he fell, and they told us it was his fault. Why?" she asked. "Why was he at that height? Why did he not have a safety harness? My brother asked the same questions, over and over…and now, I've not seen him, heard from him for more than a year. My mother, she keeps hoping that he will show up. He won't show up, my brother. My elder brother, they wouldn't give him a job anywhere, too afraid he would also be an activist, so he moved out when he got a decent job up north. So far that he doesn't even visit. Now I'm the only one left. I should be there, Martin, with her, but I can't find a job in my town… And to think it had been you, the reason I lost my job, had to leave my family, I just don't know what to think anymore."

Martin had apologized as sincerely as he could, but it hadn't felt nearly enough. She had been cordial about his apology, what else could she have done, trapped as they were in the close confines of an economy flight. She had refused his offer to drop her at home, insisting that she could find her own way in her hometown, but thanking him, nevertheless.

The formality was excruciating, yet he hadn't known how to break through the barrier that was his own making. Was it, really? At some level, he still wanted to believe that he couldn't have acted any other way, that it was his job and therefore he was absolved, but the voices in his head contradicting that were getting louder and louder. In the world's natural order, the one who benefits from something pays its cost. Setting up structures to upend the natural way could fool economic systems, but it was hard to deceive one's conscience.

Martin was good at his job, adept at the game he was expected to play. He knew that. But there were days when he envied the casual confidence of his colleagues at CBX Corp. He was never quite able to quell the dissonance he felt in the ivory towers of Holland. Which is perhaps why he chose field postings in distant countries, where he excelled. In the adrenaline of conflict and rebellion, there was little time for uncomfortable questions or inconvenient contradictions. But it was getting harder, he had to admit, to deny his own complicity, his own contribution to consequences, intended or not.

He wanted the pain to stop.

Martin picked up the phone many times to call Ansara. But every time, he hesitated. He knew it would be inappropriate for him to disturb her during the one weekend she had with her family. Martin wasn't even sure whether the number he had from her employee details was a phone in her own home or a neighbor's. Besides, he wanted to see her. Talk to her, in person. In a few days, after he had sorted out the situation in Port Harcourt, he would be back in Lagos.

And perhaps in the interim, for once, he would listen to the grievances that the protesters were bringing to him. Really listen, not just as the representative of CBX Corp, but as a human, as Erika had written, in this interconnected web of humanity.

CHAPTER 15

Ayo dropped off Erika at the airport late at night. He had been unhappy at first with Martin's request to be her local guide, but soon he discovered that she was an excellent tipper. She was keen to see and experience Lagos and the sights, providing him with unexpected opportunities to make money. And nothing could make Ayo happier than unexpected money.

Until she wanted to visit the shantytowns of Lagos. He had taken her to one closest to his apartment, one of the better ones in Lagos in his opinion, but she had been visibly troubled by the poverty and destitution. He had waited while she photographed and spoke with local children, gave them candy and gifts. His main job was to make sure she didn't get robbed or conned. At least not by anyone other than himself. He tried to hurry her along, but she didn't want to be rushed. She was, he tried to tell himself, just being kind to the slum kids, but it made him uncomfortable.

Not just that, but the visit to the shantytown brought back memories. They had started to surface after the visit from Mgbeke, but with his usual debauchery, he had managed to put a lid back on them. But the familiarity of a shantytown, even though not his own, brought them back with a force that was hard to ignore.

That night, Ayo tried to numb himself, but when the sun rose the next day, despite his throbbing head, he knew he could escape it no longer.

It was time.

He woke up earlier than usual, feeling a strange nervousness in his lower tummy. The morning was not yet fully bright outside the window. There was peace and quiet. The relentless throb of vehicles outside his window would not start for another hour or so, birds and animals were still enjoying their nightly bliss, women in the neighborhood had not yet begun their nonstop chattering, and men had not yet woken up to their work or to their fights and petty quarrels. It was just a peaceful and silent morning, and he wished that moment could last forever.

He got out of bed and brushed his teeth. How odd, he thought, I am becoming like the rich people. He didn't remember brushing his teeth or having a morning routine when he was a child. The first thing he did on any given day, as far as he could remember, was run outside. The house was like a makeshift shack that could barely house the family, and the first instinct was always to get out. He would go running to his friends, if they were up, or just hang out and do nothing in the neighborhood for a while, and then he would head back home. On good days, his mother would have something for him for breakfast. On bad days, an empty stomach was all he got.

It was well past ten by the time Ayo left his house to go to his shantytown. It was hard to predict how long any drive in Lagos would take, not to mention that the old secondhand Honda he was driving could not be relied upon to not break down in the middle of a drive. But he was lucky today. It was almost as if the universe was rooting for him, as if it knew that Ayo would make any obstacle an excuse to turn back.

By noon, Ayo found himself at the shantytown that he had called home throughout his childhood. He parked his car outside, hesitating to drive in along the narrow roads that could barely be distinguished from the front or back of the shacks that lined them. It was hard to call them roads really; it seemed more like a giant had decided to pass a comb right through a plot of land that had shacks after shacks lined up against each other.

Without much effort, Ayo found the little shack where he had lived. Just outside his door, there were two women sitting and cleaning plantain. They seemed to be chatting amiably, comfortable with each other and the routine of their actions.

"Where is Akeeba? She lives here," he asked.

The women looked surprised to see an unfamiliar man approach them.

"Who? Who're you looking for?"

"Akeeba. Old woman. She lives in this shack."

"Here? No. This is my home. I live here," the younger

looking of the two answered.

"Ok, but do you know what happened to her?"

"No, I don't. I moved here a few years ago. But my husband used to live here before. There was no old woman."

Ayo nodded his thanks and moved away. The women genuinely did not seem to know anything about his mother.

He walked aimlessly through the shantytown. In a distance he spied some boys playing *Sansa Kroma*. He smiled; it was a game he and his friends had popularized, a Ghanaian game they had learnt from an immigrant boy and made their own. A group of boys were passing stones —quite skillfully, Ayo thought—to the beat of the Sansa Kroma song that a few others were chanting loudly. He felt pleased to see that the game had survived into the next generation.

A further walk brought him to the little bridge that stood in the middle of the shantytown. He remembered a time when there used to be a quarrel between the two sides of the shantytown, the north and south sides, separated by the bridge. It amused Ayo that people, no matter where they lived, liked to pick fights with their neighbors, who were probably more similar to them than enemies far away. Yet it was the neighbor that annoyed, inspired the most jealousy, and eventually prompted them to take up arms.

Ayo stood on the bridge, surveying the two sides. He was surprised how little had changed. He still recognized most of the shacks, the place where he used to play with the boys still functioned as a playground, the shops hadn't moved, and the water under the bridge seemed as dirty as ever.

Ayo heard a commotion coming from the playground. He turned around to see that the kids had abandoned their game and were now all running and shouting after a hunched figure in the distance. The hunched figure at first seemed oblivious to the excited kids, but then turned and tried to shoo them away with a long stick.

Ayo saw that the hunched figure was an old woman. Her frame was rather large, like that of a man's, but her gray hair was long, and her wrinkled face showed remnants of feminine features. She was wearing a man's shirt that jarred with her *iro*, which extended well beyond her feet; it had either belonged to someone taller than her or her hunch had made her own clothes ill-fitting. Both the shirt and *iro* were tattered, muddy, and dusty. She had a half-eaten apple in one hand and a stick in the other, which she was using to support her walking. Even with the stick, she dragged her leg at every step, her face cringing with what might have been pain.

Ayo looked at the woman carefully. He didn't want to believe what was becoming more and more clear to him. The destitute woman who seemed to have become the shantytown's lunatic was his mother. He stood watching her for a few minutes. He wanted to run away, run away as fast as he could. Away from the woman who had given birth to him, and back to his life where the harsh reality of his childhood, and now his mother's insanity, would disappear into nothing but a few bad nightmares. But Ayo stood rooted to the ground as if some invisible rope had risen out of the water to tie his feet to the bridge.

For a moment, Ayo thought that his mother had looked up. He could not be sure whether it was his overactive imagination, but he felt there was a moment when she saw him and a glimmer of recognition had crossed her face. He must have been imagining it, because now she seemed to be engrossed again in trying to scare away the kids. The kids were louder and rowdier, and a couple of them were picking up stones to throw at her.

Ayo wanted to leave. He had made that choice sixteen years ago and nothing had changed in what he wanted. But despite himself, he ran down the bridge toward the playground, instead of away from it.

"Oi, you kids, get away from her, or I will kill you all," Ayo shouted.

The kids looked startled, unsure what to do. But Ayo's booming voice did not leave them any doubt about his intentions, and they scattered as quickly as they had abandoned their game.

"Are you alright?" Ayo asked the woman who was standing looking at the running kids. She turned to him, but she looked puzzled.

Ayo sighed. "Mama, it's me. Ayo, Ayomide." Ayo wanted to believe that there was a flicker of recognition across her face, but he could not be sure.

"Mama, do you remember me?"

Again, a mindless stare.

After a long pause, she walked to Ayo and gently touched him on his cheeks. She looked into his eyes for some time, somber at first. But then, her thin mouth widened into a toothless grin that gave way to a loud laugh, just like that of a child amused by something he had seen, except that the child's innocent sound was replaced by the croaking voice of an aged woman.

She let go of his face and walked away toward the river, without turning back even once.

"Mama, where are you going?"

Stop! Don't go! Ayo tried to shout after her, but the words would not form in his mouth. It was all too much to witness. He did not know what he had expected, but this was certainly not the image he had pictured, even in his worst nightmare. Insanity was not something he could associate with his mother. He could not imagine his stoic, powerful, and sometimes downright scary mother as the object of the village children's teasing. He wondered when it had happened, and whether that was how she had lost her house, or had it been the other way round. He felt a seething anger at the woman who sat in front of his old house peeling vegetables, although he knew that was misguided. He had to find out what happened. He headed to the shantytown's tea stall, hoping to find someone there who knew him from years before.

Just to the side of the bridge, close enough to the river so that they could use the polluted waters as a source for all their water needs and as a dumping ground, was a row of shops. It would be hard to call most of them shops in the general sense of the word; some did not even have wares displayed and were more of a resting area and a place for doing business for their proprietors. In the middle of the shops was the tea stall, and it was still exactly the way Ayo remembered it.

Bunches of plantains in various stages of ripeness hung outside the shop. A few glass jars of candy lined the countertop. Flies seemed to be crowding both the plantains and the jars, and every once in a random while, the proprietor, who sat behind a high counter, would half-heartedly swat at the flies. The flies would take off momentarily but then be back again just as determined as before.

Ayo did not recognize the proprietor. He was a young man, maybe a few years younger than Ayo. He wondered what happened to Ahmed, the old guy who used to run the place, and the many regular patrons, some of whom had been constant fixtures in their shantytown.

He went into the rather rundown shack and sat on one of the two broken benches. There was no one in the stall except a lone figure huddled on one end of the other bench. He did not seem to be eating or drinking anything, or doing anything else for that matter. Ayo's presence did not interest him enough even to turn around.

The young man behind the counter looked up, eyebrows

raised in a question.

"Tea." Ayo was surprised at the exhaustion in his own voice.

The young man went behind a sheet hung at the end of the shack. It hardly took him more than a few minutes to come back with tea. The tea was steaming hot, and Ayo did not even notice that it was in a rusted steel cup that looked like a better wash would do it a world of good.

"I haven't seen you around. Are you new here?" The man plonked the teacup on the long wooden desk in front of Ayo.

Ayo was amused to be thought of as "new" in the neighborhood. Did sixteen years away make him new? The idea piqued him; go away for good and then you come back as brand new.

"I used to live here before. Many years ago."

"Oh, it must be before then. Before the cleanup. Welcome back."

Ayo nodded. The young man went back to his place behind the counter, back to randomly swatting at the flies and looking out of the window.

"Ayo."

Ayo was surprised to hear his name called out. The voice was gruff and croaked with age, and Ayo turned to see that the little hunched figure in the corner was now peering at him intently.

"Ahmed. You're still here." Ayo recognized the old shop owner who used to wheeze behind the counters when Ayo was still a kid playing in the grounds outside and trying to figure out ways to steal a plantain or candy from the jars without getting caught.

"You've changed. But it is you." Ahmed was looking him up and down.

"Ahmed, it's good to see you. I haven't seen anyone else from the old days." Ayo remembered that that was not technically true, but his mother might just as well have died and come back as a different, unrecognizable person. "What happened here?"

A dejected look came over the old man's face. He drew in a long breath of air and went into a coughing fit. The young man looked up from behind the counter but did not make any attempt to come and help. The old man settled down after a bit and stroked his chest.

"The asthma. The cough. I can hardly breathe. Some things never change."

Ayo smiled politely.

"They came one day and made everyone clear out from the shanties. It was part of a Clean Lagos campaign or something, get rid of all the shanties in the neighborhood. New initiative by the government. One by one, they destroyed our lives. From Oshodi to Amuwo Odofin, they were going to take down all the shanties and make it into one big neighborhood. They wanted to make the mainland look beautiful. Those idiots, they thought they could move the shantytowns over and build pretty parks."

The old man laughed, as if calling them idiots was a big joke. Ayo joined him, more out of his need to keep him appeased enough to get the story out of him rather than any politeness.

"And then, after many months, after they disrupted enough lives, after they destroyed so many homes, they just disappeared. Poof, gone. Must have made all the money they could make from the exercise by then. They gave a lot of reasons, excuses. But we all knew. They had milked the system enough by then, and they moved on to the next big thing."

"So what happened, what happened to everyone here?"

"We were the last ones. The last ones in the unfortunate lot. If they had decided to stop just a few weeks earlier, we would have been spared. But if they had decided a few weeks later, we would have been completely finished."

Ayo sat there sipping his tea, thinking of the vicissitudes of circumstance that used to define his old life, and why he had been so eager to escape it.

"Many of the people had already packed their belongings and left even before the thugs arrived," Ahmed continued. "They had heard enough horror stories about what happened in the shantytowns before and were not going to just sit around and wait for things to happen. No one knows whether the stories were true, but anyone who had a friend or relative anywhere else was not going to find out on his own. Over a few days, our shantytown went from being one of the biggest, to having very few people.

"A few of us stayed, waiting for the tractors and the bulldozers. We had nowhere else to go. Usually, the thugs come in first and they go shack by shack and drive people out. They throw things out of the house and beat people if they don't clear up. After that are the big vehicles. But somehow for us, between emptying the people and the bulldozers, something happened. They just stopped. Never really came back."

"Why did they stop?" asked Ayo.

The old man went into a coughing fit before he could answer.

"Follow the money, the reason is always money," said the young proprietor, who brought some snacks to go with the tea. "There was more money to be made somewhere else. What else?"

"Who knows why they stop, why they start. We are just pawns in a game for them," said the old man, his coughing abated. "It doesn't matter why. What matters is that the harm was started. The downward spiral."

Ayo clenched his fist over the cup of tea, nearly breaking it. Being cavalier about what was catastrophic to others was the hallmark of power. Ayo had seen that repeatedly, as he hobnobbed with the rich and powerful, but it never stopped irking him.

The old man didn't seem to notice Ayo's consternation. "Most people had already moved out before the campaign paused. Many wanted to come back when they heard that it had stopped. But before they could come back, new people, I don't know from where, took over. Some tried to fight for their old houses, but the new people were more powerful and better organized, and our people didn't stand a chance. Some of us still, old people really, stuck around. Me, Ismail, Isioma,

Amadi… We gave up our houses and whatever else we had, but we still stuck around." The old man hesitated before he said, "Your mother too. Your mother, she…"

Ayo was not sure whether he wanted to hear more.

"Your mother was alright till something happened to her leg. No one knows how it happened. But from a small limp, in the blink of an eye, it went to an inability to walk. We could hear her groaning in pain when she had to walk. She couldn't work, they fired her, she couldn't leave her house anymore. One day we heard she'd chopped off her own leg."

The shame and repugnance Ayo felt made his face contort into a frightful expression. Ahmed stopped talking.

Ayo got up abruptly and walked to the counter. He had heard and seen enough.

"Ten naira."

He pulled out a ten-naira note from his pocket, put it on a candy jar, and left without looking back.

166

CHAPTER 16

It was well past midnight by the time Ansara reached her home. The flight was just over an hour, but she was glad when they finally landed and she stepped out into Port Harcourt.

It had been only five months since she left for Lagos, but it felt like she had been gone forever, and she felt so happy to be home.

Her mother was bewildered to be woken out of her sleep, and after some assurances that all was well, and that she had just come home for a surprise visit, mother held daughter in a tight hug, tears of joy streaming from her eyes. Ansara's heart was full as she tiptoed over to Femi's cot. Her son barely stirred with the noise, and she snuggled right next to him, tears streaming from her eyes as well.

"Ansara, you're here!" It was Chidera who woke her up the next morning. The sun was well above the horizon, and her mother had left for work. Femi was still asleep next to her.

"Ha, Chidera!" Ansara said, trying to sit up in the cramped cot.

"I heard you came in late last night. Your mama stopped by ours before work. I thought I'd pop by and bring you some breakfast," said Chidera.

Femi stirred out of his sleep as well, his eyes growing wide in surprise and joy as he reached over. Mother and son embraced each other. She had missed him so very much, thought Ansara, as she tried not to tear up again.

"Femi must be so very happy to see you, he has missed you so much," said Chidera, pinching his cheeks. "I've got *okpa* for you too, little man. Are you ready to eat with your mama?"

"Thank you, Chidera, come on, sit," said Ansara. "Let's all eat together! And I have gifts for you all too!"

Love, camaraderie, family, home—how she had missed it all!

Chidera wanted to hear all about Lagos and Ansara's life there. Femi followed Ansara around the whole day, hardly letting go of her hand. And when Ansara's mother arrived in the evening after work, she told her stories all over again, and Femi and Chidera hung on to her words again as if hearing them for the first time. The evening passed with neighbors dropping by, and by the time the noise and bustle had died down, it was well into the night.

After her family had retired, Ansara still couldn't sleep, her mind not settling down enough though her body was tired. She looked at her son, peaceful in his sleep but just as quiet in his waking hours. His delight at seeing her was obvious, but she wished he could express it in words.

She wondered, as she often did when she looked at his

small and frail body, whether she had failed him in some way. It was one of those days—and there were many of them—when she felt it was all her fault. Somehow, she had forgotten, in her misery and self-doubt, to give him enough care and attention, and he had decided that this was not a mother worth speaking to.

She was convinced on such days that things would have been different if Ikenna had not left her, if she could have somehow managed to convince him to stay. She knew she shouldn't, but she kept playing the events of her life in her head ad nauseum in the hope that she would find something that, when undone, would reverse Femi's withdrawal into silence.

Ikenna.

Femi's father.

Her first boyfriend.

She had been so giddy with love.

Young and full of hope and naivety.

It was around the time that Ansara started work at the Anderson household that she met Ikenna. Ansara must have been sixteen, and Ikenna just a little older at eighteen. Even though Mrs. Anderson's kids studied at the International School, she was a member of the local school committee and regularly volunteered, either by talking to the school children about socially relevant topics or by donating whatever she could: books, clothes, or sometimes even food.

Ikenna worked at the local school as a peon, the one that

the school principal sent to Mrs. Anderson's house to pick up the stuff. He told Ansara that they had made him a peon even though he had the qualifications to teach in the school, because he did not have the money to pay the bribes. Ansara was not sure whether that was entirely true, but with all the naiveté of a teenage girl falling in love for the first time, she had believed him. Ikenna may or may not have had all the qualifications, but he was definitely the most well-read man Ansara had ever met.

At first, Ansara had not thought much of the sickly young boy from the school who came to collect the clothes, food, or other donations that Mrs. Anderson regularly made to the school. But over time, he started spending more and more time at the house, often watching her fold the clothes or pack the food or just go about her daily chores, all the while entertaining her with stories about the school.

"Oh, Ansara, you've no idea what happened in school today," Ikenna said one day while Ansara sat by the window, cutting vegetables for the evening meal.

"What?" Ansara asked, excitedly expecting another of Ikenna's stories.

"I have told you about Mr. Obieze, haven't I? The one that the kids call Polkadots? He came to school in a complete daze today. He had just started reading to the kids about English literature, he was quoting some poems, and then just as he was standing in the middle of the room and reciting, his voice slurred, his arms flailed, and he just fell over."

"Oh my God! What happened?"

"Some of the kids got really scared at first. They came running to me. So I go over with a bottle of water. It was not the first time this had happened to Polkadots, so I knew what to expect, and guess what!"

He paused for a moment, relishing Ansara's captivated attention.

"By the time I got there, someone had painted a large mustache below his nostrils as usual. This time, one of them had gotten very creative and drawn a few lice creeping down his forehead. It looked so real, it was oh-so-funny!" Ikenna laughed out loud, little tears forming in the corners of his eyes.

"But was he alright? Why did he faint?"

"The man was stone drunk. I could smell the alcohol from miles away," Ikenna continued, seeing Ansara's worried expression. "Nothing to worry about it. It happens to him every once in a while. Whenever he wins some money in his lotto, he gets drunk. Luckily for us, he loses more than he wins."

Ansara laughed. Ikenna's stories amused her. He would tell her many stories about the school, about the kids who came to school, and how you could always make out by the lunch they brought in what their parents did for a living; about the teachers who would often protest and refuse to teach whenever the principal could not get enough money to pay their salaries on time, and some who even when paid, went to the classrooms, assigned the students random readings, and promptly fell asleep.

He told her about how he controlled the order of the entire school by making sure the bell rang on time—two long ones to mark the beginning and end of the school day and short ones between each period—and how without his punctuality and attention to detail, the whole world of the school would cease to function.

School was a world that had been shut to Ansara ever since her father died and her mother found it impossible to send the children to school. Ansara, along with her elder brothers, had dropped out of school to work and earn money. But she had always enjoyed learning, and in the years that she was in school, she was easily the best student in her class. She lapped up the little tidbits of information that Ikenna willingly provided her with the enthusiasm of a starving vagrant who hadn't had food for days.

Eventually, she gained enough courage to ask him to bring her a book or two from the school library to read, and he gladly obliged, each time reminding her that she needed to be careful with the book and to return it in exactly the same condition as he gave it to her in.

One day, he brought her a book, *Nigerian History in Pictures*, with its cover in tatters and the pages ready to come off at the slightest touch. Ansara had stitched back the pages, hoping that Ikenna would be pleased. But instead, he was very upset, fretting for about a month that someone in the library would notice that the book had been illegally borrowed. But she was exhilarated to get hold of books again, and no amount of trepidation on Ikenna's part would make her less enthusiastic. She managed to convince him to get back to his routine of bringing her books every week.

Every day, she would finish all her work by noon, and soon after lunch was served and the dishes cleared up and Mrs. Anderson had retired for her afternoon siesta or to read a book, she would sit in her favorite spot in the garden, in a low branch of a safou tree, and read for a few joyous hours, interrupted only by soft calls of the birds overhead and the low whistle of the afternoon breeze.

Many of the stories Ikenna told her were clearly exaggerated, and some were even just plain lies concocted for no other purpose than to keep the attention of a beautiful woman, but Ansara noticed none of it. She was grateful to him for providing her with a window, however tainted, into a world she desperately wanted to gain entry to but could not. She did not realize anymore that he was still the sickly child she had not even spared a second glance when she first met him. To her, he was the connection to the world of books, the keeper of stories, the stoker of dreams, for every time she heard those stories, she imagined some miracle by which she would be able to get back to her life as it had been before her father's demise.

It was a rainy afternoon when Ikenna kissed Ansara. The school was closed due to the threat of floods and Mrs. Anderson was far away in the main house, sleeping and safely away from any sounds from the kitchen. They were sitting side by side on the kitchen floor, watching the thick and heavy raindrops splatter against the windowsill and chatting casually, when quite suddenly, Ikenna leaned in, almost startling her.

Ansara could not remember much of what happened next—perhaps there was a part of her that did not want to remember—but after a period of time that now seemed both short and long, she was lying next to him on her bed in the servants' quarters, the buttons of her blouse half undone, her lower body smarting with a searing pain between her legs, and an awkward silence hanging heavily in the damp air. The sound of rain falling on the tin roof, combined with Ikenna's heavy breathing, made the small room so full of sounds that it made the lack of words almost deafening. After a while, Ikenna turned over to her, gently held her head in his arms, and whispered, "I love you, my Ansara." She wanted to reciprocate. She remembered trying to say something, but the words never came. Ikenna left the room while she continued to lie on the bed, listening to the rain and the fan, letting the confusion and bewilderment she felt take over her entire body, before eventually falling into a tired sleep.

The next two years passed by in romantic harmony. Theirs was not a relationship given to erotic frenzies; it carried on at the slow, gentle pace at which it started. Now, years later, Ansara could see how wrong everything had been. How she had been like a little rivulet, led on by the forces of nature, flowing as the lay of the land dictated, unaware of the thundering waterfall she was just about to join. But at that time in her life, everything had seemed just right. She had a good job; she had a man who loved her; and she had the opportunity to read and learn, even if it was from stealthily borrowed books. The future looked as bright as she could have ever hoped for.

It was about a month before the summer break—the long holiday when the school would be closed and the Anderson family would spend their days "soaking in the tropical sun in the white sands of Accra," as Mrs. Anderson liked to put it— that everything started falling apart. She remembered the days leading up to it had been filled with a strange happiness. She was looking forward to spending the break with her family, relaxing at home and playing with her brothers.

Gradually, she noticed that the smell of boiling rice was making her retch. Slowly, she realized that anything and everything made her vomit. An unexplainable tiredness and listlessness were overtaking her. That, and the fact that she hadn't had her period for almost two months, which she had ignored and could no longer ignore. It was time to tell Ikenna.

"Ikenna, there's something I need to talk to you about." She had started the conversation cautiously.

Ikenna was loitering around the kitchen, looking for tidbits to eat, hardly looking at her. "Hmm?"

Ansara blurted out, "I'm pregnant."

Ikenna stopped in his tracks for a moment, and then continued his quest for food. "Where are the potato peels that you keep in a jar? Wasn't it somewhere around here?"

Ansara sighed. "Here, here are the potato peels." She turned him around with her arms and repeated, "I am pregnant."

"Are you sure?" Ikenna looked resigned, like someone who had tried to run away but nevertheless got caught when they reached the corner.

"Yes, as sure as I can be. As sure as I need to be."

"I just remembered, I need to leave. I've to meet someone."

"Ikenna, wait, I—"

But Ikenna was gone.

Ansara was not sure what she had expected, but she was disappointed that he had not been happier. For, despite all the impending social disapproval of the situation and the inauspiciousness of a child conceived outside of wedlock, what she really felt, if she was honest with herself, was happiness. Happiness that a human being was growing inside her. Happiness that God had decided to bless her with a human life. Happiness that there would soon be someone to call her Mama.

But to Ikenna's credit, he came around pretty quickly. Before the end of the month, when they were planning to leave for their respective homes, he came and told her that he would marry her. He wanted to do the right thing, and he wanted to take care of his child.

"I promise, my Ansara, I will go to my *umunna*, tell them the news, bring them to your house for a wine-carrying ceremony. Before the end of the year, we'll be married, my love."

Ansara was overjoyed. And on that happy note, she left

the Anderson household and headed back home to celebrate the holidays.

"Ansara." She heard her mother's voice. "You're still awake."

She could see her mother sitting up on the cot, the bright flares of the sky throwing light through the open windows.

"You didn't sleep, Mama?" she asked.

"Oh, I did, but I often wake up in the night these days. Just an old age thing, nothing to worry about. As you get older, you sleep less and less, they say."

Ansara nodded. "I'd almost forgotten how the nights never quite grow dark here. The flares, we don't have them in Lagos," she said absently.

"Ah, just for us, just for us here," her mother said. "Tell me, Ansa, is something bothering you in Lagos? I'm very glad to have you back, but you came…I don't know, so suddenly. And earlier, you looked distant sometimes. Disturbed."

"Did I? I shouldn't have," said Ansara. "Nothing to worry about." Thoughts about her last exchange with Martin had been on her mind throughout the day, even when she tried not to think about it. She thought she had hidden it well, her anxiety, but clearly her mother had noticed.

"Ansa, you're my child, my only daughter," she said. "You don't need to be strong for me. What is it, dear?"

Ansara was silent.

Her mother came by and sat with her, holding her close. As she lay her head against her mother's shoulder, Ansara felt like a little girl again, and though she had decided not to burden her mother with any of her troubles, it all came tumbling out: Martin, what she felt about him, how she was certain he felt something too, but he didn't say anything, but how he was her boss, an *oyibo*, how he had fired people at the refinery, how Emeka always said *oyibos* couldn't be trusted, but Martin was not like that, she felt certain. He was different. Or maybe not. After all, how good a judge of men was she?

It was a relief to get it all off her chest, and her mother listened, holding her, hugging her close. Ansara was quiet too after a while, feeling lighter, as if she had just needed to tell someone. If anyone wouldn't judge her, that person was her mother, and she knew she was lucky to have been blessed with a mother like that.

"What should I do, Mama?" she asked, after a while.

"You know, Ansa, I'm not from here," her mother said. "I don't talk about it often, and I don't know if I ever told you, but when I met your father, my entire family was against the relationship. You've heard bits and pieces of the story, I know, but not the full extent of it."

She paused. Ansa looked at her mother, the flare highlighting the wrinkles on her face.

"I was born an Ogoni, and we were proud people. No one married outside of the tribe, so you can imagine the wrath when I fell in love with an Igbo man."

She smiled, and Ansara saw her mother's eyes light up.

"But he just swept me off my feet, your papa. He was tall, dark, handsome, charming, and kind. I had never met anyone like him before. My head, my family, my friends, neighbors, everyone and everything told me I shouldn't. But there it was, my heart, doing its own thing."

"We never go back to your family. We never did," said Ansara.

"Yes, it was a long time ago, and when I chose to marry your father, your grandfather made it very clear that I was no longer welcome. I was not part of the family anymore."

"I'm so sorry, Mama," said Ansara. "You never told us this."

"Yes, I know. I didn't want to relive the past, so when we moved here, I erased it. Moved on. We raised you all Igbo, and no one asked anything. We told you that your grandparents had passed away, which by the time you were born, was probably true anyway."

Her mother's eyes had filled with tears. Ansa reached over and wiped them.

"Do you regret it, Mama?"

"Regret? No, never!" she said. "When your heart sings, my daughter, you must dance. Not everyone gets to hear the song in their heart, and if it ever happens to you, don't quiet it down. Get out there and dance like there is no tomorrow." She had a faraway look on her face, as if remembering the good times she had had. "Because when you find that joy, there is no need for tomorrow. All you need is today."

Ansara tried to picture her mother eloping with her father, happy and in love.

"I would have given up anything for the years I had with your papa, and I did give it all up. Everything. The price was heavy. But I would not have done it any other way."

"But Mama," Ansara started. Her situation seemed to be so different. How could she forget all that Martin was, what he stood for? And her past choices in men didn't leave her with much confidence. But she couldn't find the words to ask.

"Ansara, I can't tell you what to do. No one can," her mother said. "But don't be afraid to see people for who they are. Don't mistake them for what they stand for, or for who they belong with. See with your own eyes, not through the eyes of others."

Ansara reached over and hugged her mother tighter, feeling a flicker of hope.

"And listen to the song in your heart," she whispered in Ansara's ear, "however faint it may be. Remember what I said. When you hear that tune, dance. Dance like there is no tomorrow."

CHAPTER 17

It was midweek before Martin could make his way back to Lagos.

The weekend demonstrations by the activists had been more peaceful than the company had feared. For the first time, Martin felt that he was gaining ground with Blessing, Udo, and other leaders representing the workers. He felt pleased with his progress as he walked into the Port Harcourt airport.

In an unprecedented move, he had agreed to set up a joint working group to tally up the environmental consequences. He knew it was a risky step, something he would not have ordinarily done. It would require all his charm and maneuvering skills to get it approved by headquarters, but at the very least, with such a joint working group, they would begin to get a clear picture, not blurred by the exaggerated emotions of the protesters or the downright denials of the corporation. At this point, he was not sure that anyone other than he wanted to see the clear picture. But it had felt the right thing to do, and Blessing and Udo had recognized the gesture for what it was, an atypical and momentous measure that Martin was making at personal risk to his own career.

Besides, he asked David to offer jobs back to all those who had been fired a few months previously. David was surprised and seemed unsure what to make of it.

"Don't. Don't make it a big deal, David," Martin said. "Tell them the safety review is completed, and the plant is now ready to run at full capacity. And if they want to come back, they are welcome. Keep it simple."

"But, but—" David had begun to protest, and Martin reminded him that he was getting what he had wanted in the first place, and in such a situation, the smartest thing to do would be to take the win. David left, still confused but content.

But work, however challenging it had suddenly become, was not the cause of Martin's restlessness.

He had not heard from Ansara for days. He had not expected her to call, of course, and he was hesitant to initiate a call. But he couldn't stop thinking about her, and about their last conversation.

From the moment he met her, if he was honest with himself, he had been distracted by her beauty and grace. As he came to know her better, he had learned to admire her grit, wisdom, and kindness, even when life had been incredibly hard on her.

Martin prided himself on being a self-made man. He had dreamed passionately, planned meticulously, and toiled diligently for everything he had achieved. But listening to Ansara during those evenings, the evenings that he, consciously and subconsciously, had made a part of their routine, had given him an entirely new perspective. Listening to the way she described her life, never with a complaint and always with a smile, he had, for the first time, felt a sense of humility and gratitude for his own fortune, a recognition of his privilege.

He had never felt for anyone the way he felt for her. He was sure of that. Yet he had been so lost in his own world, in his own concerns—what did it mean for him to have feelings for his cook? How would it affect his job? Was he really sure or was this just a fleeting feeling?—that he had never quite realized how much harder it must have been for her. That from her perspective, he was someone who looked entirely different from who he imagined himself to be.

Had he taken her for granted? Someone who would unquestioningly spend her evenings with him, though he felt sure that she seemed to enjoy them just as much as he did. But did she really, or did she feel obliged to?

Martin shuddered in his seat.

He considered himself the worldly-wise sort, well-traveled and culturally conscious, not to mention a firm believer in the equality of all. And here he was, acting just like any other stereotypical white man.

"Sir? Sir?" A young black man was trying to get his attention. "Can I clear these, sir?"

Martin was grabbing a quick bite in the lounge of the Port Harcourt airport, at a terminal that was in a state of disrepair. "Yes, sure," he replied, adding, "thank you," as he got up and walked away.

Martin looked out of the dusty glass windows. Port

Harcourt was one of the busier airports in Nigeria, as the gateway to one of the richest regions in the continent, but it had been shut down just a few years before due to safety concerns. Rebuilding had been going on for some time, and it was still not entirely finished, although the authorities had deemed it safe to be reopened. Martin was glad about that. With trips to the company's facilities every week or two, without this airport, his travel would have been more tedious than it already was.

He looked over toward the runway. It looked new or at least recently repaired; a long grassy patch looked freshly mowed and well maintained. He could see tiny specks of black and white flitting about on the green. Martin peered at them.

A mischief of magpies.

"One for sorrow, two for joy." Martin only had to close his eyes to hear his mother's unfailing refrain whenever she spotted a single magpie or more. He smiled to himself.

The memory of his Aunt Marta's wedding came to his mind, as clearly as if it had happened just yesterday. Martin must have been about ten years old, but the day left an indelible mark on his young mind.

His mother had been nervous, as she often got before social occasions. The boys were dressed smartly in black tuxedos. Martin's mother looked elegant in her flowing beige dress. The gift had been packed in beautiful silver-colored wrapping paper and safely placed in the trunk of the car. Food and drinks had been packed in case the younger boys got hungry during the drive. The three boys had been bundled into the back seat of the old Volkswagen. But his mother was still flitting about nervously, convinced she had forgotten something. After a while, his father finally managed to calm his wife's anxiety and they were ready to go.

His mother put her palms to her mouth just as his father started the engine. She cried, "Oh no!"

"What is it, Marieke?" Martin's father was worried.

"One for sorrow." Martin's mother pointed at the lonely magpie that had found its way into the driveway. It was almost fall, well past the mating season for most birds, and most magpies moved about alone.

Finding a pair of magpies was just as unlikely as something sad happening just because a single magpie had been seen. But his father had not pointed out how ridiculous such superstitions were, how stupid it would be to be late just because they had spotted a lone magpie, how lame it would be to go in search for the second magpie, especially when they were already late.

Instead, he had done just that. He had driven around the neighborhood and then driven through the park nearby till they spotted a pair of magpies and his mother sighed in relief. "Two for joy!" She had leaned over and kissed her husband, overcome with love and gratitude.

Martin had known, probably as early as then, that he would settle for nothing less. Nothing less than what he thought was perfect love. To go beyond reason to make someone happy and to feel unconditionally happy yourself when you saw them smile. To have someone who would make you want to do that, he thought wistfully, must be the ultimate happiness.

Martin looked on at the magpies on the tarmac. At that distance, he couldn't be entirely sure they were magpies, but he could be sure there were at least a dozen pairs of them, and that, surely, must be a good sign.

He looked at his watch, eager to get back home to Lagos, and to Ansara, just as the boarding call sounded over the intercom.

As his car pulled into the driveway of Rose Villa, Martin noticed a dim light from the kitchen. The rest of his household, even the guards, seemed fast asleep.

As he walked in, he could hear sobs, soft and muffled. He could make out Ansara's outline, sitting in a corner on the kitchen floor with her head tucked between her knees. A moonbeam shone on the floor nearby, as if guiding him toward her. She didn't seem to have noticed him.

A sense of panic came over him. "Ansara, is everything ok?"

She quickly stopped crying, as if startled by his voice, wiped her eyes, and tried to get up. "Yes, I'm fine. I didn't realize you were coming tonight," she said "I'm sorry. I was... I... Can I get you something?"

Martin was astonished by her abrupt transition from a woman lost in tears to a person inquiring about his welfare. He wished the barriers between them weren't so very high, but he also knew that he was the only person who could bring them down.

"Ansara," he said, his voice soft and low. He had to push back the facade she had donned. He moved closer to her, his hands gently supporting her as she stumbled.

"We don't have to get up," he said gently, sitting beside her on the kitchen floor. "Ansara, what is it? Why were you crying?"

"Oh, it's nothing." She tried to smile, but her formality seemed to have softened a little. "Don't worry about it." Her words did little to dispel the deep sadness in her eyes.

"Ansara," he said, "you don't have to tell me if you don't want to"—he took her hand in his—"but I've been thinking about you, about us, ever since… and I just want you to know, I'm here for you. Whatever it is, what I feel for you is so very deep. I'm here for you." He couldn't find the right words. He knew he should be doing better.

Ansara didn't pull back her hand, but she kept her head turned away.

"Is everything ok at home?" he asked. "Your mother, your son?"

"Yes," she said, her voice a whisper, "they're fine. Everything is ok. I had a good time there. I was so happy to see them. So happy."

"And you miss them?"

She nodded, sobbing again, unable to stop.

"I came back," she said softly, in between her sobs.

Martin looked confused. He wasn't sure what he heard. Or what that meant.

"They, the manager from the refinery, he called me and said I could have my job back," she clarified, "but I…"

"…came back," said Martin, his heart nearly skipping a beat in his joy. "Ansara, about last week, I'm sorry, I—"

But he couldn't continue. Ansara put a finger gently to his lips and whispered, "You said that already."

Martin moved closer to her, and she toward him, her head almost resting on his shoulders. The faint whiff of jasmine in her hair, the scent of lavender from her body… Martin closed his eyes. He had wanted her for so very long. But he couldn't just…

Ansara turned, a light giggle escaping her. Her tight curls had caught against his short beard, the two-day stubble new on his face, and she couldn't get loose.

She looked at him, her face glowing in the moonlight, her lips slightly parted.

Almost against his own will, Martin moved in, pulling her closer to him, and gently kissed her on her lips. She pulled away slightly, looked into his eyes for a moment, and then leaned in to kiss him back. He kissed her again, turning to face her, his arms drawing her closer, his lips hungrier this time, his tongue seeking hers, and he could feel her respond, her back arching, her mouth closing in. As he laid her gently on the floor, he could feel the moon smiling from the sky, playfully lighting their bodies as he stripped off their clothes.

He knew he had wanted this for so very long, and as she pulled him in, he knew that she had wanted him too. On that night, time stood still for them, the stars stood guard, the world outside disappeared, and it was just the two of them, falling in love. Body, mind, and soul.

PART III

CHAPTER 18

A bouquet of sunflowers stood tall at the center of the dining table. Ansara ran her fingers over the bright petals that surrounded the meticulous pattern in the middle made of hundreds of dainty, densely packed florets.

"Sunflowers for my sunflower," Martin said when he brought them, proud of himself that he had discovered the meaning of her name. Her father told her once that she was named after the sunflower because her birth was such a happy occasion in their family. Ansara was not a traditional name, and her father had found it in a book he liked. He said that he knew she would be a cheerful child, bringing joy to all around her. "Sunflowers remind me of my family too," Martin had said. His mother had been an admirer of van Gogh, and she took her sons to his museum, often lingering in front of his painting of sunflowers.

Six months had passed since their first kiss. A period of bliss, when it seemed as if the outside world paused, granting them a brief respite from reality.

The kitchen was still Ansara's favorite part of the house, the one place where she felt completely safe and free to make it her own. It was also shaded by the trees in the back garden and was cooler than the rest of the house. The weather this year was predicted to be exceptionally hot, and the summer that had just arrived had already begun to bare its fury.

Ansara walked to the window at the opposite end of the kitchen. It opened to a small courtyard. One side of the courtyard was flanked by the servants' quarters, another by a part of the wall of the main house, and the third side was a small room that housed the generator. The slender leaves of the mango tree near the kitchen wall peeped in through the top of the window. She loved staring into the courtyard. It was an enclosed area and, except for the occasional whir of the generator, nothing stirred the peace of this self-contained space.

She could see Ayo moving around in the generator room. The electricity supply in Lagos often seemed to have a mind of its own, and ever since the news of a heatwave started to come in, the electricity had been more whimsical than usual. The official story was that people were using their air-conditioning more than ever, causing some of the transformers to fail. But in Lagos, it was more likely to be just a circumstantial cover-up for a new corruption scheme.

Ayo looked up, saw her at the window, and shouted, "Ansara, bring some water down here." Sometimes she felt that Ayo liked to give her work just to show that he was the boss. She brought him a bottle of cool water, not showing any sign of her annoyance.

"Ansara, have you talked to your mother lately?"

"No," she replied, surprised. Ayo usually acted as though

it was beneath him to have a conversation with her. Admitting that he knew her from a social setting outside the house was out of character for him. "I tried to call her last Sunday at Mohammed's shop. But she hadn't come to the shop at the usual time. I thought something might have come up."

"Hmm..." Ayo seemed to be hesitating.

"What? Is there something wrong?"

"Well, it may not be anything, but…" The lack of gruffness in Ayo's voice unsettled Ansara.

"Do you have any news from my mother?" she asked.

"I spoke to Chidera yesterday. She said they have not seen your mother for a few days. She asked me to let you know."

"What?? What happened to my mother? Where is my son?" Ansara's voice was almost a high-pitched scream. She wanted to shout at him. Why had he not told her immediately?

"Look, it may not be anything," said Ayo. "The heat there is much worse than here, maybe she just decided to get out of the city."

"Get out of the city?" asked Ansara. "My mother would never do that. My son is with her."

"Your son is with Chidera's mother. Your mother left him at their house for a few days. Nothing to worry about," said Ayo.

"But she wouldn't leave Femi with Mrs. Jideofor. She would have said goodbye before leaving. She would have told me before she left. It makes no sense," said Ansara, her words coming out in a rush.

Ayo did not reply.

Ansara arrived at the bus station at a quarter to six in the morning, almost an hour before the bus was scheduled to depart. It was the main bus station in Lagos, and in just a few hours, the place would be a sprawling ground of chaos and cacophony with honking buses, shouting passengers, jostling vendors, persistent beggars, and on market days, bleating goats and cackling chickens. But for now, it was still dark and the place was quiet, except for the snores from people who had spent the night there and had yet to rouse from their slumbers. In just a few minutes, when the first bus started, they would have to get up or risk being under a hurried commuter's feet.

Ever since she got the news from Ayo the previous day, she had counted down the minutes, vacillating between hope and despair. She had tried to leave immediately after the conversation, but then found out that most of the regular buses had stopped running; just a few were still operating.

As soon as Martin arrived home and heard her news, he tried to book her a flight. Ansara listened to Martin's half of the conversation with a sinking heart. All flights to Port Harcourt had been canceled, she could hear the distant voice of the travel agent say even though the phone was pressed to Martin's ear. Martin tried to convince the agent to get them tickets through any route, but apparently, it was not possible. The quickest way to get there, she said, was by road. A car or a bus were the only options. Martin thanked her and hung up.

Ansara sighed. "It's ok. I was planning to take the bus anyway."

"No, Ansa. Let's take the car. I will call Mohammad now."

"I think I should go alone. And the bus is fine. They travel much faster than cars, actually."

"I want to come with you. It may not be safe, and I can help search for your mother."

Ansara touched his face gently with her hand. "*Nkem*, it is best if you don't come. Don't worry about safety. It's my town, I grew up there, remember? I'll be fine."

"Are you sure?"

"Yes, sure. I don't know what has happened, or what is in store for us there, and a white man driving up there with me in a big car will attract more attention than necessary. In times like these, it's safest to keep a low profile."

"I can always come with you on the bus."

Ansara smiled at Martin's earnestness. "No, *nkem*, I'll go alone. Besides, you have your work here. I will be fine." She did not tell him that she could not even imagine Martin traveling on Nigeria's public buses. Besides, she felt that having Martin around, despite his best intentions, would be more of a hindrance than help. People would expect more bribes with an *oyibo* around and it could even alienate those who may otherwise help her. This was a trip she needed to do alone.

The bus to Port Harcourt came in at about 6.30 a.m. There were ten people waiting to get on. Ansara was surprised. Usually, buses to Port Harcourt were packed to the brim.

"What happened? Why are there so few people?" Ansara asked the woman next to her. She had the bored look of a regular commuter, but her eyes betrayed a kind of curiosity that indicated that if there was anything to know, she would be the first to know.

The woman looked at Ansara suspiciously, as if she must be mad that she could ask such a question. After looking her up and down, she seemed to decide that the question was genuine and Ansara was really expecting a reply.

"You mean you don't know what's going on there? The heat! It's unbearable there! People are dying. You don't know, and you've packed your bags to go, you silly woman."

Ansara did not particularly care for being addressed as a silly woman, but she needed information. For two weeks now, she had had no news except for snippets gleaned from Martin's English newspapers. But the *Wall Street Journal* and the *Financial Times* carried very little local news. They had all reported about the heatwave striking Africa that could turn into a major disaster, but the articles had not sounded immediate or threatening, only like a white man's typical response to a higher-than-usual increase in summer temperatures.

"I'm going to find my mother. She lives there, with my son. I haven't been able to get in touch with her for a few weeks now."

The woman's eyes mellowed in sympathy, and she said in a slightly softer voice, "I hear many old people are in hospital. They couldn't stand the heat. Check hospitals first."

Ansara nodded, any suggestion welcome. "How bad is the heat? I haven't been out of Lagos in many months, and here it's not that different from a very hot summer."

"It's terrible, girl. Very, very terrible. I was there a month ago, everything was normal. Then I went just last week, and it was all so different. The heat was like that in the middle of a desert. They say an angry jinn from the Sahara has come down to devour the people. It sleeps for five hundred years and then it comes out to eat people before it goes back to sleep again."

Ansara nodded again. She would have to listen to the jinn story and probably many more stories like that, if she hoped to get any useful information.

The man sitting in front of them turned around. He had been listening, and by now, considered it a sufficiently interesting conversation to join in.

"My daughters, they lived in Port Harcourt. The eldest one came home to Lagos last week. She thought the weather was already terrible. I'm going now to fetch my younger daughter, help her get her things together. It's no good. The place is no good in this weather."

The man, with his wrinkled body, missing teeth, and scarred face seemed to be the kind who would not be fazed by a slight change in weather. It could not be a good sign that he was going all the way to Port Harcourt to help his daughter.

Ansara resolved to bring her mother and Femi with her to Lagos. The servants' quarters were small and all she had was a tiny bed, but her mother could sleep in the room behind the kitchen. Femi could sleep with her in her bed. Ayo would not be happy, but this would be the one time she would ask Martin to overrule Ayo's decision. She would think about the consequences of that later; for now, she had bigger worries.

"It's good that your daughters are leaving. Did you know that people are going mad? Men and women are running through the streets stark naked," the woman next to Ansara continued.

"Yes, the heat makes people lose their mind. The hospitals are overflowing. None of them are taking new patients. If you're sick, you've nowhere to go," the wrinkled man added.

"I still have business there. People still need to buy things. But I said this is my last trip till the jinn goes back. Last time I sell things for some time. It's bad for business, but I value my life."

"Yes, of course. The streets are no longer safe. Guns are coming out much faster. The other day, I heard someone shot a young girl just to get the bottle of water she was carrying."

"A bottle of water, a space in the shade, a morsel of rice… These days, you don't need much to get shot at."

Ansara stared out of the window, hoping the bus would get moving soon. All this depressing talk was not getting her anywhere. And she had a long way to go.

A few hours into the journey, the weather began to change noticeably. It was getting hotter and hotter, as if they were driving toward an active volcano. The lush green that usually adorned the roadside had begun to give way to dried-up plants that stood limply, refusing to accept that their will to live would not be sufficient to win against the vehemence of the heat. The plants reminded her of spirits who, according to ancient beliefs, lingered on Earth long after their death, never quite getting around to starting their journey to the nether world. Even the stray dogs and cats dawdled, neither bothering to disturb the other, as if they were all suffering together in the grip of a deadly lethargy.

In the bus, passengers were getting jittery. Those who had managed to sleep despite the rumbling noise and the bumpy ride were roused by the suffocating heat. Rolled-up newspapers were up in the air, going back and forth in a desperate attempt to cool the air. The enterprising driver tried to sell bottles of water at an exorbitant rate of five hundred naira a bottle. No one was buying it yet, but he knew it was only a matter of time before someone would be ready to shell out hard-earned money for a few sips.

By the time the bus rolled into the main station at Port Harcourt, the sun had begun to set.

CHAPTER 19

'Beautify Lagos campaign to resume, more destruction ahead' The headline screamed out at Ayo from the last page of the *Daily Herald*.

It was not a newspaper he usually read, but the page fluttered just on top of his head, irritating him, while he was paying for his beer at the local roadside shop. The headline caught his attention: It was bold and big, and accompanied by a full-page article and pictures, one of which he was sure he recognized.

He pulled the newspaper out from the clip that held it to the thin thread above the shop, partly because of frustration and partly because of curiosity. He had barely glanced at it when the man behind the raised counter cleared his throat and said, "You want to read, you need to buy. People behind you also must buy things."

Ayo grunted impatiently and paid for the beer and the newspaper. The picture that had drawn him in was part of a set of four. The first was of Shamiya, a shantytown situated to the west of Lagos. It focused on a young girl of about ten with bewildered eyes, holding a broken bucket. The water leaking from it formed a jagged line tracing the path she had followed. She was presumably running from the river from which she had collected the water toward the burning shanty that lay in front of her. The photographer must have called to her, because it looked like she had stopped in her tracks and turned around, perhaps expecting help or relief, but instead receiving nothing but the bright light of a large flashlight held by an unnamed intruder.

The second picture showed a bulldozer about to start moving toward a shanty. It was hard to recognize the shantytown from the picture, but the caption below identified it as Abuska, which lay to the east of his own shantytown. The houses still looked like they had people in them, or had been recently abandoned: Clotheslines still had wet laundry hung out to dry, the mud had markings from a children's game just deserted, small flames still peeped out from the sides of a pan of fresh meat left to cook on a block of bricks. A crowd was gathered to the side of the bulldozer, but no one dared to step in front of it to stop the demolition of their homes. In all likelihood, the driver had instructions to go ahead with his task regardless of whether there were protesters in front of him.

Ayo peered at the third photograph. He did not recognize the place, and the caption did not say where it was taken. It showed the aftermath of a bulldozer having passed through a shantytown, almost as if it was taken after the second photograph, but there was nothing left to make such a recognition possible. The walls of most of the shacks had been crushed. Some remained, trying in vain to preserve the privacy of a place that no longer existed, as if they were the last remaining soldiers in battle, forging ahead while refusing to accept that the war had already been lost. In the distance, if he looked carefully, he could see a family of five with heavy loads on their heads walking away from the scene.

The fourth one, the one that had caught his attention, was that of his own shantytown. It was, he decided, the least depressing of the four. It just showed a well-dressed man in blue jeans and a t-shirt that had the letters *Armini* sprawled across it, holding a microphone toward a thin, haggard fellow. Behind the two men was Ahmed's old teashop, complete with the hanging plantains and the swarm of flies. Ayo recognized the man being interviewed as the new proprietor of the shop, a happy grin radiating across his face, the joy of being interviewed and photographed overshadowing the gloom of his shop and the shantytown being obliterated.

He read through a few paragraphs of the article.

Authorities have so far destroyed nearly twenty shantytowns in southern Nigeria as part of an urban development plan, displacing at least 25,000 people from their homes without compensation, human rights groups said on Monday.

"I'm stranded. I don't know where to stay now," said 28-year-old Jide Adeyemi, crying as his wife salvaged pots and pans from their house, destroyed by government bulldozers in recent days.

When the campaign was launched three years ago, the focus was on Lagos where the destruction was especially brutal. Most of the damage was done in the western and northern parts of Lagos, before the campaign was mysteriously stopped in the middle of its operations and moved to other part of the country.

While rumors have been abundant about the reasons for its sudden stop in the main city, the residents of the shanties that were spared were relieved. Now it looks like the relief might have been short-lived.

He groaned as he read the list of shanties that were next in line. His own was on the list, and according to the article, it would not be long before the residents would be displaced.

Without compensation, without sufficient warning, and without an alternative place to stay, the article went on to say.

Ayo crumpled the newspaper in disgust and threw it to the side of the road as he headed back to his apartment.

Ayo had been sixteen years old when he left the house he grew up in for good. It had been a typical day: He woke up early, hung out with his buddies in the shantytown smoking whatever it was he could get his hands on, holding on to the one beer bottle he could afford to buy, and making sleazy remarks to the girls that passed by. His mother had prepared dinner, and he had come home to eat. His brother had already stopped coming home, even though he often saw him hanging out at the other side of the shantytown, mostly with a crowd of drug lord's cronies. They never acknowledged each other beyond a brief nod.

Ayo could not even remember what it was that had instigated his mother that day—it must have been something small and inconsequential—but he remembered clearly the mood changing without even a moment's notice. His mother leaned over, took his bowl from his side of the table, and threw it against the tenuous walls of the shanty. The bowl broke into tiny pieces while the *garri* in it made stains on the walls. His mother took out the log she kept in a corner and started beating him, all the while cursing him and his brother and their good-for-nothing father. He tried to protest, but she was too strong and had too large a log for him to do anything. He somehow managed to run out of the house, but only after a large part of his body had been bruised.

He limped back home well past midnight. His mother was fast asleep, with an innocent, almost babylike smile playing on her lips. He stared down at her and at that moment, decided that if he were ever to remain sane and perhaps even alive, he needed to leave. He needed to get as far as possible from the woman who clearly seemed to have the devil in her.

Many years later, with time lending a forgiving hand, Ayo could see that she had been doing the best she could. Drawn to extremes of happiness and despair, love and anger, the loneliness and hard work must have been too much for her to bear. But at that time, he could not even comprehend, much less forgive, the mother who would take out her frustrations on him. He could no longer live with the uncertainty and the volatility and the constant fear of not knowing what lay ahead, not knowing when a happy meal would turn into something violent, not knowing when a hug could lead to a slap, not knowing whether any day would end in peaceful slumber or a slew of ruthless flogging.

That night, while she slept peacefully, he packed up his meager belongings and left. Never to look back.

But now, as he lay on his cot, relaxing on a weekend evening free of responsibilities, his stomach satiated after a hearty meal and his mind blissfully numbed by a six-pack of beer, his memory succumbed to the trickeries of time. He let it paint the less painful events of his past in happier hues while allowing the torturous ones to fade away further into oblivion.

He thought of the many happy meals they shared on the days she was not violent, of the roof she provided above his head, and of the sacrifices she must have had to make to offer him and his brother a living that was decent by the standards of his shantytown. If he dug deep enough, Ayo still had some respect for the strength and resilience of the woman who was largely responsible for giving him his life and for making sure he stayed alive, at least for the first fifteen years. She may not have been the most affectionate or the most consistent of mothers, he reasoned to himself, but at some level of consciousness, she must have cared about him. He had more to be grateful for than to be bitter about.

By the end of that week, Ayo had decided to make his second trip to the shantytown.

This time, he wasted no time going to his old home, but headed straight to the bridge. He must have waited about twenty minutes and was about to give up, when he saw the harassed figure approaching from the distance. She carried a gunnysack with her and stopped at regular intervals along the river to pick up something or other.

Ayo hesitated, but not for long. He had come this far to meet her, and now he could not just go back. He walked down the bridge to the riverside.

"Mama," he said.

There was a moment of surprise on her face. But it was soon replaced by a look of fear. If there was any sign of recognition, it was too fleeting for Ayo to notice. She must have been so plagued by tormentors ever since she went mad that her first reaction to anything unfamiliar was terror. She tried to hide her gunnysack and move away.

"Mama, it's me. Ayomide. Remember me? I'm your son."

Again, just a blank scared stare.

"I'm not here to hurt you. I don't want your things. You can keep them." He tried to gently take her arm. "How about I buy you some food?"

To his surprise, she did not resist.

He led her to old Ahmed's shop. The shop was crowded, with many people standing beside the counter, listening to the new proprietor loudly talking about the details of his interview with the newspaper reporter.

Ayo's mother's eyes shone with anticipation at the sight of the plantains—it must have been weeks, or even months, Ayo had no idea, since she had a decent meal. Ayo reached up and plucked a plantain for her. The proprietor looked at him briefly, not bothering to break the flow of his conversation, and Ayo nodded to acknowledge that he would pay for it later. She ate it up in a few large bites and looked at him with gratitude.

They walked inside the store, where Ahmed was still sitting in the corner. Ayo called out to the small boy who seemed to be an employee and ordered a midday meal.

"Only one?" The boy looked at him in suspicion.

"Yes, one for now." Ayo shooed him away. He watched as his mother gobbled up the food.

"Ah, good that you're back. Your mother is eating good food." Ahmed turned around from his corner. He adopted a louder voice, as if speaking to someone who could not hear or comprehend and spoke slowly, enunciating each word. "Akeeba, how are you? Do you remember me?"

The loud voice and the increased effort brought on a coughing fit, and he turned away. Akeeba looked up for a moment and then went back to her food, ignoring the old man.

After a while, the old man looked up again and said, "Quite a crowd here. Everyone thinks Kachi knows something about the demolitions. He's enjoying his few moments of fame. Good for the business, I say."

"Does he know?"

"No, not much. I was here when the reporters came. They didn't tell him anything."

"So they're going to bulldoze the place, huh?"

"Bulldoze shulldoze, I say it's just some publicity shit. The weather has been so hot these days, they would wait till the weather is a bit better. By the time they come around to doing it, it'll be a while." He raised his voice and said, "Our shantytown, it never dies, I say."

The raised voice set him coughing again, and this time he was at it for a while.

As Ayo sat there watching his mother devour the food, he tried to think of what he could do with her. He didn't want to take her with him. The obligation of taking care of someone was not something that he wanted at the moment. And it was probably something that he couldn't ever fit into his lifestyle. He spent most of his days at Martin's house, where his evenings were for drinking with friends. It was only on weekends that he made a trip back to the one-room apartment on the mainland, and that because he would have a girl or two in his arms and he needed a place to spend the night. Having his mother at Martin's place was out of the question, and having his mother at his own apartment was not something he wanted. Besides, he couldn't leave her alone in his apartment for most of the week; he couldn't forget that she was already insane and incapable of taking care of herself. Ayo sighed. He wanted to be that young boy again who had, without a second thought, left home and never looked back. He hated himself for feeling this dilemma. It should have been easy for him to ignore his mother and walk away.

His mother was so intent on eating she did not notice as he got from up from the bench. He paid for the lunch and the plantain and left the shantytown.

But he kept coming back. Every few weekends, he would come back and repeat what had by now become a ritual. He would wait for her at the bridge. She would come by after twenty, fifteen, or sometimes even just five minutes. And together they would have a meal at old Ahmed's shop. Ahmed had become more and more chatty over the visits, reminiscing about the good old days whenever his wheezing would let up long enough to embark on a monologue.

It must have been the fourth or the fifth such visit. As usual, Ayo was on top of the bridge, and his mother was ambling toward him. She looked extraordinarily tired that day. The temperatures were continuing their steady climb up, and like most elderly folk, she must have begun to feel the effect of those rises. When she came up to him, Ayo was sure there was a look of recognition on her face. She stood maybe a few inches away from him and caressed his face with her palms, outlining his face with her fingers.

"Ayomide," she said gently, "it's you. It's really you."

"Mama. Mama." Ayo did not know what else to say. "How are you?" he said after a pause, as if he was meeting her for the first time after so many years. In many ways, it felt like he was. It seemed that the woman he had been meeting on all those weekends was someone else, and now finally his mother was here.

There were tears in her eyes. She seemed to recognize, for a few lucid moments, what had become of her life. Was it shame that he saw? Was it pain? Or was it a deep sense of loss about the dignity that had long deserted her?

"Ayomide. You've grown so much," she said, looking him

up and down. "I'm tired, my son. Very, very tired. Can you do me a favor? One last favor."

"Yes, of course, Mama."

There was no time for small talk or pleasantries; it was as if she wanted to tell him whatever she wanted to before she lost grip on her mind again. "I want to end my struggles. I want to end this torture, and I can't. Will you help me?"

Ayo could not believe what his own mother, after she had finally recognized him, was asking of him. "Mama, no, I can't do that. I just cannot do that." Ayo had seen many murders in his life and had also been party to some. But to kill his own mother, even if it was at her own request, was something he could not bring himself to do.

"Yes, I understand. I'm sorry I asked. Sometimes, just sometimes, the pain is unbearable. I wish I would just die." Her eyes, dry by now, looked sadder than if she had tears streaming down her face. "I'm glad to see you. Happy. Very, very happy."

Those were the last words Ayo remembered her saying in her lucid state. After that, she rested her head on his shoulder for a few minutes, resting, relishing, absorbing the moment to stash it in a memory that seemed not to obey her anymore. When she lifted her head again, she remembered nothing of the past.

She seemed to have a vague recollection of an association between Ayo and lunch, and she eagerly pointed toward the tea shop, her eyes lighting up like a five-year-old's. Ayo sighed and led her to their regular haunt, where they would order a midday meal and she would relish it, leaving him to contemplate the gravity of the favor she had asked of him.

That night he shocked himself by seriously considering putting her out of her misery. He could not even imagine what it must be like to lose your ability to think, and if his mother wanted it so much, he should find a way to get her to heaven. But how could he? She was the only family he ever really had, and ever would have, and no matter how much strangers' blood had spread on his palms, he did not want his mother's to be among them.

CHAPTER 20

Ansara looked around the bus station she had just stepped into, the gateway to her hometown, exclusively for the unfortunate who could not afford the speedboats, the planes, or even the cars. Unlike the bus depot at Lagos, this place was still crowded. Long queues of very tired people, many of them with overflowing Ghana bags, the kind that could hold a family's entire belongings, were waiting for buses to take them to places far away.

As Ansara stood amidst the bustling bus station, myriad emotions welled up within her. She felt a wave of warmth sweep through her. After the alienation and anonymity of Lagos, it was nice to be home. But she shuddered with fear as she thought of her mother. Where could she have gone without telling anyone?

Port Harcourt had always been a bustling city; it was the epicenter of activities in the Rivers State. Today, the city was still a busy place, but it seemed to be fueled by pessimism and anxiety rather than optimism and ambition. Young men and women did not run and shout at each other clamoring to get the best deals. Instead, they walked around with shoulders drooped, heads hung low, their will to live held by thin threads of vague hope. Unlike every other time that Ansara had been at this bus station, no vendors offered her reduced rates in an attempt to clear their wares before the end of the day, no young boys offered to be her porter for exorbitant rates they would expect to be negotiated down, and no hooligans hooted or shouted sleazy comments at the beautiful young woman. The relative silence felt more conspicuous and real than the raucous noises of a regular day.

Ansara took the exit at the west side of the bus station and walked toward her house. The sun had gone down, leaving just a faint glow to guide her through the walkways. She hastened her steps, not wanting to be out on the streets when darkness fell. If even half of what she had heard on the bus was true, the less time she spent out the better.

Her neighborhood was shrouded in an eerie quietness. There were no kids playing in the background, no women coming back from work, no men swatting flies while lounging on makeshift beds outside. The foreboding silence, with the occasional flicker of candlelight coming from some of the windows, terrified her.

"Femi, Mama is here!" Ansara called out, panic rising as she realized the house was empty. Despite Ayo's message, she had retained a faint hope that perhaps her mother would have returned, and all would be back to normal by the time she got to Port Harcourt. Ansara went into the kitchen. The stove, though not cleaned out, looked like it had not been used for a few days. She ran through the back door into Mrs. Jideofor's house.

Mrs. Jideofor was resting on the cot inside her house. Chidera was sleeping on the floor, and Ansara saw two children lying next to her, her son among them.

"Femi, you're safe! Oh, thank God!" She went over and hugged him tightly, kissing him all over his face. He smiled in his sleep and opened his eyes briefly, but they were glazed with sleep. Or fatigue. Ansara smiled back at him and laid him gently down, feeling sheepish about disturbing a sleeping boy.

Mrs. Jideofor got up slowly. Ansara wondered what had happened to the energetic lively woman. She seemed to have been replaced by someone weighed down by stones, struggling even to get off the bed.

"Ansa, you're here. Thank you, Jesus. We were wondering how to get in touch with you. In the end, Chidera managed to send a message to Ayomide. Are you alright, my child?" Mrs. Jideofor was looking at her as if she expected her to be broken or injured, worrying that something may not be right.

"I'm ok. Thank you. What happened here? Where is Mama? Is she ok? Ayomide was not clear what happened to her. The house is empty."

"Sit down, my child."

Ansara did not want to sit down. She just wanted to know what had happened to her mother. But Mrs. Jideofor was tugging at her elbow, and it was easier to just give in and sit on the cot beside her.

"Kisi left, Ansa. She left a few days ago. We don't know what happened."

"Left? Where did she go?"

"It was getting so hot here, it was very difficult. She fainted at her work a few times, and after the third time, they fired her. She couldn't do much around the house either, she was tired all the time. It comes with old age, my child." Mrs. Jideofor sighed. "I told her to go to your brother up north. She didn't want to go, but anyone with family outside is getting out. I told her she must go to you or your brother."

"But she didn't tell me anything about it. What about Femi? Was she going to take Femi to Makurdi?"

"She was going to ask you, Ansa. It was just a few days ago. She went to Mohammed's shop to call you and then… Femi was playing here with Inni." Mrs. Jideofor paused and wiped the sweat on her brow before she added softly, "She hasn't been back since then."

Chidera was by now awake and sitting up, leaning her head on the cot. She looked up and said, "We looked everywhere, Ansa. We went to Mohammed's shop later, but he said your mother didn't show up. We don't know where she went. Maybe she left for Makurdi?"

"No, of course not, she wouldn't leave just like that. That's impossible." Ansara felt a silent rage, but at what or whom it was directed, she was not sure.

"Ansa, we looked in all the streets, we asked whoever we could find. No one had seen her," said Mrs. Jideofor, her words barely louder than a whisper, as if apologizing for being the bearer of bad news.

Ansara nodded. She walked over to Femi again. He slept peacefully, unaware that his grandmother was missing, believing Mrs. Jideofor's words that she had gone to Makurdi to visit his uncle. Ansara bent down and kissed him gently on his forehead, careful not to wake him.

She stood up and said to no one in particular, "I'll check all the hospitals tomorrow. And look through the streets and shops. And the refinery too, and the church." She realized, even as she said it, that none of them provided an explanation to why her mother would have been gone for days. "I'll also check at the police station." She left out the morgue; it was too painful even to form the words.

Ansara had a lot to do the next day. A good sleep was what she needed, but it kept eluding her through the night. The heat was like a thick dark blanket that would not budge, weighing her down and soaking her body in sweat. Open windows brought in mosquitoes and flies rather than any wind. Water was so scarce that it would have been treason to think of using some to cool her skin. There was nothing to do except lie down and hope that tiredness would take over.

As she slipped in and out of consciousness, images of her mother kept streaming in. She imagined her mother walking to the shop, with a bag to carry back the shopping and Ansara's phone number on a piece of paper safely tucked into her wrapper. All of a sudden, her mother was at the edge of a cliff, and not noticing the abrupt change in landscape, she walked right off the cliff. Then suddenly, she was walking down the street again and turning into an alley she had never been to before—one that could have made a perfect scene setting for a movie in hell—and getting completely lost. She had no idea where to go and kept calling out for Ansara.

After each abrupt ending, Ansara woke up with a start. As the night progressed, her dreams became less surreal and more unnerving. She saw a car come out of nowhere, open the door, and pull her mother right in. The hooded men drove off before anyone in the street even noticed them. In another variation, she saw the same car with the hooded men, but the men shot her mother in the chest three times before grabbing her bag and speeding off.

Ansara woke up again, sitting up in her bed this time. Femi was sleeping beside her, his nostrils flaring slightly in tiny regular snores. She decided to get herself a drink of water. The water supply was still running here, even though it was only for a few hours a day. Mrs. Jideofor had told her there were rumors that even that would stop soon. Ansara was grateful for the soothing cold of the water, the clay pot having protected it from the heat outside.

She decided not to go back to sleep, instead using the time to look through the meager belongings in the house, packing her mother's and Femi's clothes in anticipation of their trip back to Lagos. It did not take her long to decide what to take, but she went about the task slowly, wary of the restless sleep that lay ahead if she were to finish packing too soon.

Finally, just as she finished throwing things into the two Ghana bags her mother had kept in a wooden box and was thinking that this night could not get any longer, she heard the cock crow, and the first rays of the sun came in through the cracks in the window.

Ansara's first stop was the City General Hospital. It was located on a busy street near the bus station, and even as she approached, she could see a large crowd outside the hospital. Some were crying at the wayside, while many just stood and stared, and a luckier few were walking as if they still had some purpose in life. There was a long queue at the information and inquiries desk, which was manned by just one person who looked tired and irritated.

There must have been at least twenty others in front of her, all in different levels of despair. It didn't take long for Ansara to realize that they were all there for the same reason: to search for a missing loved one. It was tedious to have to listen to the same conversations, repeated on a mirthless unrelenting loop.

"Next!" the attendant would say.

The next in line would move forward, holding on tighter to their bag as if the harder they clutched it the more support it would provide in case the news was bad. "I am looking for 'name-of-missing-person.'"

"Who?" the assistant would ask, either slightly deaf or to make sure she got the name absolutely right before she gave them news, good or bad.

The name of the person would be repeated, louder this time.

The attendant would flip through pages and pages of a long list, filled in a scrawled handwriting with names added to the end as and when new patients were admitted. If they could still remember their names, that is. The names were not in any particular order other than the order in which they were admitted, and there didn't seem to be any way of removing names if and when the person was discharged, or more likely, dead.

The answer would come after minutes of incessant flipping. "No such person here," or "He came in a few days ago, check the ward inside."

The ones who got the first answer would hang their head, dipping one more level in their desperation, and head to the next hospital. The others would head inside, advancing to the next stage of their search, where they would peer at the rows and rows of sick people lying down wherever they could find an inch of space.

After a few names had been searched, Ansara tried to tune out her thoughts, the repeated performance plunging her further into hopelessness. Just then, she heard a commotion up front. She peered ahead and saw that a woman a little ahead of her in the queue had fainted and fallen to the floor. The woman looked as thin as a stick but with a protruding belly. She was too old for *kwashiorkor*, so pregnancy seemed the more likely explanation.

As Ansara watched in growing horror, the queue just moved forward, neatly stepping over her. A woman a bit down in the line felt an iota of pity and moved her slightly, so people could move past without really stepping over the body on the ground. Ansara was just about to rush over to the woman when she heard a voice from behind. "You leave your place in the queue, you don't get it back."

Ansara looked back. By now there were at least ten more people behind her in the queue.

"But she has fainted. She needs help."

"We all need help. She'll get over it."

Ansara hesitated for a moment. Going back to the end of the queue was not an appealing thought, and this was just the first stop in her search. Then, chiding herself for having thought that, she stepped forward and helped the woman to the curb.

She let the woman's head rest in her lap and tried to shake her into wakefulness. She remembered the bottle of water that Mrs. Jideofor had insisted on putting into her bag and took it out. She had barely sprinkled water onto the woman's face when Ansara felt a rush of air behind her. Before she knew what had happened, someone had snatched the bottle from her hand. She looked up, angry and shocked, to find a toothless man staring back at her. He wore ragged clothes that covered some parts of his upper body, his torso and scraggly legs left bare for all to see. He grinned at her. The heat had deprived him not only of his modesty but also his sanity. Before she could think of what to say or do, he disappeared into the crowd.

The water brought the woman back to consciousness. She muttered something and clutched her belly. Ansara helped her sit up on the curb. And then, without a word and without turning back, she walked to the end of the queue, startling Ansara with her abrupt recovery. Ansara shook her head in disbelief and then took her position behind the pregnant woman, settling herself for a long wait.

It was more than an hour before Ansara's turn came up. "Kisi Okafor," she shouted as loud as she could. It seemed like an eternity to Ansara while the attendant flipped through the pages and finally the verdict was out. "No. No one by that name in this hospital."

Ansara stood there stunned. It seemed rather unreasonable that such a long wait in this hot weather would yield nothing but a negative answer delivered in one short phrase.

"Next," came the attendant's booming voice, and Ansara was roughly moved aside by the next person who had been eagerly awaiting his turn.

Ansara spent the rest of the day going from hospital to hospital, visiting each of the five main hospitals in Port Harcourt, but the results were the same: a long wait and a negative answer at the end.

She tried the police station, her mother's workplace, the church, and even the morgue, but there was no sign of Kisi Okafor. It was as if she had disappeared from the face of the earth, and no one had even noticed. Dejected, Ansara headed back home.

For three days, Ansara kept going back to all the places she could think of. She went back to places she had already been to. She tried to think of new places. Any place that her mother could have gone to. She tried asking people on the streets. Had they seen an old woman with curly black hair and possibly wearing a yellow wrapper and a white t-shirt? Either the answer was a straight out "No, don't bother me" or "Yes, I have seen many." After all, old, curly black hair, and a yellow wrapper could describe many a person in Port Harcourt.

The last time Ansara had felt so helpless was the summer of 2004, a few months before Femi was born. She was home then too, for the summer, on a break from her work at the Andersons, while the Anderson family were away on holiday. Ikenna had left for his village after asking her to marry him.

The days were passing in a joyous bliss. Ansara was nervous yet excited about meeting his family. She had been waiting for him to call or send a messenger to let her know when they would arrive for the wine-carrying ceremony. Instead, he surprised her by showing up at her door.

It must have been late afternoon. Her mother had finished her morning shift and was free for the rest of the day.

"Ikenna, what a surprise!" She ran to him and hugged him. She ignored the slight resistance she felt when he hugged her back. "I'm so glad to see you. I was beginning to think you would never come. Let me go tell Mama."

She turned around to leave, but he caught her by the wrist.

"No, wait. I've to talk to you."

"Yes, yes, I know, you want to talk to me. I want to talk to you too. I missed you. But let me just tell—"

"No, wait." Ikenna tightened his grip on her wrist.

"Is everything ok? You are scaring me. What happened?"

"Ansa, I don't know how to tell you this…"

Ikenna was struggling for words. Ansara interjected, "Tell me what?"

"I spoke to my *umunna*. They don't want us to get married now."

"Oh, when do they want us to get married? After our child is all grown up?"

"No, no, that's not what I mean. They want you to get rid of the child. And we can get married a bit later. They won't let me marry a woman who is already pregnant."

"What? They want to get rid of our child? Are they crazy?"

"Well, it makes the most sense…" Ikenna tried to pull her closer.

Ansara pushed him roughly and pulled back her arm that he was still holding on to. "Makes sense? You think it makes sense? You agree with them?" She put her head in her hands. "Oh my God!"

"Ansa, listen to me. It's all going to be alright. I'll take care of you."

"Ikenna, we can't get rid of the child. He's our baby."

"How do they know it's mine?"

Ansara felt a shiver of rage pass through her entire body. It was as if every emotion she had ever experienced had decided to culminate now in her person and was exploding at that exact same moment.

Ikenna said, "I'm sorry. I didn't mean it that way."

She sat down, suddenly, as if something had pushed her down. The weight of her own body was too much for her legs to bear. Silence hung in the air between them. After a while, Ansara spoke, calmed by the few moments of quiet. "We've to keep the baby. I'm not getting rid of it. It's too late, Ikenna. We can't just kill our own child."

Ikenna did not say anything. She continued, "Ikenna, let's get married anyway. We don't need our families. We can live our lives, and we'll have our child."

A look of shock came over Ikenna's face. "No, I'll not go against my *umunna*. You must destroy the child. I cannot marry a woman who already has a child. I can't take care of a child now." Ikenna did not even look at her face as he spoke.

"Ikenna, this is our child. A life. God's gift. We cannot kill it."

"You have to. You have to destroy the child." Ansara noted the use of the word "you." As if he had nothing to do with it. Ikenna kept shifting from one leg to the other.

"I cannot. I will not." She tried to look inside herself and find a reason to keep loving him. A reason to want to do as he asked her to do. All she felt was revulsion. A growing hatred toward the man who was asking her to take her own, his own, child's life.

A look of horror came over his face, as if he was suddenly helpless in the face of her resolve. He turned around and left, not saying another word.

Three days of relentless searching had been in vain. Ansara was resting at home, resigned and exhausted. She watched Femi eat the meager dinner she could put together.

Mrs. Jideofor came by and sat next to her. They sat there for a while, watching the child eat, each thinking about the misfortunes that had befallen them, one missing a beloved mother and the other a dear friend.

"Ansa, you've searched a lot, my child. It's time to stop." Mrs. Jideofor's voice was low and husky.

Ansara did not respond. Even when you know something is true in your heart, sometimes it is easier to pretend it is not true till you hear it spoken by someone else.

"You should go back to Lagos. I'm sure Kisi wouldn't want you to risk losing your job. Take Femi with you, he's getting thinner and thinner in this heat."

Ansara stared at the walls of her childhood home. She knew what Mrs. Jideofor was suggesting was the only sensible option. The whole evening she had been grappling with what else she could do to find her mother, and the truth was that she had come up with nothing else to do and nowhere else to search. It was unlikely that she would lose her job, Martin wouldn't do that to her, but she had to think of Femi. She was struggling to provide him with food here. She herself had barely eaten more than a few handfuls of rice a day since she arrived, and the exhaustion was beginning to make her delusional.

Femi would soon finish his food, and she would have to tell him about what lay ahead. The boy was very fond of his grandmother, and she was not sure how he would fit into life in a Lagos mansion.

She was glad that Mrs. Jideofor was sitting next to her, someone to share the weight of the silence.

"Ansa, I know this is not the right time to ask, but there is something I've been meaning to ask you."

'Yes, Mrs. Jideofor, what is it?"

"It's about Ayomide. I know you work in the same house as him. He has not come around for a few months now. He used to call in the beginning, but these days, he doesn't even do that. Do you know if everything is ok there? Does he have another wife there?"

"I don't think so, Mrs. Jideofor. As far as I know, he doesn't have another family. But I'll keep a look out and let you know if I hear of anything." Ansara added, "It's probably just the heat, it's difficult to travel here."

"Yes, I wish we could have the wedding soon. If I can make sure Chidera is safe with her man, I can close my eyes in peace. This damn heat is going to take all of us, and I just want to know my daughter will be safe."

"Don't say that, Mrs. Jideofor. You'll be fine. We'll all be fine." Ansara consoled her with a confidence she did not feel. "I'll ask Ayo the next chance I get and let you know."

Mrs. Jideofor sighed and fell silent again. The two women sat side by side, each lost in their own thoughts and worries but glad to have someone beside them.

After a while, Mrs. Jideofor got up to leave. Ansara

looked up at her.

"I'll leave tomorrow morning. As early as I can. The buses out are very crowded, so the earlier I leave the better the chances of getting on one of them."

Mrs. Jideofor nodded. "You take care, my child. Till my last breath, I'll make sure you'll have a home here to come back to. May the Lord be with you."

They hugged each other goodbye.

Ansara arrived at the bus station before dawn the next morning. Luckily, the crowds had not yet gathered in full force. She managed to get on a bus leaving for Lagos and even got a place in the last row. Femi fell asleep as soon as he could get a place to sit. She smiled at her sleeping son. At least he was still young enough to be blissfully oblivious of the full gravity of the situation.

Unlike her journey to Port Harcourt, the people in the bus were unusually quiet. The heat had already taken its toll on their energy. Besides, each of them was leaving behind a home, a history, and in many cases, family. Ansara leaned back and closed her eyes, trying to push away the unwanted thoughts crowding into her head. She was unsure of what she was leaving behind or for how long, but she was certain that it was best not to think about it.

CHAPTER 21

2 to 27: With those odds, would you bet on our survival?

Posted on 13th April, 2010, Tuesday. By Erika Smit.

When heat hits you, it hits you hard. There are, the experts say and we witness here, 27 ways that heat can kill you. Who would have ever thought?

Our body is like a light bulb: When you are at a rest on an average day, we give out as much heat as a 100-watt bulb. Which is fine if the temperature around us stays close to our body temperature. But when it starts rising, we start sweating. But why? Because sweat evaporates, and this cools our skin. To make use of this, the blood capillaries near our skin expand, making us look red like a beetroot—Hot Flush—the first sign.

But what if the weather is muggy, not dry? High humidity means the air is already full of water, and our sweat won't evaporate. So our body doesn't sweat. Instead, our heartbeat increases, we start breathing faster, we get tired, light-headed, exhausted. We feel nauseous, we vomit, our head feels like it's about to explode. Like mine feels as I'm typing this right now. That's Heat Exhaustion.

I'm sitting indoors, the fan is on at full speed, and I still have some water with me. But what about those stuck outdoors now? Organs start to shut down. Cells deteriorate. Cardiac Arrest. Commonly known by the less gruesome name, Heat Stroke.

God bless them, for at that stage, there are 27 roads ahead. Kidney failure, brain damage, respiratory failure, heart failure, liver failure, pancreas damage, intestine damage… You get the picture. Twenty-seven paths that all lead to the same destination: death.

And our odds of two, you ask? Well, we have exactly two natural defense mechanisms against extreme heat: breathing and sweating. That's it, folks, that's all we got.

Pray for us. We're in Diobu, a village in Rivers, and trying to get out of here, but the asphalt roads have buckled under the heat. Expanded, rutted, and cracked, and it's unsafe to drive over them. Less safe than being cooked to our deaths? I don't dare ask.

Martin had a choice to make: Violently grab the newspaper from the old man who was using it to fan himself or just continue to stare enviously at him and thus maintain his last shreds of human dignity. In this crisis, just like in most others, speculation was rife and information was scare. The newspaper was very tempting.

After a moment's hesitation, and probably due to his Christian upbringing, Martin chose the latter. He squinted at the words that were moving back and forth in tandem with the slow motions of the old man's arms. He could make out the numbers 4 and 8 staring back at him. Forty-eight degrees Celsius, that was how hot the day was.

The headlines in the newspapers these days were about one topic only: the heatwave that was sweeping all over north and Sub-Saharan Africa.

"Communications across Eastern Nigeria shut down."

"Airport in Abuja taken over by the army."

"Family killed over struggle for a bottle of water."

"US and UK continue to evacuate their citizens."

The headlines did not offer any comfort. But when the heat threatened to suck the last breath out of every living soul, there was not much else anyone cared about. In Nigeria, it had started in the southeast, near the Niger Delta, and was now moving steadily north and west. Authorities were still debating whether to pronounce this a national emergency, but the ordinary man on the street had no doubt that these were no ordinary times they were living in. At 48 degrees Celsius with humidity, death was rampant. Without access to shade and water, chances of survival were slim.

Martin saw the water truck approaching from a distance. He had been sitting at the gates to his house for almost an hour now, and this was the first vehicle that had passed by. Ordinarily the street would have been filled with hundreds of cars all trying to get ahead through a combination of unruly driving, continual honking, and violent verbal assaults by the drivers. The result was usually a traffic jam where no one got ahead. But today there was peace and silence. That and the cool shade of the large banyan tree made the spot even more appealing than the concrete walls of his mansion beyond the gate.

Martin could not bring himself to shoo away the random vagabonds who sought shade under the banyan tree, motley folk who were emboldened by the heatwave to break the usual rules of propriety and social conduct. The tree may have been outside the gates, but on most days, the homeless and the nomads of Lagos kept well away from it, wary of Ben's and Chinua's possessive protection. But today the guards were resting in the guardhouse, their tiredness overcoming their desire to throw out the unsightly loiterers. It intrigued Martin, though, how the old man managed to get hold of a recent newspaper when his own newspaper boy had been lax in his daily deliveries.

The water truck was almost here. Martin looked around for Ayo. Ayo had been acting a bit strange of late, distracted and distant. When Martin asked him whether everything was alright, he had elusively blamed it on the heat. Martin curbed his instinct to think that Ayo was just using the heat as a convenient excuse to cover up a scheme. After all, the heat was making inroads into Lagos and steadily and stealthily taking its toll on its residents, and it was reasonable that Ayo would be affected by it.

Ayo made his appearance just as the water truck stopped in front of the gates and promptly engaged in what seemed to be fierce negotiations with the water guys. About three days after the fiercest heatwave in human history struck Lagos, the city's water supply had succumbed to the fury of nature. In a country where water shortages were a daily occurrence even in the normal course of things, this was no surprise. After a while, Martin saw Ayo hand over an obscenely large wad of cash in exchange for eight bottles of water. With a noisy rumble, the water truck crawled along to the next rich man's house.

Martin still found it difficult to think of himself as rich. At home in Amsterdam, he had lived in a modest apartment that could barely hold his bed, a desk, an old television set, and an antique sofa. Getting a job at CBX Corp had made him an instant celebrity in his working-class family, so much so that an aunt who had not even known his name decided to leave him her prized sofa upon her death. But somehow, the feeling of being rich had never quite sunk in. In the race for success, running wasn't the hard part. It was knowing when the finish line had been crossed.

Martin headed inside the house to get a sip of water. He found six bottles neatly lined on the countertop. *What happened to the other two?* At some point, he would have to confront Ayo over the consistent inconsistencies. But that would have to wait. For now, he had a more pressing concern: to get out of this ovenofaplace, alive and sane. With Ansara, if he could convince her.

"Martin, are you alright? You don't look so well. You should probably spend more time inside. The sun is going to burn your skin." Ansara's voice, weary from the continual heat and recent events, exuded concern.

"I'm fine, Ansa. Just had to make sure I was there when the water truck came. Didn't want Ayo to tell me again that the water truck didn't come today."

Ansara was standing by the window, staring into the courtyard. Ever since she came back from Port Harcourt, she had been swinging between hope and despair. She would think of some new way to try and find her mother—a distant acquaintance that she had forgotten to contact, a new government agency that had sprouted up to help locate victims of heat-related casualties, or a newspaper advertisement about an old amnesiac—then get hopeful and be preoccupied with that lead for a while. But when that ended in a dead end, she would spend the next few days in frantic activity, busying herself with household chores, cleaning, washing, cooking elaborate dishes, rearranging the bookshelves, anything she could think of. On such days, sometimes she would run out of things to do, and Martin would catch her mulling or staring out of a window or just sitting motionless. Today seemed to be one of those days.

"Ansa, how are you doing?" Martin asked, looking at her intently.

Ansara avoided his gaze. After a while, she replied, "It's not easy, Martin. With each passing day, it gets harder and harder to believe that she's safe somewhere. I feel that I should be doing something, but I don't know what else I can do."

"I'm so sorry, Ansa. I can't even begin to imagine what you must be going through. But you're doing everything you possibly can."

"Maybe I should go back to Port Harcourt. I don't know."

"Ansa, we've gone over this many times. It wouldn't help for you to go to Port Harcourt. If your mother comes back, Mrs. Jideofor will contact you. You've to think of Femi. You can't take him into such heat. Besides it's not even safe to go there anymore."

Ansara turned around from the window. "Thank you, Martin, you've been so good with Femi. Letting him stay here, making him feel welcome. You've—"

Martin cut her off mid-sentence. "No, don't thank me, please," he said. "You know I enjoy having Femi around. He's a good kid."

It was true. Martin enjoyed having Femi in the house, his childhood innocence a welcome break from the bleak events unfolding around them. Perhaps comforted by the presence of his mother, Femi seemed to have adapted to his new surroundings and the increasing heat with a serenity most adults would have found difficult. Martin liked to spend time with him, reading or playing, a respite from thoughts about work and weather.

Her eyes were dry, but her voice was uneven. "Martin, she's my family. My mother..." She let the words trail off.

Martin wished he could hold her close. He could not bear to see her in such pain and not do anything to comfort her. But none of the house staff knew about their relationship, and they had decided that it was best to keep it that way, at least for a while longer. In the evenings, when the house staff went back to their own houses and Ayo was out with his buddies, they were free to be themselves, but during the day, they had to keep their distance.

Martin looked out of the window. The silence in the courtyard was calming. He thought of how their relationship had changed over the last months. He remembered the first time he kissed her, in this very kitchen, on the cold floor. He had deliberated for days on every possible ramification of their relationship. He had thought about the vast social differences that separated them, he had fought every doubt that it was just an infatuation, he had wondered what the future could possibly hold for a relationship between people from as different backgrounds as theirs. All those nights of deep thought and agony seemed so trivial now, when everything they had taken for granted was overturned, when even simple daily routines had been shattered, when everyday existence was not assured. The answers to the questions he struggled with at that time had come to him with a startling clarity. He loved Ansara more than he knew he was capable of loving someone. Nothing else mattered. He knew that he would risk everything, including his life, for her, for her happiness, for just being with her.

He turned and looked at her standing beside him, staring into the same courtyard, and he could feel her pain cutting through his own chest, he could feel his eyes hurting from the tears that she refused to shed, he could feel every fiber of his body wanting to somehow channel the pain away from her body and into his own.

Ansara broke the silence between them. "Martin, you should go back to Europe. All the houses around here now only have house staff in them. The *oyibos* have all gone back to their countries. Just go to the airport, they will get you on a flight out of here. You need to leave while you still can."

"Ansa, you really think I'm going to leave you here? I've

told you before, if I go, we go together."

Ansara sighed. "Your skin, *nkem*, is not meant for this weather. Look at my skin. I can survive this. I'll never forget you, and when all this is over, you can come back and look for me. Please think it over."

Martin relished every instance that Ansara referred to him as her *nkem*, one of the few terms of endearment she used. In the months before the heatwave, he would be home only in the evenings, and they would be alone. When they were together, her passion for him was unbridled; he felt like he was the only man in the whole universe and the only thing that occupied her mind. But recently, Martin had been around more and more during the day as work had slowed considerably and the commute to the office had become increasingly dangerous. It felt awkward to be with each other yet behave so distantly. Even though he knew why she showed no signs of affection, it often left him with a strange sensation of losing something that was so close, of something precious slipping away from his grasp.

"Ansara, I'm staying with you. When you want to go, we'll go. Together. Till then, I'll be here, right beside you."

Ansara smiled, and her eyes lit up with warmth and love. Martin felt his unease ebbing. Looking into Ansara's eyes, he knew that her love was genuine and pure, and he knew, beyond the shadow of any doubt that despite heat or cold, scorching or freezing, fireballs or snowstorms, this was a woman worth living and dying for.

"I should go check on Femi," Ansara said. She looked

around to make sure they were not being watched and then leaned over and gave him a quick peck on the cheek before leaving the room.

Martin sighed. Lagos was one of the few places in Nigeria with some infrastructure remaining. He had made a final trip to Port Harcourt about two weeks earlier. He was alarmed by what he saw and hoped that the situation in Lagos would not deteriorate to a similar state. What he had seen at Port Harcourt terrified him. As he walked out of the plane, Martin had found it hard to breathe.

The air was heavy, and wading through it took every ounce of strength he could muster. His skin was burning and his mouth parched. The streets were littered with corpses. The living looked at him with vacant eyes, as if their souls had succumbed to forces beyond their will. The deep foreboding silence was punctuated only by distant gun shots, and the void left behind by the dearth of vibrant activity was filled by a heavy, putrid cloak of a stench that seemed to originate from nowhere but permeated everywhere.

Martin had come to Port Harcourt to attend a workers' meeting, usually loud, boisterous affairs that often left him wishing for ear plugs. But this time, he was struck by the quiet calm room that welcomed him. Each of the speakers took turns to speak, and in low voices. If he did not know any better, Martin would have sworn they were from any country on Earth but Nigeria. He had come to the meeting prepared to exhort the workers back to work and to remind them that, regardless of the heatwave, they had to keep the refinery open. But as he listened to their stories—people slipping into unconsciousness while in the middle of their jobs, some disappearing on their way to work, and a few dying because they had not dared rest for fear of losing their job—he decided to shut down the refinery temporarily and to grant paid leave to all employees. He would decide how to square this with headquarters later. If it cost him his job, so be it. The men and women thanked him for his kindness and left, the relief in their eyes conveying the gratitude that they could not muster enough strength to verbally express.

"Martin, that was…kind. Thank you very much."

Blessing stayed back after the meeting to talk to him. Blessing and Martin shared a love-hate relationship. Martin admired that she was dedicating her life to fighting for workers' rights. On the face of it, Martin, the corporate golden boy, was everything Blessing despised, and she had made no attempt to hide it. But then, over time, Blessing had acknowledged, grudgingly at first and gratefully later, that Martin was different and that he had, over time, taken a real interest in local realities and brought to bear some measure of socially responsible behavior. They may be serving different masters, she once told him, but their ideologies and philosophies were not that different. And he had considered that high praise, coming from her.

"It's the least I could do," Martin said.

"Martin, I would like to apologize. We've not always treated you well, assuming that you want to take advantage of us. But today, in our darkest hour, when we need you the most, you came through for us. The company has shown us its human side and we're grateful."

Martin was dreading how "the company" would react. He had been burning through his good will with Teun Bergman fast, ever since his decision to allow a working group on environmental consequences. The sheen of being Teun's favored protégé, groomed as his heir apparent, which had been instrumental in Martin's success until now, was swiftly dimming. But standing in the scorching heat, with death and devastation all around him—which, despite his repeated appeals, was no more than a sentence in the company updates in Holland—he could not care less. He knew there would be consequences to his decision to pay workers who were not at work, for shutting down the refinery when the demand for fuel was higher than ever, for the lost profits that would definitely get tallied by the accountants in Europe, but somehow, he didn't feel as scared as he knew he should be.

Blessing seemed to notice his silence. "Martin, I'm aware of the difficulties you'll have justifying your decision. Of the risks you're taking. Please do know that you've helped to save many people's lives."

"I'm glad to be of help. I personally know someone who is from Port Harcourt, and her mother has been missing for a few weeks now. I may not live here, but I can imagine the hardships. I'm sorry that we can't do more."

"If you like, I can help you. There are many missing people and it's hard to trace them, but if you like, I can come with you to look for them. I've contacts in most of the places around here."

Martin took Blessing up on her offer. He postponed his flight back and combed every hospital, every morgue, every police station in the city in search of Ansara's mother. At every place, as he made use of Blessing's connections and bribes to cut through the queues, he thought of Ansara, how she must have been at that very place just a few weeks ago, standing in the heat in the unending queues while desperation bore deeper and deeper into her as each place turned out to have the same answer that he was now receiving: "No, we don't have anyone by that name here."

CHAPTER 22

The heat bothered Ayo. It bothered him even more that it bothered him.

Everyone everywhere was talking about the heat and how it would lead to the collapse of their country. *This is Nigeria, we have seen so much worse*, he would think irritably every time he heard those doomsday predictions. Summers in Nigeria were meant to be harsh, definitely not for the fair-skinned and the delicate, and now it seemed to him everyone was acting as if they were an *oyibo* worried at the slightest increase in temperature.

But in the safety of his room, while he tried to catch an afternoon nap, it was hard not to admit that the heat was making a visible dent in everyone's daily routine. Even after a hearty meal and some beer, sleep eluded him. He felt as if worms were crawling all over him as sweat beads settled into the crevices of his body and trickled toward the bed. He could see little puddles forming on his pillow. There was not even a rustle of trees or buzzing of insects; the only sound seemed to be an echo of his own heavy breathing, as if the air was mocking him for panting like a dog.

Thoughts about his mother kept haunting him. He remembered his childhood at home with his mother and brother. Pain, resentment, happiness, and joy were all part of the mix. He thought of the mother he took to Ahmed's shop for lunch, the woman who gratefully gobbled up her lunch and smiled sheepishly, a far cry from the mother he had known in his childhood. Her few moments of lucidity and her request to relieve her from the drudgery of her life popped into his head despite his attempts to keep it out. Ayo could not quite decide which was worse, a woman who he knew was his mother but who acted like a little child and was interested only in the meals he provided her, or his mother who was so desperate that the only thing she asked in her moment of sanity was an escape from her worldly torture.

Ayo kept his eyes firmly shut, determined to drive out his demons and get some rest.

There was a slight rustle in the air. Ayo could sense someone was about. Instinctively, his hand rushed to the knife under his pillow and once he had a firm grip on the handle, he slowly opened his eyes.

"Oh, it's you! What the hell are you doing here?" Ayo was surprised to see a five-year-old boy peering curiously at his sleeping face.

Ayo had been annoyed when Ansara brought Femi back to Lagos. He wanted to send the boy back immediately, but Martin had not even let him voice his concerns fully, shutting him up and insisting that Femi was welcome to stay with his mother. Ayo had thought it entirely inappropriate that Ansara would be accorded such preferential treatment. He had, after all, got her this job and should have the final say on matters relating to her. But Martin was having none of it.

Ordinarily, he would have found a way to wrest more control over the household staff, but if he was honest with himself, his mind had been elsewhere for some time now. In any case, he had seen the boy around once or twice, a quiet and harmless fellow who didn't really bother him, so he let it pass.

Now, the boy smiled at Ayo, apparently amused. Femi extended his hand and gently touched the scar on Ayo's forehead. Ayo was surprised at the boy's fearlessness, and mildly impressed. It was not every day that someone casually felt up his face.

"What are you doing here, boy? Where's your mama?"

The boy pointed toward the kitchen. He could see part of the kitchen from the door of the servants' quarters, and as he looked, Ansara came briefly into view, carrying a heavy pot, then disappeared again.

"I forgot you can't talk! But looks like you can understand what I'm saying." Ayo sat up on his bed. It was a rudimentary sort of bed, a piece of soft rattan tied by four strings to four wooden poles. The rattan had started fraying at the edges, but its decrepit condition was hidden by a thin mattress and a sheet on top, which he used to cover himself when it got a bit chilly on rainy nights. He felt rather superior though. He was the only one in the servants' quarters who slept at an elevated level. The rest of the staff just spread their mattresses on the floor every night.

"You know what, boy, you're just the kind of person I like talking to. I talk, you listen. No questions. No interruptions," Ayo continued. The boy continued to peer at him, looking amused.

"What do you have there?" Ayo asked, noticing the boy's tight-fisted hand, which he had carefully hidden behind his back. The boy did not move, continuing to just look up at him. "Come on, you can't hide things from me." He gently pried open the boy's hand. He opened it to find two mangos, both small in size but ripe and ready to eat.

"Oh my God, you little thief! These are from the neighbor's house. You stole them, didn't you?" The boy looked a little bit scared and edged away from Ayo.

Ayo laughed. "Who would have thought the little mute boy steals mangos? Way to go, I say. There is plenty of fruit in that house. You want something, you take it. No one is going to get anything for you, I tell you. You have to make it, all on your own. Come here, you little bastard. You don't have to be afraid of me." Ayo slapped the spot next to him on the bed, to indicate that he could come closer.

The boy obediently moved closer and sat next to him. He extended his hand tentatively and offered one of the mangos to Ayo.

"You're not bad, not bad at all." Ayo was guffawing by now. "You get caught, you offer a bribe. You're a lot smarter than I thought." He accepted the mango and bit into it. Femi bit into the mango he had kept for himself, and for a few moments, they sat there on Ayo's cot, side by side, enjoying the sweet taste of the stolen mangos on their tongues.

"Boy, let me tell you a story. When I was your age... Oh wait! Maybe a few years older," Ayo said, turning to look at Femi, trying to gauge his age. "Or maybe you're just a shortie for your age?" He tousled the curly hair on Femi's head. "Let's just say when I was a child and still living with my mama," Ayo continued, "there was a big bad man who came to live with us. You see, my papa left us when I was very, very small, just like your father. So bad men, they came and went in our house. But this man, he was there for a long time." Ayo paused, as if wondering whether the pain of the memory was worth it. Then, he said, "This man, he was very cruel. When Mama was around, he didn't do anything. But when he was alone at home with me, he would beat me. With a long metal stick. I think he used it in his shop. He worked in some place where they pulled out parts of cars. Anyway, he would make me do all his dirty work, and if I didn't do it, he would beat me bad. Real bad. Till I started screaming and turned black and blue. Black and blue, you understand?" Ayo turned to Femi to see whether the boy comprehended the full severity of the situation.

The scared expression on the boy's face pleased him. "I tried telling Mama, but she wouldn't listen. She just said I was lying. And every time I told Mama, the bad man found out and the next day, when Mama was out at work, he would beat me even more." Ayo continued, "So one day, I decided I had had enough. I couldn't take this anymore. How much beating can a boy take and still live quietly? I thought of a plan." Ayo leaned over and whispered in a low growling voice, "A very clever plan. When Mama was back home that night after work, I slid up to her and took some money from her. It felt like a rather thick bundle. She must have had a good day and that was good, Mama would definitely miss the money. And then when no one was looking, I put it into the pocket of the bad man's pants.

"When Mama wanted to go out the next morning, she looked for the money. Of course, it wasn't there. Oh man, what a ruckus she created! She got hold of my brother—the idiot didn't have the sense to move away—and started beating him, asking about the money. When she realized he didn't know where it was, she turned to me.

"You know, kiddo, that was the moment of truth. The bad man was watching. But I had to take a chance. If he heard me accuse him and Mama didn't get rid of him, I was as sure as dead. But I took my chance. I pointed at him and said that I saw him take the money.

"Now Mama, she may not like her kids so much, but money she liked a lot. Even more than men. So she let go of me and looked in the bad man's pockets, and there it was, the thick wad of cash."

Ayo laughed, obviously pleased with himself with what he had managed to do.

"Mama went mad. She took the machete she kept in the kitchen and went straight at him. She is a big woman, my mama, and when she goes crazy, she is crazy like a bull. Like a bull charging straight at you. The bad man was so surprised and shocked he nearly couldn't move and caught the edge of her machete. But sadly, only the edge. He managed to move away soon enough. He threw the money back at her and tried to accuse me. He knew I had put it there. But Mama was in no listening mood. She grabbed the money and told him to clear off. I think the whole neighborhood heard her. She told him never to show up at her house again. And when my mama gets that mad, you listen. Everyone listens. And the bad man never came back."

Ayo laughed in satisfaction. He looked over at Femi, who was listening attentively.

"You know what it means, boy? It means, you got to take care of yourself. No one will take care of you. You want something, you do it yourself. Don't run to your mama, don't run to the others, because they really don't care. You look after your own self."

Femi nodded.

Just then, the door flung open and Ansara came bursting in. "Femi! I've been looking all over for you! You had me so scared!"

Femi got up from the cot and walked to Ansara. He glanced back in a silent goodbye to Ayo.

But by then, Ayo was back to his normal self.

"This is why you shouldn't have kids in your workplace. They get lost, distract people from work, won't let others sleep. Can you tell him not to come here again!"

Ayo ignored the hurt look that passed over Femi's face. Ansara hugged her son close and went out of the room.

Ayo settled back onto his bed. He had some things to attend to, but they would have to wait till the evening. The afternoon sun was getting hotter and hotter, and he was in no mood to brave the heat. Enjoying the relative coolness of his room and the lethargy of lying in bed was all that he wanted to do right now.

Ayo was slowly drifting off to sleep when the loud lyrics, "*Do me! Do me! Girl, I love the way you do me,*" filled the room. It was a new Nigerian song that left little to the imagination. It took him a moment to realize that it was coming from his mobile phone, then he grinned. He had just changed his ringtone that morning and felt particularly pleased with it.

It was Prince. Ayo grumbled as he picked up the call. "Arrrgh! Damn people won't let me have an afternoon of peace."

"Hey, am here, at your house."

"What! You can't come here to see me. Not when the *oyibo* is in. I've told you many times."

"Ayo, it's no time to argue. Are you in your room? I'm coming over!"

Ayo hung up the phone and looked around his room. Was there anything he did not want Prince to see?

Born Bunkechukwu Belonwu, Prince had changed his name the moment he got his first gun. Prince. No last name. Just Prince. Once you have a gun in your hand, people will call you anything you want them to, and Prince had decided to take full advantage of that. And now, he didn't even need to brandish the gun; not many people remembered his original name in any case.

Prince was one of Ayo's friends who helped him in the underhand dealings he needed to make. There was only one reason Prince would visit Ayo at this time of the day: to ask him for money. It was important to keep the cogs in the maChiderary well oiled. It was hard to predict when he would need to call upon Prince for help, but he wasn't keen to part with money without notice.

He pushed back the tip of the knife that was jutting out from below his pillow. He then went over to his wallet, emptied it of all the cash except for ten thousand naira, and tucked the rest of it into his shoe. And just in time, as Prince walked in.

Prince was one of those who was born to violence. There was nothing in his face that did not look sinister. It was as if all his features joined forces to give him a unified look of evil, which he then compounded by his own addition of scars and broken teeth. Prince had dark, narrow, close-set eyes that could not hide their meanness even with the help of the thick bushy eyebrows that hung onto his upper eyelids. When he opened his mouth to speak, you could see a few yellow teeth left behind, the ones that had managed to survive the many fistfights and bar brawls. He wore a khaki uniform that was badly in need of a wash and army boots that were covered almost entirely with caked mud. His gun, though, was gleaming, as if it had just been wiped and cleaned and was itching to get some action.

"Come in, come in. How are you?" Ayo feigned an enthusiasm he did not even begin to feel. They exchanged pleasantries while Ayo took out two bottles of beer from under his bed, opened the caps, and handed one to Prince.

"I haven't seen you around for some time, Ayo. We need to get together and have some fun, what do you say?" said Prince. "Madam Wong's has a few new ladies, I hear. How about we go down there this weekend?"

But Prince was insistent when Ayo declined. "Is everything ok, Ayo? You never turn down a visit to Madam Wong's." He slapped Ayo hard on the back. "Oh, I know why. It's your new bride, isn't it? You are not even married yet, and she is already making you stop seeing other women."

"No, of course not. That will never happen to me," said Ayo.

"Yes, I thought so too. I can't imagine you ever stopping your trips to Madam Wong's," said Prince. "But still, I was surprised you found yourself a bride at all. Whatever for, it's just a distraction."

"Oh well, it's no big deal. It came through a distant relative. And she's in Port Harcourt. My boss makes a lot of trips to Port Harcourt, and I need to go with him. And nothing like a woman waiting for you in a new city, is there?"

"Ah, a woman in every city. That's more like it, Ayo."

"Now I'm having second thoughts though. The *oyibo* flies economy, never takes the car, and he comes back the same day most of the time. No time for fun. Besides, after the heat started, the woman has gotten irritating, calling me often, complaining about the heat there. I think she wants to come here, to Lagos. It's not like I've married her yet. After I get what I want, I can always back out of it," said Ayo. "But let's talk of something else. There must be more to life than a marriage to some girl."

"Listen, I'm in a bit of a fix. I need some help." Prince took a large gulp of his beer. "My brother, he got into a bit of debt, with his gambling, you know. I need to help him out. And I need some money real quick."

"Again? Your brother, he likes to gamble, don't he?" Ayo knew very well that the one with the gambling problem was Prince himself, but if this was the game he wanted to play, Ayo was willing to play along.

"I know. I keep telling him. Every time he says he'll stop, but then he continues. Like nothing ever happened."

Prince paused and looked at Ayo. Ayo was not going to give up the money that easily.

"This is how the business runs, man," continued Prince. "Today, I want to help my brother pay off his debts. You help me pay. Tomorrow, I help you. What do you say, Ayo? Are you going to help me or not?"

"I don't know, man. Money has been tight these days. How much do you need?"

"Thirty. You have it?"

"Maybe twenty I have. Let me check." Ayo got his wallet out of the drawer, emptied it all, and counted. "Ten, man, ten is all I have. It's not payday yet and I am out. I can give you what I have for now. But that's all I can do."

"Ten, huh?" Prince casually got up and walked to the other side of the room and pulled open the chest of drawers. He glanced at the windowsill and ran his eyes around the room, looking for possible places where Ayo might have an additional stash. "Guess this will have to do for now. Thanks, man."

Ayo reluctantly parted with the ten thousand naira. He didn't have much hope of ever getting it back. At least not as money. But in Lagos, Prince was an asset to have on one's side, and if it cost Ayo money once in a while, he just had to part with it.

"I've to get going soon. But I tell you something, Ayo. This heat, they say, this heat is going to burn our country down. Anyone who can afford to is running. If you can put together a million naira—sell your house, sell your woman, I don't know what—if you have that kind of cash, call me. I'll get you out of here."

Ayo laughed. This was most likely the latest of Prince's con schemes. "Where do you think I have that kind of money from?"

Prince shrugged. "I don't know. Your *oyibo* friend there, he seems loaded and also a bit naive. Nothing you can get from him?"

"A bit here and there, but not much. And that kinda money, I don't think he has it with him. If you ask me, I think this heat is going to blow away. It's just a bad summer, man. All the white people, they are running away. But it's not going to do anything to us. We'll be fine."

"I hope you're right, Ayo. I hope so. But that's not what I hear. If you change your mind, call me." And with that, Prince left, leaving Ayo to ponder the many things he would do if he could indeed swindle a million naira off Martin.

CHAPTER 23

It had been over an hour since Ansara got Femi to his bed. The boy just would not sleep. The heat was perhaps too much for him. Or perhaps with the intuition of children, he knew that things were changing, the world around him was changing. Or maybe it was just that he missed his grandmother and the familiarity of their home at Port Harcourt.

She looked around at the tiny room, trying to think of some way to make Femi more comfortable. The room they were in was much better than the one she used to have in the servants' quarters. When Femi joined her, Martin had insisted that she move into the room behind the kitchen. It was part of the main house, slightly bigger and away from the servants' quarters, but still far enough from the main house not to warrant any suspicion of special treatment. The room was well kept and dry, unlike her old room, and it was definitely better than the small, cramped house at Port Harcourt that Femi was used to. But on days like these, the lack of windows made it as hot as a sauna, as the heat that bore down on the room during the day could find no way to escape the confines of the walls.

She lay on the bed next to Femi and smoothed his crinkled hair. "I know, pumpkin. I know it's very hot. But try to get some sleep. I'll stay with you till you fall asleep. Now, close your eyes."

Ansara could hear Martin move around the main house. On most nights, she would put Femi to bed and make sure he was sound asleep before heading to Martin's room. She was glad and grateful that Martin was so understanding about everything, her distracted moods since she came back from Port Harcourt, their decision to keep their relationship a secret, and even the intrusion that a five-year-old created in such a relationship. In fact, he seemed to enjoy having Femi around. Just today, while she was cooking, she heard noises from the main garden and was surprised to discover Martin and Femi having a game of throw-ball. She had not wanted to interrupt the game and watched from behind the curtained window. Seeing Martin play so patiently with her son had filled her with a sense of love deeper than she had felt on any night she spent with him.

Femi tossed and turned in his bed. Sweat dribbled down his face. Ansara wiped it off with the end of her wrapper. He tried to get out of bed, but she nudged him back in. "If you get up now, you're going to lose whatever sleep you have. Close your eyes and try not to think of anything." Ansara picked up a rolled-up newspaper and used it as a fan, trying to create some movement of air around them.

After a while, she could hear Martin's footsteps just outside the door. She left Femi and went out, gently closing the door behind her.

"*Nkem*, he's still not asleep. I'll stay here with him tonight. I think he may keep waking up in this heat."

"It's really getting insufferable, isn't it?"

Ansara nodded.

"Ansa, why don't you bring him up to one of the bedrooms upstairs? It has air conditioning and he'll sleep well through the night."

"Oh, I couldn't… It'll raise suspicion."

"Who will be suspicious? No one is around. Ayo has asked for this weekend off and won't be back till Monday. As for Femi, I think he would appreciate a good night's sleep. He's your son, Ansa. At some point, he needs to know about us."

Ansara hesitated. "No, it's not that I'm worried about him finding out. Just, is it appropriate?"

"Don't worry about it. It's really hot, Ansa. A child needs a good night's sleep. All those rooms are unused, you're not hurting anyone by using one. Besides, I would hate to sleep comfortably in my room up there while you both are suffering in the heat here."

She roused Femi gently and led him up the stairs. Femi was amazed at the coolness of the air-conditioned bedroom and gave his mother a questioning glance. "It's ok, Femi. It was hot and you couldn't sleep. Martin has said you can use this room tonight. Now try to get some sleep."

After a while, his eyes were still wide open, and he was not loosening the tight grip he had on her. Ansara sighed. "Femi, let me tell you a story. My grandmother used to tell it to me when I was a little girl."

Femi's eyes widened with excitement. His grandmother used to tell him stories before he went to bed, but his mother did not seem to have such a ready stock of stories for every night.

"But there is a big curse on the story. You have to sleep before the end of the story." Ansara's voice assumed a menacing tone. "If you're still awake when I finish my story, the big sleep monster will come and take you away to his kingdom. He'll keep you prisoner for the whole night, with all the other naughty children. He's a very scary man, and they say he's not very kind to naughty children." She smiled as she remembered how scared she used to be every time her grandmother brought up tales of such curses. Her heart sank a little when she saw Femi's scared face, but she told herself that that is just how stories ought to be told.

"Are you sure you want to hear the story, Femi?"

Femi nodded.

"Ok, my brave boy. I'll tell you the story of the Bini people."

Ansara settled into a comfortable position next to Femi, stared at the ceiling, and started her tale. "Many many years ago, before your grandma was born and before Grandma's grandma was born and even before her grandma was born, there lived a people called Bini. They were tall and black and healthy and strong.

"Their land was beautiful and had many trees and rivers. But the most special of all was their sky. The sky in the land of the Bini was not so far away as our skies are. It hung very low, so low that even little kids like you could just stretch up their arm and touch the sky. And it was not just any other sky. The land of Bini had a very special sky. Femi, you need to close your eyes or you won't sleep by the end of the tale, and the sleep monster will come after you."

Ansara smiled as Femi obediently closed his eyes, and she continued.

"So, as I was saying, the sky was very special. The sky was made of food, real tasty food that tasted different every day. If you felt hungry today and wanted to eat mutton stew, you could just reach out to the sky, take a piece, and it would taste just like mutton stew. If you wanted to eat your favorite *jollof* with meat, then the sky would give you just that. So the people of Bini, they never had to work and they never had to hunt. They had all the time in the world to sing and dance and paint pictures and make art, just as God wanted them to.

"But then, as time went by, the people of Bini started getting more and more greedy. They would take food even when they were not hungry. Sometimes, they would grab the food, just take a little bite, and throw away the rest. The sky was getting smaller and smaller. There was enough for all the people in the land to eat well, but not enough for them to waste. But the people of Bini, they were so used to always having a sky full of food that they didn't even notice it."

Ansara looked up and saw Martin standing by the door. She hesitated for a moment, but he smiled reassuringly. She continued. "One day, the sky got very angry. It grew very very dark, just like it does before it starts to rain. So the Bini people looked into the sky and they heard a loud thundering voice. It said, *Oh people of Bini, for a very long time, you have enjoyed food from me. Whatever you want, I have given you. When you wanted plantain, I gave you plantain. When you wanted corn, I gave you corn. When you wanted meat, I gave you meat. But now, you don't care for me anymore. You ask for too much, and you take too much. And you don't even use most of it, you just throw it away.* The people of Bini were frightened, the sky looked so dark and scary.

"The sky continued. It said, *People of Bini, I will give you one last chance. If you waste any more of the food, I will go away from your land. I will move far far away and you will never be able to touch me again.* The people of Bini were terrified, and they promised that they would never waste the food again.

"A few years passed, and by then, the people of Bini had forgotten all about the sky being dark and scary. They started eating too much and wasting food just as they had done before. The sky got angrier and angrier. So one day—"

Ansara heard a small snore. She looked down to see Femi's eyes closed and his breathing calmer.

She was just about to get up when Martin mouthed the words, "What happened next?"

She smiled and continued. "So one day, the sky moved away just as it had warned, and it settled into a place so far away that nobody could touch it. And to this day, the sky remains high up, far far away from human hands. And the people of Bini, and all the people who came after them, had no more food from the sky. They have to work very very hard to get food from the earth, or they would starve to death."

Martin walked into the room and sat on the bed, holding her from behind. Ansara leaned back against him, wishing the moment would last forever. Femi smiled in his sleep, the sweet innocent smile of a child in the comforting lap of slumber. Perhaps he was relieved that he'd managed to outwit the sleep monster that night.

"Did you know, Ansa," whispered Martin, "he smiles exactly like you? This is how you smile when you sleep."

"I smile in my sleep?"

"Yes, and I could spend hours looking at you smiling."

She reached up and stroked his hair gently, the soft golden curls against her palm.

"Do you know how I imagine our life to be?" he asked.

"No, what is it like?"

"There will be five of us. You, me, Femi, and two more kids."

Ansara let out a small laugh. "Two more? You're thinking of kids?"

"Yes, wouldn't it be nice? We'll have a girl first. She'll look just like you, with wild hair that has a mind of its own." Martin brushed aside a few strands of her hair that had found their way onto his face when she turned around. "She will be our little princess, beautiful and royal, and we will shower her with everything she needs."

"Oh, we're going to have a spoilt little brat," Ansara whispered back.

"And then we will have a son, maybe a bit of me, a bit of

you. He'll be funny and smart. He'll make everyone laugh and be daring and adventurous and go where no one has gone before."

"And you plan to make a nomad of our son?"

Martin ignored her. "And Femi will be the big older brother, kind and responsible as he is now, and looking out for the younger ones. Imagine, we would all be on one large bed just like this. The three children will be sleeping, and we can just sit and watch them sleep. And they will all have those angelic smiles, just like yours. I can't imagine anything that would make me happier."

Ansara turned around and kissed him gently on his ears. She felt his hands slide down and trace the curvature of her hips.

"I think he's fast asleep. We should get some sleep too." Ansara said, getting up and pulling the sheets over Femi. Martin's imagination of their family offered her a bit of hope, but mostly it amused her. Her own life so far had made it hard for her to believe that such good things could come to her. She knew that the realities of life were harsh. She wanted to forget her pain in a peaceful sleep. It may not be as blissful as that of a five-year-old's, but at least sleep was more peaceful than her waking moments.

She bent down, kissed Femi on the forehead, switched off the light, and went out of the room, with Martin behind her.

"You know, I think I'm going to refuse to sleep without a story every night from now on. It was a very nice story that you told Femi, about the sky moving away," Martin said.

Ansara playfully poked him, but her voice was tired as she said, "It looks like our sky has moved away too, doesn't it?"

Martin hugged her close and gently led her to his room next door. "Maybe it will come back and give us one more chance."

She hoped he was right. Perhaps, unlike her story, the sky had not moved away for good. Maybe, just maybe, it was hiding until it found a fitting time to come back and give them one last chance.

PART IV

CHAPTER 24

There are many ways to kill a person, and three factors determine which one to choose: Do you want the person to suffer? What resources do you have? And how do you plan to hide the body?

Ayo preferred a gun shot, one direct hit right to the temple. It was the most painless and the quickest way to die. He knew that if he ever wanted to commit suicide, that's what he would choose for himself. A gun was a commodity in Lagos. If you were in the right circles, a gun could be easier to acquire than a bottle of import-quality rum. Then the question remained of how to hide the body. Truth be told, it didn't quite matter. Ayo would have liked to give his mother a proper funeral, but he wasn't sure it would be appropriate to shoot her in the head and then wrap her in her best clothes and call the minister to do the last rites. That would be risky too. He would have to dump the body. Probably in an unobserved part of the river.

That pained him, that he would have to dump the body. He briefly considered hiring an assassin to kill her, just so he could claim her body later and give her the last rites. But then he decided against it. He couldn't trust an assassin to ensure that the end would be as painless as possible. Once they took the money, they did the deed, no matter what, and Ayo couldn't reasonably insist that it was either one shot to the temple or no harm done. Moreover, it would be a waste of money, which his mother certainly wouldn't approve of. It would be the ultimate insult to his upbringing and her ideals to flounder money on her assassination when he could do the deed himself. After all, she had asked him to do it, hadn't she?

It was a Saturday night that he chose for the deed. It had to be a weekend, so he would be at his one-room apartment and not at Martin's place. He would need time alone, before and after. And a whole lot of rum.

By ten o'clock that night, Ayo was drunk enough not to question his own decision. Driving would not be that easy; he wished he had thought about that earlier. Driving to the shantytown and drinking on the bridge would have been a safer option. Oh well, it was too late for that now.

He staggered to the car with his gun safely in his coat pocket. He patted the thick wad of cash in his trousers. They were for greasing fingers in case he got caught for drunk driving or anything else. It was good that Martin had asked him to exchange money that very day, otherwise he would have had to find other sources of back-up cash.

The drive would have taken him about two hours on a typical Lagos day, but ever since the heat started setting in, there was a relief to the heavy traffic. It was almost as if people had found the perfect reason not to go to places where they were supposed to be. Maybe it was true that the heat was claiming many victims, but as always, statistics in Nigeria were not something to trust. It took him under an hour to reach the shantytown.

He parked the car at the outskirts of the shantytown and walked to the bridge. A cool breeze offered some relief from the heat, but it also swept the smells from the river right up his nostrils. Ayo heard the clock from the church tower. He counted eleven strikes. Good, it was not the witching hour.

He got off the side of the bridge and walked along the river. He saw a few homeless people, those who could not afford even the shanties just up the road, lying curled up below the trees. Some of them had newspapers to cover themselves with, whereas others lay exposed to the cruelty of buzzing mosquitoes.

It wasn't difficult to spot his mother. She was still up, sitting with her back against the bark of a tree. A cane and a bag lay to her side, and a stray dog had curled up next to her. She saw Ayo approaching and smiled. For a moment, his heart skipped. This would be harder if she recognized him, then he would have no chance of pretending it was a stranger she had asked to kill her. Then, he realized that she had no idea he was her son. To her, he was probably just the nice guy who bought her lunch every once in a while.

Ayo wanted to get it over and done with. He imagined himself walking back along the river, with the clock chiming twelve. That gave him slightly less than an hour. The thought of a deadline, however arbitrary, was reassuring.

He smiled back at her.

"Mama, today is the day. Are you ready?"

She nodded, probably thinking she was to have another meal.

"Will you come for a walk with me?" He helped her up to her feet. He noticed she was frail and her leg—the one she had not cut off herself —looked like it had been chewed at. There was still some blood sticking to it. He looked at the dog curled next to her. It could not be this sickly creature, probably a more ferocious version. She could not walk properly, so he let her lean on him and he led her along the path. In less than fifteen minutes, they were in some dark undergrowth, well shielded from curious eyes.

Ayo looked at his mother. He tried to think of it as a job. It had to be done and he knew it was for the best.

"Mama, are you sure of this?"

The old woman did not reply. Instead, she reached up and traced the outlines of his face with her fingers. She gently pulled his face toward her and kissed him on the forehead.

Ayo kissed her on the top of her head. He then turned her face away, so she could face the water. He placed the gunpoint on her right temple, looked away, and fired the shot.

There was no other sound for a while.

No one came to check what was going on. No one cared. He closed her eyes, wiped the blood that flowed over her face, and sat with her on the ground next to the river. His shirt was getting soaked with blood and his trousers were caked with mud. He must have been there a while when he heard the church bells chime. It was time to leave. He kissed her forehead one last time, muttered the few prayers he remembered, and let her body float down the river.

He turned around and walked back to the bridge, remembering to take off his bloodstained shirt. He climbed back onto the bridge and watched as a dark mass floated farther and farther away.

Ayo remembered very little of the next few days. They passed in one drunken stupor. He remembered, though, going to the liquor shop often, shelling out the money Martin had given him. He would need to explain that. But that would be later. For now, he needed the alcohol. The demons in his brain just refused to go away.

Everywhere he looked, he saw his mother, sometimes limping while a dog tried to chew the rest of her leg off, sometimes scolding him for coming home with a bruised eye, sometimes standing up with her eyes looking straight ahead and blood flowing from her temple, and sometimes just as a dark mass floating in the water.

He closed his eyes. He felt as if he were standing on a freeway with cars coming straight at him at full speed, but as they got closer and were about to hit him, they turned out not to be cars but images of his mother.

He threw the empty beer bottles at the wall. They would hit with a loud clatter and smash onto the floor. Little droplets of beer hung on the wall. He felt better for a moment, but soon the pain and the images were back. His mother was standing by the wall, on the beer bottles, the shards of glass cutting into her already chewed-up leg. Blood was flowing down her face, but she smiled at him and put up her hand to trace the outline of his face.

Ayo put his hands on both sides of his head and tried to press down the throbbing headache that surged through his veins. He opened his mouth and let out a loud noise. But when the voice came out, it did not sound like his own. He felt he was floating outside his own body, looking at someone who was making a racket.

After a while, there was a knock on his door. It was his neighbor.

"Ayo, my man, what's the noise up here? And what's this, you drinking alone?"

Ayo took out his knife and pointed at the guy, threatening probably, or maybe being just downright silly; the floating Ayo couldn't really ascertain.

"Cool it, man. I just came to share a drink. You've had way too much, now let me in and let's drink some together."

He tried to take the knife away from Ayo and step into the room. Then, he saw the bloodied shirt lying on the back of the chair.

"Shit, what have you done, Ayo?"

Ayo snarled and pointed the knife at him again.

"Ok man, I'm leaving. I'm leaving."

Ayo closed the door behind his neighbor, emptied the remaining rum in the bottle, and floated away with his demons.

It must have been a few days before he got a call from Martin.

"Ayo, how are you? I didn't see you today and wanted to check on you. Is everything ok?"

He could still feel the throbbing in his head. His stomach felt empty and queasy. The bright light coming in from the window was hurting his eyes.

It was Tuesday. He had forgotten about work.

"*Oga*, I'm down with a fever, a nasty one. Can hardly lift up my head." At least the second part wasn't untrue.

"Sorry to hear that, Ayo. Do you need anything? Shall I ask Mohammed to bring you some medicine?"

"No, I'm fine. Thanks. I'll need to take a couple of days off though."

"Yes, of course. You rest. Call me when you feel a bit better."

It was not until two days later that Ayo felt a little better. Better wouldn't be the right word. The truth was that he had run out of money, and the effect of alcohol was slowly but surely wearing off.

He wanted to get away. His first instinct was to run, run as fast as he could. Away from everything.

But that was not going to take him far. The heat would get him before he got far enough. He would just end up collapsing, exhausted, in some alley. If someone did not consider a lunatic a good target for gun practice, that is.

He would need to find a way out. He wished his head felt less muddled, so he could think better.

Prince. He remembered the offer from Prince. He wondered

if a ticket and a visa out still cost a million naira. He dialed Prince's number.

"Prince, my friend, how's your day?"

"Ayo, is that you? You sound totally wasted. It's Thursday afternoon, I'm impressed, my friend. What's happening to you?"

"I want to know what's happening to you. And I'm not wasted."

"Haha. You are in the middle of a lot of fun, aren't you? Do you have women there too? I have to be on this job till four. But I'm coming right over after that. It's been a while since we had some fun, isn't it?"

"Prince. I—"

Prince had hung up.

"Dammit."

The next thing Ayo remembered was the loud thuds on his door.

"Bloody hell! Who is it? I'll kill you if you break down the door."

"Cool down, man! It's me, Prince. Remember you called me?" Prince walked in and surveyed the room. "You alone in here? Geez, Ayo, what's going on?"

"Nothing. Nothing much. But I need your help."

Prince may have been disappointed at the lack of women and the many empty bottles, but the mention of the word "help" was sure to lift his spirits. A favor would almost definitely mean some cash in his hands.

"I need to get out of here. I've to go. And you said you could arrange for that. Out of this goddamn country," said Ayo.

"Yes, I can do that. But are you sure? You didn't seem so keen the last time. If it's something that's bothering you"— Prince glanced at the shirt caked in dry blood—"we can take care of it. That'll be cheaper."

"No, that's not it. I just need to get away."

"So do you have the money?"

"No, not yet. But I'm ready to do what it takes."

Prince guffawed, a combination of mockery and incredulity. "Man, you're something. You call me here to tell me that you're ready to do what it takes. Let me tell you something, There are many people who are ready to do what it takes. But a million naira is not that easy. You need a lot more than just being ready."

"Prince, you know I'm not the many people. I want to get out, I will get out. A million naira or not. Are you going to help me?"

Ayo looked at Prince. Prince was looking at him carefully, considering. The fake visa business was one of the most profitable schemes Prince was engaged in. The margins were high enough for him to overcome any scruples about conning his friend. He knew Ayo well enough to believe his claims, and there was something about him—a sense of obsession, or was it desperation?—that made him believe Ayo would do what it took. Perhaps it would not be a complete waste of time, after all.

"Ok, man, let me see what I can do. It'll take maybe a

week, maybe ten days. Have the money then, and we'll get you out of here in a jiffy."

"Thanks, man. I'll have the money by then."

"Anywhere you want to go in particular?"

"No, as long as it's out of Africa."

"No problem," Prince said. "So, what about we drink a bit to celebrate?"

Ayo looked around apologetically. There wasn't a drop of alcohol left, nor a cent of money to buy some. "I'm completely out. Maybe next time."

As Prince was getting ready to leave, he added, "If you see any good jobs that'll get me a million naira, let me know. No harm having an extra pair of eyes looking around."

Prince nodded, and after a customary goodbye, headed out of the door.

CHAPTER 25

A descent into hell: Life in Lagos amidst heatwave havoc

Posted on 2nd May, 2010, Sunday. By Erika Smit.

If you had told me, just a few months ago, that I would consider a ride to Lagos an entry to heaven, I would have laughed at you. Heaven may still be hyperKisi, but I certainly regarded the opportunity to reach the safety of Lagos as an exit from hell. The last few weeks, you read my stories from the front lines in the Niger Delta, and I thank you for your support. I am out of there, finally, and in Lagos, and I had intended this to be a happier report, one of hope after the catastrophic chaos. But alas!

The situation in Lagos is on a steady downward trajectory. I stand here, witnessing the failure of the infrastructure right before my eyes. It comes in small incremental steps, but the direction is unmistakable. Down, down, and further down.

First to cave was the electricity supply. It started with two hours of blackouts a day and has steadily increased to more than half the day with no electricity. The water supply has completely stopped. Unsurprisingly, a black market for water has sprung up, but the prices demanded are so excessive that one wonders how the common man could afford this basic necessity. The milkman, the paperboy, the fishmonger, the garbage man, all those regulars to whom we never paid attention before, have stopped *working. And the effects on daily life are devastating. It will not be long before the whole country shuts down.*

Who is responsible, I ask?

As we plundered…

Martin didn't read the rest. He picked up the phone and called Erika. He hadn't been able to reach her for weeks, but her posts had been regular enough that he knew she was alive, though in precarious situations. And now, it was a relief that she was in Lagos.

This time, though, she picked up almost right away. "Van Oost!" she said. "You're still here? I thought you would be back in Holland by now."

"You're in Lagos, Erika?"

"Just leaving…I'm at the airport," she replied.

Pleasantries and catch-ups followed for a few minutes. Erika had been stuck in one of the villages in the Niger Delta for a few weeks, unable to drive out, but she finally hitched a ride to Port Harcourt and then to Lagos. "An inferno on Earth," she described her time in the delta, "the worst you can imagine."

Martin told her that CBX Corp had already asked him to leave Lagos, but he had bought some time citing personal reasons. But it wouldn't be long before the request to leave became more forceful.

"And for once, they would be doing something sensible," said Erika. "You need to leave, Martin."

He hesitated.

"Look, I know why you're staying," she continued, "and I get it. But the answer is to bring Ansara. That's her name, right? To Holland. Get her out of here. Not you stay here with her."

"I wish," he said, "but it's more complicated than that. She has her family here, and she isn't going to just leave them."

"Take them all with you," Erika said. "My friend, the one from Amnesty International I told you about, he did just that. He took his wife and her family back with him to Europe. Visas are coming through for spouses and families of spouses exceptionally fast, under these circumstances, I'm told."

"Ansara is not my wife," said Martin.

"Dude, marry her then! Whatever are you waiting for?"

"I don't know, it's a big decision, and I don't even know if she wants—"

"Martin, you haven't seen the hell I've seen, and let me be clear, that hell is not far from your doorstep. It's banging on the doors of Lagos. Don't stay here."

Martin acknowledged that it was not reasonable to stay, but he didn't want to explain the whole situation, about Ansara's missing mother and their hope that they would find her soon. His rational mind knew that he should leave before it was too late. There was no telling when the airports could close for good; the frequency of flights had already decreased significantly. But it almost felt like travesty. Injustice. Why should he get to leave, when millions of people had no choice but to stay put and suffer?

"These are extraordinary circumstances. Wartime, if that

works for you, or worse really," said Erika, "and you must do what you must do. Listen, I've a contact in the embassy here, Tunde. He helped me get a few of the field workers who were with me in the delta out of here, with expedited visas. I'll text you his contact. Get in touch with him, and if Ansara is your wife, I'm sure he can arrange to get her and her family out of here soonest."

Martin could hear the boarding call for Erika's flight. Through hurried goodbyes, she reminded him again to get the hell out. ASAP.

Erika was right. He could not stay in Nigeria. Neither could Ansara nor Femi. Their chance of survival here was slim, at best.

Ever since he realized he was in love with Ansara, Martin had known this was the woman he wanted to spend the rest of his life with. He had been surprised by the suddenness and surety of his feelings, but somehow it seemed right, in a way that could not be explained. But he had not expected everything to happen so quickly.

If ever there was a time for quick decisions, this was it, Martin told himself. He knew, with no doubt in his heart, that he would not leave Ansara and head back to Amsterdam by himself. If they stayed here, none of them was likely to survive the heat. And if getting married was the way for them all to leave, he thought, there was really no reason not to.

Except, he would need to ask her, and she would need to say yes.

Martin absently started dialing the numbers of every contact he had in Port Harcourt. He knew it would be futile. Everyone had left the city, and most, even the country. But he dialed anyway, listening to the tones that told him either no one was answering the phone or that the phone was disconnected.

He was startled when someone finally picked up.

"Martin, is that you?" It was Blessing's voice. "Are you there?"

"Yes, I'm here. Sorry, I was just surprised to hear your voice."

"Well, you called me."

"I know, I'm sorry."

"Is everything ok, Martin? I'm surprised you're still in Nigeria."

"Yes, everything is ok. I was just wondering whether you had any news about the woman we were searching for. Remember, when I was last in Port Harcourt? Kisi Okafor."

The line was silent for a while. Martin wondered whether Blessing really had some news, or she was just trying to remember. Martin prayed silently that there would be news, good or bad. He did not need the truth necessarily, but he needed an answer, any answer.

"I'm afraid I don't have any news, Martin. She worked in one of the other refineries for a brief while before she disappeared, didn't she? I had the workers search for her after you left, as well, but nothing came up. I'm sorry."

"It's so strange, isn't it? How can someone disappear like that?"

"I wish I could tell you, Martin. But when you've no way

of tracking people, it happens. People are disappearing everywhere. Especially the elderly and the sick. They can't stand the heat, but they still push themselves to go to work. And they just collapse. Who's going to take care of them if they collapse on the streets? They're left to die and rot on the roads. If they're lucky, someone takes them to the hospital. If they're very lucky, they make it out of there alive."

"It's so sad. I've no idea what else I can do."

"What can you do, Martin? Nothing. There's nothing any of us can do. It's been a long time since she went missing, isn't it? If you haven't heard from her since then, I'm sorry to tell you, but chances are she's not coming back."

"It's just..." Martin hesitated.

"Martin, if this person, Kisi, is close to someone you care for," said Blessing, "and it seems like you care for them very much, I suggest you prepare them for bad news."

"What do you mean?"

"I'm going to suggest something you may not like. But take it as advice from a friend who means well," said Blessing. "She, Kisi, is most likely not coming back. You should tell her family to accept it."

"I guess. The uncertainty is hard to handle."

"I have seen it so many times now, with relatives of people who go missing. They just live in a limbo for so long, and in the end, for what? The news is most often bad. Sometimes I think God is cruel in not letting them know early."

"I just wish we could find out something. That there was

some way of getting information."

"Well, there isn't. You have tried everything you can. It is time to tell them that she's not coming back."

"Would it help if I, or her family, came to Port Harcourt?"

"Are you mad?" said Blessing. "It would be absolutely a stupid thing to do."

"So, you think I should tell her, the family, that she is dead? Kisi is dead. Is that what you're saying?"

"Yes, Martin, that's the only way they can move forward. And they need to move on, for their own sake. You need to do this for them."

"I cannot possibly lie..."

"It's up to you, of course," said Blessing. "All I'm saying is, it's very hard when people have no news. They keep going between hope and despair. I think in those situations, it is easier if they get some news, any news, even if it is bad news. And then they can move on, focus on their future, on their own survival, which is pretty much all the future any of us can hope for at this point."

Martin thanked her for her help, for checking on Kisi.

"Goodbye, Martin," she said, "I hope to see you again. We'll catch up when all this is over."

When all this is over… It seemed so far away, yet it felt good to hear those words. Blessing's optimism, however guarded, gave him some hope, and he let the words linger in his mind after he hung up the phone. It was hard to imagine now. He had thought many a time, especially in the first few months in

Nigeria, that life in Lagos couldn't really get any worse. And now, it was truly something worse that his worst nightmares. Every day, when he thought that this was rock bottom and it couldn't possibly get any worse, something happened that made him wish for the day before.

But then, he consoled himself, it must be over someday. There is an end to every road, a light at the end of every tunnel. How many casualties it would cause before they reached that end, only time would tell.

CHAPTER 26

Ansara stood in front of Martin's bookshelves. Tall, broad, and overflowing with books, they covered one whole wall. She found it fascinating that a single person could possess so many books, just for his own consumption. She let her fingers slide along the spines. Argentina, Brazil, Curacao, Denmark... It was the travel section, and she had arranged his *Lonely Planet* series in alphabetical order. She tried to imagine a world beyond Nigeria. Coming to Lagos from Port Harcourt was already an adventure for her; what must it be like to travel across the world, country to country, culture to culture?

"It gets tiring after a while," Martin once told her when she asked. "At the beginning, I used to be excited about each place, of meeting new people, of new cultures. I suppose that's why I took up this job in the first place, to see the world, but at some point, it becomes routine. Mundane. And all the places start to look the same, blur into each other."

Ansara had nodded as if she understood. But she did not.

She took the books out, carefully looking at the pictures. They looked so different from each—myriad landscapes, skin colors, food—she felt certain she would never tire of seeing the world, if ever she got the chance. She hadn't told him that though.

Even as the external world kept changing, he had said, the buildings that looked different, people who dressed differently, the food that tasted different, there was something fundamentally similar across all the places. "Like ice, water, and steam, Ansara. At first, you might think they are different things, but really, they're just in different states. The countries and cultures that you see in books may look different, but beneath the surface, they are all the same, in different states at different times. And they move from one to the other when the cycles of fortune reverse, which they almost always do. We just don't live long enough to see it." Martin had sounded convincing when he said that.

But Ansara was not sure. She had never known her country to be anything but chaotic and poor. Her father had told her that when they first found oil in the delta, people thought their lives would get better. Much better. But the state of the nation, of their lives, had not changed for them. Or for anyone she knew. And now with the heatwave… Ansara's eyes welled with tears as thoughts of her mother came rushing in. She sank to the floor, her back against the shelves, her face lowered between her knees.

Ansara was still on the floor when Martin came in. Her tears had dried by then, but her heart was still heavy. He sat down beside her, holding her close.

"I wish I had told her," Ansara said.

"What do you mean?" asked Martin.

"About Emeka," she said, "my brother." Martin didn't probe, but she continued. "I should have told her that he's never coming back."

"Isn't he with the activists?" asked Martin, "I'm sure…"

"He was," she said. "He joined them after Papa died. After one of the protests, the police took him away and we never heard anything for many months. We didn't know where he was. We kept waiting for him to turn up.

"And then one day." Ansara paused, gathering her words, and her strength. "They asked me to come to the morgue to identify his body. They said it was an accident. He had been in police custody, and then he was in the morgue, and they said it was an accident."

Martin was silent, letting her take her time. "I'm so sorry to hear that, Ansara," he finally said.

"He was just a regular guy till our father died, you know. Then something in him changed. He had always been a bit hot-headed, but after Papa's accident, it was as if something snapped. He spent hours and hours fighting for the families of the injured and the dead. He joined environmental groups. He fought against the free use of arms. He was a peaceful protester though, vehemently against violence of all kinds. But that didn't matter."

Ansara hesitated. It felt odd to tell Martin about Emeka.

In the beginning of her relationship with Martin, Ansara had often imagined telling Emeka about him, and how her brother would have reacted. When Emeka learned about

Ansara's pregnancy, he threatened to kill Ikenna, wagging his machete in the air. If there was anyone her brother would have hated more than Ikenna, she thought, it would be an *oyibo*. Emeka could not stand Ikenna, but his hatred for the West was in an entirely different league. Her brother blamed the Western corporations for the evils that had befallen their land. He blamed them for the death of their father, for the pollution, for the violence rampant in the refineries. She often thought about how he had taken her to see acres and acres of land burning, sending thick plumes of smoke and light flares into their night sky. He told her that it was all the gas that came out when the oil companies drilled for oil, and since they didn't need the gas they just burned it at night. The flares were killing the children, he said, burning through their lungs, blinding their eyes, depriving them of a healthy childhood.

But try as she might, Ansara could not reconcile the image of the evil white man that Emeka insisted on painting, with gentle and generous Martin. Compared to some of the Nigerian bosses she had worked for, his kindness and patience with all the house staff was striking. Except for his occasional annoyance with Ayo, but Ansara thought a lesser man would have fired Ayo long before. Martin even cared for the plants and trees and the gardens, watering them himself on some weekends when Raphael was not around. But Ansara was sure Emeka would see nothing but the devil in Martin. Life would have been so different had Emeka not become part of the extremist groups. Tears prickled Ansara's eyes as she thought of her brother, and she wiped them off. How she missed him!

And how she missed her mother too.

Martin put his arms around her, sitting on the floor beside her.

"Mama still thinks her son is alive," she said. "Everyone thinks he is alive. They think he is living in hiding. I couldn't let her see him like that, Martin. His body…" Her voice trailed off, and Martin held her closer. "He would want to be remembered as a hero, as a strong man, not as a mangled piece of flesh. I told them it wasn't him. I paid them with whatever money I had to give him a good funeral, but I didn't take the body back with me. And no one else knew. Mama didn't know. She kept hoping, every day, waiting…"

An almost inaudible sob escaped her.

"The waiting," said Ansara, "is so very exhausting. I wish I had told her. I should have."

She leaned against Martin's shoulder and closed her eyes, tired and resigned, shutting out the colorful, unattainable world that the travel books strewn around them promised, but finding comfort in the immediacy of love in the arms of a man who was waiting too. For her. With her.

CHAPTER 27

The next morning, Martin woke up with a deep sense of foreboding.

The previous evening was still fresh in his mind, how Ansara had talked about her brother and his death. It had rattled him more than he let on, to learn that Emeka had died presumably at the hands of local authorities. He tried not to recall the number of times he had asked David to call the Mobile Police, the *MoPo*, that they regularly employed to keep him and his company safe and whose methods they never questioned. To him, they were the enforcers of the law, and even though he knew about the bribes he approved every month as "miscellaneous expenses," and he had heard about their unsavory methods, he had preferred not to dwell on them, chalking it up to just a different way of doing business in a different country. He had convinced himself that calling the police was always the right thing to do, and never bothered to find out what happened after the police cleared the protesters or the activists.

Martin had always believed that, when it really mattered, he would do the right thing. But he realized now that doing the right thing is the easy part. Discerning what was right in a world where virtue depended on perspective was the hard but worthy feat.

Ansara's words continued to haunt him: *The waiting,* she had said, *was exhausting.* He could feel the depth of her pain of a truth concealed that she feared she may no longer be able to reveal.

Martin sat on the side of his bed, not ready to face the day.

A part of him wanted to follow Blessing's advice and let Ansara believe that her mother was no longer alive. Martin knew that if the heat continued for much longer, the casualties would be very high. In a country where more than half the population had guns, and many of them did not need much of a reason to use it, irreversible descent was dangerously close. If the heat did not kill them, there was a very good chance that the ensuing chaos would. To let that happen to Ansara and Femi when he had a chance to save them from that fate was unthinkable.

The waiting, in this case, was not just exhausting, it could be fatal.

But on the other hand, he could not bring himself to lie to her. Definitely not about something as important as her mother's life. But Ansara would not leave the country if she thought her mother was alive, out there somewhere. Every rational bone in his body wanted to protect the woman he loved, to do so at all costs, but he also knew that he would never forgive himself if he lied to her. Could he wake up next to her every morning, knowing that, had she known the truth, she may not have chosen to be with him? Could he live with that?

Decisions are rarely about making a choice between right

and wrong, but most often a choice between two wrongs.

If saving Ansara from the heat meant living with guilt for the rest of his life, perhaps, he told himself, that was what true love was about.

"Ah, there you're! Breakfast is getting cold," Ansara said as she walked into the room.

"Ansa, how are you? There's something I want to talk to you about."

"I'm fine, *nkem*. Is everything ok?" She looked surprised by the grave tone of his voice.

Martin hesitated.

"Martin, what is it? You're making me worried."

Suddenly, he was not sure that he wanted to do this. He had convinced himself that it was the right thing to do, but now, looking at Ansara's anxious face, he was wavering.

"*Nkem*, tell me, what is it?"

He had to. He had to say it. It was the only way.

"Ansa." He held her hands as he spoke. "We have bad news about your mother. I had asked people at Port Harcourt to check about her, and I'm afraid the news is not good."

"Bad news? What does that mean?" Ansara took her hands away from Martin's. He looked away from her staring eyes.

He remembered Blessing's words: *It's very hard when people have no news. They keep going between hope and despair.*

"Ansa, she has passed away."

"That's not possible. Mama has to be okay. She'll be fine.

She has to be."

"Ansa, it seems a lot of older people were missing, because of the heat. They collapsed, and many of them didn't make it."

"But we don't know for sure, do we? Did they find the body? Maybe they made a mistake."

"Ansa, I'm sorry. That's the news I've from Port Harcourt."

Ansara sat back on the bed, held her head in her hands, and cried. Softly at first, and then loudly. Uncontrollably. Martin held her tentatively, and later he hugged her hard as the intensity of her sobs increased. He told himself that it was the right thing to do. The uncertainty was not going to help anyone, and this was the best way to help Ansara move forward and think of what was best for herself and Femi.

"I want to go. I want to go to Port Harcourt." She looked up after a while, her eyes glinting with tears.

"Ansa, it's not safe. It's too hot, there are shootings everywhere."

"Martin, I need to bury my mother. It's important. I need to see her one last time. I should never have left her. I didn't even say goodbye."

Martin didn't respond.

"I need to go… I really need to go…" Her voice trailed off into sobs.

"Ansa, you've to think of Femi. You can't take him there. You know it's not safe."

She sank back and continued to cry. Martin looked away, guilt already beginning to weigh on him.

That afternoon, after lunch, he decided to go to church, something he had not done for a very long time.

"Can I join you?" Ansara asked as he was dressing.

"Sure, of course. I didn't know you go to church."

"I don't usually, but..."

"Of course. Mohammed will be here in a few minutes."

Mohammed seemed surprised by this rather curious event. Martin thought of offering an explanation but decided it would only make matters worse. Besides, he did not think Mohammed could do any harm. People tend to gossip more when they are living together and when they have plenty of free time. It seemed unlikely that Mohammed, appreciating the time he got to spend with his family and probably worrying about how to get his family safely through the heat, would have the time or energy to think about Martin and Ansara's sudden interest in religion. Martin hoped that in a few days, all this would be over, and he would not have to keep his relationship with Ansara a secret.

Martin still kept his distance from Ansara in public. He chose an aisle away from her and Femi while they were at church. He was glad that they arrived at a relatively quiet time, morning mass already finished. He had visited a few African churches in his time, more as a way of socializing with clients and suppliers, and had been surprised by the vigor of their prayers. He definitely needed his quiet prayer and contemplation, especially at a time like now.

Martin closed his eyes. In his mind, the modern African

church transformed into a sixteenth-century European one. St. Stephen's was the main church in Rijswijk. It was an impressive Gothic building with high arches, stained glass windows, and vivid images of sin and hell painted on its walls. He could not remember the last time he visited the church. It must have been when he was ten.

In his mind's eye, Martin saw a little boy walk timidly to the confessional at the far end of the church hall. Father David, who taught him catechism, was at the other end of the booth, with only the brown of his coat visible through the net of the confession box.

"Son, what brings you here today?"

"Father, I've sinned." Martin was surprised that the little boy in his imagination had the voice of a grown-up man.

"What have you done, my child?"

"Father, I've lied. I've lied to the woman I love." He paused. "I told her that her mother died, when that may not be true. And now she's here, crying. Mourning a woman who may still be alive."

Martin did not wait for the priest to respond. "I did it because I wanted her to have closure. I want her to move on, for her sake and for her son's sake." He sighed and let his head drop onto his palms. "And I did it so that she would leave the country with me."

Martin did not know what he expected. Perhaps that the priest in his imagination would say that what he did was ok, that God would descend from the heavens and forgive him, or he would suddenly come up with a way to forget his sins. Whatever it was that he had expected, nothing happened. He just sat there with his head in his palms for what seemed like forever but could not really have been more than half an hour. Eventually, the confessional, the priest, and the little boy faded from his mind.

The weight of his lie still hung heavily. He knew it would be his cross to bear for the rest of his life but, glancing at the crying Ansara, he hoped he had done the right thing, that at least the burden was worth it for what it had saved. He got up and left the main church hall to wait outside for Ansara, hoping that she was having better luck finding some peace.

"Is everything ok, sir?" Mohammed's voice startled him.

"Yes, I'm not too much of a church person. Just that when you're struggling with the heat, a bit of help from God doesn't seem so bad. I thought you were in the car, Mohammed. Or were you inside the church?"

"Oh, just for a peek. I used to come here with my mother, when I was a child. My father was a Muslim, a converted one at least. But my mother could not give up the church entirely and once in a while, she would sneak us kids in here. I still associate church with something I shouldn't be caught doing."

"Let's wait in the car. Looks like Ansara may be a while."

"Is everything ok with her? She seems very sad," Mohammed asked.

"She got news that her mother died. She had been missing

for a while, but now it seems she is no longer alive."

"Oh, that's very sad. I heard that things in Port Harcourt are getting very ugly. It's good that you don't have to go there anymore for work."

"Yes, the company is asking everyone to leave. Port Harcourt is out of the question. They are asking me to leave Lagos as well."

"Oh, you're leaving? We'll miss you here. You've been a good boss to us. But I can see why the company wants you out of here."

Martin smiled. He had always enjoyed having Mohammed drive him around. The man had a good head on his shoulders, and more rarely, a good heart also.

"Is everything ok, Mohammed? You want to ask me something?"

"You like her, don't you, sir?"

"Who?"

"Ansara. I knew, sir, from the way you look at her. It's ok, sir. I've known for a while. I don't think anyone else in the house has noticed."

Martin did not say anything. He did not realize he was so transparent. And he was thankful that Mohammed was the only one who knew.

"You've to take her with you, sir. It's not safe here for just a woman and a child. If you want to, sir, of course."

"I want to, Mohammed. But she just lost her mother."

"Exactly, sir. She's alone. She needs to go with you."

Martin spotted Ansara in the distance, walking toward the car with Femi.

"Mohammed, please keep this to yourself."

"Of course, sir. You can trust me," he said, and then added thoughtfully, "but does it matter anymore?"

The scorching heat burning his skin, sweat making his shirt stick to his body, the stench of rotting living matter all around, Martin considered Mohammed's question. *Does it matter anymore?* It was hard indeed to tell what mattered anymore.

The days passed at an excruciatingly slow pace. Nothing marked the passage of one day to another, morning giving way to noon to afternoon and later to night, and then again night to morning.

It had been two weeks since Martin told Ansara that her mother had died, but it felt interminably long. Work was suspended, operations were pared down to the minimum, and he had been asked to leave Lagos. His mind was riddled with guilt; his body was ravaged by the heat.

The evening was quiet and eerie. There were no gunshots. There was no power in the house. The television and radio were out. Martin decided not to switch on the generators. There was still enough light that they could get by. When night fell and it became impossible to sleep without the whirring breeze of a fan, he would switch on one of the generators.

Ansara was in the kitchen, busy with cooking. He tried to take over the responsibilities from her, but she refused.

"*Nkem*, let me do this. I need to," she pleaded. And he let her. He pulled his chair to the window and opened the page to his bookmark, trying to make the most of the remaining daylight.

Everyone had a different way to grieve. Ansara's was the kind that Martin found difficult to console. During the day, she immersed herself in work. Food was rationed. She couldn't spend too much time cooking elaborate meals, so she turned to cleaning. Scrubbing. Wiping. Tidying. Everything in the house sparkled, in sharp contrast to the gloom he felt in his own mind.

One night, Martin had asked her, "Ansa, aren't you going to tell Femi?"

Ansara had been silent for a while. They were in bed and the lights were off, but he was sure she was not asleep.

"*Nkem*, he's just a boy, and still adjusting to leaving his home and his grandmother. I don't want to tell him now. Maybe later."

"Wouldn't he wonder what happened to her?"

"Maybe. I'll tell him later. But for now, he has just gotten used to his life here. He thinks she's back home, that he'll see her when we return, accepting that she left without telling him goodbye. I can't. I just can't tell him now."

"Yes, of course, if you think that's best."

All was quiet again. Ansara slept on the other side of the bed. When he tried to hug her, her body stiffened. He let her be. The darkness was complete. There were no streetlights visible through the windows, no neighbors had their lights on, and even the stars seemed to have joined in the conspiracy of blackness. The fresh smell of the sheets, which Ansara had washed recently, offered a respite from absolute sensory deprivation.

He woke up in the middle of the night to quiet sobs next to him. He almost turned and hugged her but stopped himself in time. Late at night, in bed, when she was sure no one was around to try and console her, seemed to be the only time Ansara let herself cry, and he could not deprive her of that.

Martin wanted to help, but there was not much he could do. He had tried to reach both Mrs. Jideofor and her brother in Makurdi, hoping they would be able to comfort her. The phones in Port Harcourt had stopped working, and it was impossible to reach Mrs. Jideofor. The man who picked up when Martin called Ansara's brother told him that he had moved north to his wife's family home. It seemed to Martin that everyone was fleeing as far as they could, as if running from an invisible monster that was slowly creeping up on them. He knew he had to leave soon too. But he had a few steps to complete before that. Even in his worst nightmares, he never imagined he would be proposing marriage to a woman in the throes of a grief brought about by his own lie.

He spent a large part of his days playing with Femi. Martin found a basketball hoop in the garage and together, they fixed it to a free wall by the side of the house. He taught Femi how to play the game, the boy displaying not just an affection but a natural inclination toward the game. At least that was something he could do for Ansara, relieving her from having to pretend to be happy. Besides, he had come to enjoy spending time with the young boy.

"Femi, that's a nice shot!" Martin called out as he ran toward the basket to get back the ball the boy had just netted.

As Martin ran, Femi deftly dribbled the ball out from right under him, and as Martin looked on admiringly, the ball found its destination once again in the basket.

"Well done! That was amazing!" Martin panted. He heard applause behind him and turned around. He was surprised to see Ansara. She smiled, the sun shining brightly on her face. She stayed and watched the game, cheering them both on and occasionally joining in when the ball bounced next to her.

Later, as Martin and Ansara walked back to the house, leaving Femi to fiddle with the ball on the ground, Martin remarked, "Ansara, I'm glad you're feeling better."

"Yes, I know. Mama would not have wanted me to brood over her. She wasn't the sort of woman who let things get her down and she wouldn't want me to either. We all have to move on, don't we?"

She smiled at him, and he realized how much he had missed her, the happy, optimistic Ansara he had come to rely on.

He reached over and hugged her, and this time she did not resist.

Later that evening, when Ansara was in the shower, Martin decided it was time to ask her to marry him and come away with him to the Netherlands. He could wait no longer, and she seemed ready to move forward. It may not be the best of times, but if he postponed any longer, he was not sure he would be able to get them all out in time.

Martin kept turning the words over in his mind. Nothing seemed right. He had no ring, he had no flowers, he had no wine. All he had was the sincerity of his words and the depth of his love for her. He hoped that would be enough.

"*Nkem*, wake up." Ansara's voice startled him. Martin didn't realize he had fallen asleep on the couch.

He could smell the faint whiff of lavender from her soap. He wanted to pull her to him. The fresh odor unadulterated by perfume, her skin soft and supple from the water, and her hair wet and wild... Right after a shower, he always found her irresistible. Ansara was beautiful and Martin felt like a lucky man. He just wished that circumstances could have been luckier.

"Ansa, there's something I want to tell you," he said. "Will you sit down?"

"Are you sure it's just something you want to tell? I know what that look means." Ansara's eyes sparkled. Martin was glad that she was in a jovial mood.

"Yes, come on. Sit down." Martin pulled her to the seat next to him.

"Oh, it does look serious. *Nkem* has his all-important look."

Martin ignored her playfulness. "Ansa, I know this is not the right time to ask, and believe me when I say that this is not how I envisioned asking you this question. But I cannot wait any longer."

He paused and looked deeper into her eyes. "Ever since I met you, Ansa, I've known that you're the one I want to spend my life with. You're the one I want to sleep every night with and wake up every morning with. You make me happy, Ansa, like no one else could and never would be able to. And I want to be the one to make you happy, the one to make you smile. I want to spend the rest of my life with you."

Martin slid off the couch, went on his knees, and took both her hands in his. "Ansara Okafor, will you be my wife?"

Ansara looked bewildered. He brought her palms to his lips and kissed them tenderly.

"Ansa, I know this is sudden. I didn't want to spring this on you now. I've no ring for you today. But I mean it, Ansa, more than I've meant anything else I've ever said. There is nothing else I'm surer of than that I want to spend the rest of my life with you. I want to marry you. I promise you I'll keep you happy and do everything I can to—"

"Shh." Ansara pressed her fingers on his lips, her bewilderment giving way to amusement at his tumble of words and joy at his love and sincerity. "Yes, I will marry you. Yes!"

Martin could not believe what he had just heard. He picked her up and twirled her around. When he set her back on the ground, he felt the whole world was turning around him. They both stumbled as they moved toward each other's lips. The world still was turning around them, but in that moment, he would not have noticed even if it had stopped.

CHAPTER 28

"Ayo, I'm in the neighborhood. You up for some drinks? I can come over." Prince's call was a nice break in the monotony of Ayo's day.

The inactivity was killing Ayo. But the thought of going back to Martin's place, back to his old life, repulsed him. He wanted to get away, and that's all he wanted right now. He still had not figured out a way to make the million naira. He no longer felt the zest and enthusiasm that came with scouring for a new con. The old Ayo seemed to have been lost somewhere, replaced by the lethargic alcoholic maniac he felt himself turning into. Time was running out. He would need to do something drastic to get so much money at such short notice—there was always money to be had for those willing to be ruthless—but he would need to make sure there was a solid escape route before he committed to a desperate job.

"Sure, drinks it is. See you soon!" he replied with feigned enthusiasm.

He would need to find a way to stock up drinks in his apartment. Prince was not going to be forgiving about not getting alcohol a second time, and that could severely impact his chances of finding a way out of Nigeria.

Ayo had run out of money. He had spent every cent of his own and the money Martin had entrusted him with. He poured some water onto the front of his shirt and staggered out to the shop down the block.

"Isaac, I need three packs. I'll pay you later." He spoke in a slurred voice, pointing at the beer. A drunk man was more likely to do rash things than a sober one, and fear always helped in getting what one wanted.

"No, Ayo, we don't do business on credit. You need to bring the money."

Ayo pulled the shiny knife that he had tucked into his belt ever so slightly and patted it a few times.

"Isaac, for old times sake, how about you call this a one-time thing?"

Isaac looked at the point of the knife and took a quick look at Ayo.

"Yes, of course. But you've to pay by the end of the week."

"Of course. Have a good day!"

It was just as well that Isaac had not insisted on payment. Ayo was in no mood for any violence. And today, he would have had no other choice.

Ayo had just got back to his apartment when Prince arrived.

"Ah, I see that you've got beers this time. We all need some fun in a day, don't we? Tell me, how have you been, brother?" Ayo was surprised to see Prince in a chatty mood. That must mean good news, he thought.

"Alright, doing well. How are you, Prince?"

"Doing well too, Ayo. Very well, you might say. Business is good these days. Everyone wants to leave the country, and that means good business for me. This country will be good, I say, with fewer people in it. You still want to leave, Ayo? Good times may be ahead."

"Yes, yes, for sure."

"Well, it's not a bad idea to go for a few years. People go to the US or Europe, and then they come back rich and famous. Never have to work again in their lives. Like all those bastards in the islands."

Prince didn't wait for an answer. He continued. "Listen, I've got some good news. I've arranged for your visa. It's yours whenever you want it. As soon as you pay, you can be on the next flight out."

"Great, great…" Ayo hesitated. "Any chance you can lower the price a bit for an old friend? A million is a lot, Prince."

"Of course it is a lot. Imagine what you're getting in return. And this is already a good price for a friend."

The bargaining went on for a while. Ayo knew that Prince enjoyed the back and forth as much as the actual money he would get. Ordinarily, Ayo enjoyed it too, but today he was tired. He felt as if a huge weight was bearing down on him and all he wanted to do was lie on a bed and sleep. But he willed himself to do this last thing. Get out of there, and he could sleep on a nice bed in a nice place. Finally, they agreed on 800,000 naira. Ayo was not sure he got the best deal possible, but it would have to do.

"So when can you get me the money?"

Ayo hesitated. Telling Prince that he did not have the money might ruin his chance of getting the visa, but on the other hand, Prince might have some lucrative jobs for him.

"You don't have the money, do you, man? I'm telling you, ever since you decided to get married, you've been a changed man. Oh, and just so we are clear, the eight hundred is for one person. If you want a visa for your new wife, that will be another million. Special price is just for you."

"Oh, for the last time, it's not about the marriage. I've had other things on my mind. You know, I'm not even getting married anymore."

"Oh, you're not? What happened?"

"It was never a firm thing anyway. And I've too much going on in my life right now. And the bloody family wanted help from me. The mother and daughter wanted to know if they can come to Lagos with me. Can you imagine? Not even married and they were making demands."

Prince laughed out loud. "That's the problem with marriages. Anyway, I hope you got what you wanted before you broke it off."

"Well, not really. But it doesn't matter. I've other things to worry about."

"Speaking of marriages, your cook seems to have done very well for herself. She was one hot bitch, but I never thought she could pull off marriage to an *oyibo*."

"My cook? Ansara? What are you talking about?"

"I don't know her name, but the woman who was working as cook in your house. Your *oyibo* is marrying her and taking her to Europe with him."

Ayo started to laugh. But he stopped abruptly, seeing Prince's serious expression. "No, no way. Are you sure?"

"I'm sure, man. You think I'd be in my business if I didn't have the right sources to everything that goes on in Lagos? My sources are reliable. And they are leaving very soon too, I hear."

Ayo got up from his chair. He picked up a bottle of beer absently and walked to the window that looked out onto the derelict neighborhood beyond. His house was one of the few with concrete walls. It may not be a mansion, but it had a functioning roof. He saw little kids running around naked, a woman scraping a banana peel in hope of finding something to eat. He saw a man with reams of magazines, some tucked under his arms, some placed precariously on his head, and the rest fanned out in both his hands. They were the unfortunates, not he. He was the one who had made it, or at least, the one who was on his way up. He was the one, not them, not Ansara.

Yes, not Ansara. He had given her the job.

He wanted out of here, and instead, she was getting out?

How had all this happened? Right under his nose? She, who was nothing more than a lowly factory worker, and not even in Lagos. All because she was a woman. A bloody woman.

He thought of Europe, the land beyond, which seemed so full of promise. The stories of wealth he had heard from those who had gone and come back, how they lived like kings after being gone for just a few years... He wanted it all. He wanted out of this place, out of the mess he had created for himself, away from the memories that haunted him in the heat. It was he who deserved to escape, not anyone else, not Ansara.

Ayo bit into the cap of the beer bottle and tugged it. The cap flew open, hit the windowsill, and bounced back toward Prince.

"Watch out, man. You ok?"

"I can't believe it. He's marrying her? Marry? When did all this happen?"

"Shouldn't I be asking you? Weren't you right there?"

"Yes, but I didn't know. How could I have missed it? How did I not know?" He let out a roar, no longer able to control the anger erupting inside him.

"Ayo!" Prince shouted back. "Calm down, man! What's wrong with you? Why do you care so much?"

Ayo stared at Prince for a moment, then he came back and sat on his chair, the beer bottle dangling dangerously from his hand. He was still panting. "Why do I care? It should be me, Prince. Not her. It should be me who gets to leave the country. I work with these bloody *oyibos* for so many years now, and no one helps me get out. This woman, this stupid idiot woman, she comes and works for, what, a year, not even two, and she is out of the country and into a wonderful life. The bloody slut!"

Prince thought about it for a moment. He said, "You know, it may not be such bad news for you after all. This whole marriage and leaving thing."

"Not a bad thing for me?" asked Ayo.

"Think about it. You need to have money real quick. What do people have in plenty when they are about to get married and leave the country?"

"Cash."

"Yes, exactly. And that has got to be more than eight hundred," said Prince.

"The *oyibo* would have cash at home. He must be keeping enough to pay the marriage and the visa people. Enough for all the bribes and fees."

"That's what I'm saying," said Prince.

"Yes, yes!" Excitement shone in Ayo's eyes. "It's so hard to travel these days, he must get it a few days before and keep it at home. I know him, he likes to be prepared. And he's a bit of a trusting idiot too. I'm sure he will keep it at home with him."

"You can just walk in and take it."

"Prince, this is a great idea. You're a genius. Thank you." He went over and hugged Prince.

"You better hurry though, before they leave. Get yourself cleaned up and call me as soon as you get the money. And if you find more in the house, remember who gave you the idea in the first place."

"Yes, of course."

Prince stayed on till the three packs of beers were cleaned out. Ayo did not care if he had all the beers. He was finally excited. He felt as if there was finally a light in the darkness that had engulfed him. Even as Prince droned on about inconsequential things, new cons that had opened up because of the heat, how women were cheaper these days, and how his business was thriving, Ayo was planning his next move.

He would go back to work as if he had recovered from his illness. He would wait till Martin was out of the house, or at least out of his library where he kept the cash. It should not take him more than ten minutes to find the cash, and he would disappear immediately. By the time they realized the money was gone, Ayo would be gone too. Finally, to the life he always knew he deserved.

CHAPTER 29

Throughout the week since Ansara had said yes, Martin had been plagued with a curious mix of feelings, happiness, excitement, relief... and, if he was honest to himself, a sense of dread.

Finally, it was his wedding day, and he couldn't think of any reason to be happier than getting married to the love of one's life. It felt like the last lap of a long run, where the red tape of the finish line was finally in sight and the end was no longer a distant illusion. There were even rumors that it might rain that weekend. The showers were expected to lower temperatures, an indicator that the worst of the heatwave could be behind them.

It was hard to deny the dread though, a gnawing feeling that wouldn't leave him. Perhaps it was because he was still struggling with starting a life on a lie. He tried to convince himself that there had been no other way to get to where he was, that giving Ansara that choice would not have been the right thing to do. Perhaps one day, when they were happily together and life felt less precarious, he might tell her the truth. And when the worst of the heat was over, they could resume the search. After all, there was nothing more to be done now in any case. The logic felt right, but he couldn't shake the knot in the pit of his stomach. Maybe it was just the heat, he tried to tell himself. But he needed to keep focus, he reminded himself. Get through the wedding and the administrative formalities and leave the country.

Martin called his mother. He spent most of the call assuring her that things in Nigeria were not as bad as the media made them out to be and that he was safe. Most importantly, he told her, he was coming home very soon and he had a surprise.

He did not tell her that he was getting married. There was so much to tell and so little time, he wouldn't know where to start. He would have liked his family to witness his wedding, but somehow it felt oddly right. Ansara was here without her family, so it was only fair that he was without his too. But he looked forward to the day he could take her home to his family. A day not far off.

The preparations for the wedding were simple, yet it had left Martin alternating between anger and amusement: anger at the registration fees, which he was sure had more to do with him being a foreigner rather than any standard policy, and amusement at the list of items he was asked to bring, which included two packs of Five Alive juice, a pack of canned Coca-Cola, one bottle of Bacchus tonic wine, and a carton of noodles. Tunde, Erika's contact at the embassy, had agreed to help him with the bureaucratic arrangements.

"A carton of noodles, did you say?" Martin had asked Tunde again, unable to believe that he had heard right.

"Yes, sir. A carton of noodles. No noodles, no nuptials!"

He got a traditional Nigerian dress for Ansara, a beautiful *buba* and *iro* with a matching *gele*, all in white and patterned with white lace and *aso-oke*. It looked so beautiful, he couldn't wait to see Ansara in it.

"*Nkem*, you shouldn't have done this. I thought we were going to have a simple wedding," Ansara protested when she saw the dress, but her eyes had shone with happiness. And for Martin, that was worth all the effort that went into finding just the right dress.

It was a hot day, but people had stopped remarking about it. It would be more of a surprise if it weren't hot. Martin prayed that he would not witness or be subject to anything unpleasant on the trip to the registrar's office. The uncontrolled violence that had been predicted in Lagos had not happened yet, and he hoped against hope that today would not be the day it would erupt. For once, the stars seemed to be aligned in favor of Martin and Ansara's union, and they arrived at the Registrar's Office earlier than planned and without much adventure.

The Ikoyi registry was as crowded as any typical government office in Nigeria. There were people standing in queues, sitting in waiting rooms, officials walking around, and in general, chaos. It seemed that hot weather did not prevent people registering their births and deaths or getting married. Fortunately, Tunde was there to welcome them, and he knew just how to get ahead of the long queues.

Within a few minutes, Martin and Ansara were in front of an official who would double as the person registering the marriage as well as a witness. The marriage itself was a pretty nondescript affair. Some paperwork, signatures from the bride and groom and two witnesses, and most important, the exchange of all the items previously agreed on, including the noodles. And that was all it took. Photographs were snapped by the official photographer which the registry arranged for, paid for by mandatory photo fees.

They celebrated with a round of champagne. And then, in a dusty government office, amidst chaos and confusion and strangers made friendly with a glass of alcohol and a lot of money and noodles, Martin kissed his new bride.

There wasn't much time for more celebrations. Martin had to accompany Tunde to the Dutch Embassy to sort out the necessary papers for Ansara and Femi, a process he hoped would not take too long. Now that Ansara and Femi were traveling with him, Martin could not wait to get out of the heat. Tunde had promised him that with a marriage certificate, it would be relatively easy. But with these affairs, one could never be sure.

Ansara decided to go home, not wanting to be walking in and out of government offices in her bridal dress.

"Ansa, my love, when you're home, ask Ayo to bring you some lunch from Cactus. You should not be cooking today."

Ansara smiled. "Ayo is not around, remember? But don't worry about it, I'll be fine."

"Of course, how could I forget? And no, you don't get

to cook." Martin turned to Mohammed and gave him clear instructions to bring his bride food from one of the good restaurants nearby.

He thought of Ayo briefly. He had almost forgotten about Ayo's illness. It seemed a rather long time for someone to be sick. He would need to give him a call. For now, Martin was happy and unwilling to let worries about Ayo ruin his perfect day.

He leaned over and kissed Ansara before she left with Mohammed, promising to be home soon, and then headed off to the Netherlands embassy in Tunde's car.

CHAPTER 30

"Are you happy?" Mohammed asked Ansara while he was driving her back to the house.

"I am, Mohammed. Sometimes, I feel like all this is a dream, and I'm just about to wake up from it. But for now, I'm happy. Very happy."

"So now you're our big boss. No longer Ansara. I'll call you Madam."

Ansara laughed aloud. "No, Mohammed, of course not. Things don't change just like that. Yes, I've a new role, true. But please don't call me Madam or anything. You'll embarrass me."

As they entered the driveway, Ben waved them in.

"If you don't need anything else," said Mohammed, "I'll leave you at the door and get you food from Cactus. Is it ok with you?"

"Oh, don't bother about the food, Mohammed. There are leftovers in the house. I'll be fine with that."

"Are you sure about that, Madam? *Oga* asked me to."

"Yes, of course. And really, don't call me Madam, please."

As soon as she reached home, Femi ran to her. Any drive out of the house was dangerous, and they had decided not to drag him into a crowded office. He hugged her tight, perhaps confused by her pretty new dress and all the events happening around him. Ansara had explained the previous night that she was going to get married. She told him that they would now be living with Martin and he would be a new dad who would take care of him. Femi had not even looked remotely surprised. He had accepted it as he accepted everything else that had been happening— the heat, his displacement to a new city, the disappearance of his grandmother. He smiled and nodded.

Ansara repeated it and explained again, but smiles and nods were all she got. She wished he could say something at least this one time, something, anything, to let her know that he understood and that he was happy about it.

"He was a very good boy." Mohammed's wife, who had agreed to stay with him while they were at the registry, came from behind.

"Oh, Femi, I'm proud of you. Aren't you my good boy, my very best boy?" Ansara hugged him tight and kissed him on the head.

"We are off then, take care. Wish you happy marriage, again." Mohammed and his wife waved goodbye. Ansara was alone in the house, with Femi. She looked around, trying to understand her new role as the mistress of this house. She couldn't. She still wanted to go and hide in the kitchen.

Ansara walked to her old room, with the damp walls and no windows. She sat down on the bed and started to cry. It was all happening so fast. In her heart, she knew this was the right thing to do and her mother would have approved. But she wished, she just wished, that Mama could be there to witness it, to be part of it, to tell her that everything will be alright, and that she was making the right decisions.

Ansara changed out of her wedding dress.

She caressed the dress, straightened out the creases, and folded it. "Isn't it pretty, Femi?" she asked her son when he walked in. The boy nodded.

She opened up her Ghana bag and started putting things into it. Femi looked on with amazement.

"Yes, pumpkin, we're going on a long trip. Away from this heat and danger. But we'll come back, one day, when it is safer. When Nigeria is beautiful and well again, as it used to be."

Martin had tried to get her to move her things to his room and move out of the servants' quarters as soon as she agreed to the marriage. But she had not wanted to jinx it. Now she dragged her Ghana bag up the stairs into Martin's bedroom, Femi trailing close behind her.

Ansara heard a thud from the library on her way. She paused and opened the door.

"Ayo, you're here! Are you feeling better?" she exclaimed when she saw Ayo in the room.

He was standing by Martin's desk, both his hands resting on it for support. The paperweight lay on the floor, knocked off the tabletop. Ayo's eyes were red and his pupils bulged out even more than usual. He moved toward the front of the desk, trying hard not to stagger, but it was obvious that his hand against the desk was the only thing propping him up.

"Ayo, what are you doing?" asked Ansara, a little shocked by his sudden and disheveled appearance.

"I'm feeling alright, better," replied Ayo. "Martin asked me to come here and get some papers."

"Oh, he didn't tell me that you were coming." Ansara immediately regretted telling him that.

"Of course. Why would he tell you? Shouldn't you be in the kitchen, cooking?"

Ansara hesitated. She decided this was not the right time to tell Ayo about the wedding. In any case, she wanted Martin to be the one telling him.

"Make me some hot soup, will you? I thought I was getting better, but my throat still hurts."

Ansara looked around at the room. She could not imagine what Martin would have asked Ayo to get for him.

"Take the boy with you. What a nuisance!" Ayo grumbled. "I told you not to bring him here."

Ansara was sure something was amiss. If Ayo was coming in, Martin would have told her. And what would he be doing in Martin's library? Ansara didn't trust Ayo one bit, but this time it seemed like he was up to more harm than usual.

Ayo rummaged through the contents of the desk.

"Ayo, what are you doing?" Ansara's voice was cold and sharp. "I'm certain Martin would not have asked you to look into his desk."

"I don't have to tell you anything. Get lost, you stupid woman."

"Ayo, I think I better call Martin," she said. The phone was on the desk next to Ayo, but she didn't want to approach him. She would need to use the one downstairs.

"I told you, he asked me to bring him some papers," said Ayo.

"Ayo, I know you're not looking for papers in there. What's this about?"

"Oh yeah, what's this about, you want to know? You want to tell me what's been going on here when I was not around?" Ayo's anger was beginning to show in his voice.

"That's none of your business," said Ansara, "and has nothing to do with what you're doing here looking through Martin's desk."

"Hey, you crazy woman! Don't forget who I am. I gave you this job. If I want, I can fire you right now."

"Ayo, you tell me what you're doing here, or I go call Martin now."

"So you're not going to tell me, huh? I know all about it, you cunt. You seduced the white man to marry you. And now he's getting you a visa, a ticket out of here." His bloodshot gaze moved to Femi. "You and your good-for-nothing son!"

Ayo was trembling. He was a sorry sight. Days of alcohol and anger at Ansara and frustration at not finding the money was making him lose his mind. Ansara tried not to let on that she was scared. Letting Ayo know that would only worsen the situation. She wished she hadn't let Mohammed go. Or that Martin would show up soon.

"That still does not explain why you are looking through his desk." Ansara was surprised at how steady her voice sounded.

"Oh. So now you think you can order me around? You can do whatever you want, and you'll be out of here in no time? I've news for you, sister, you're not going anywhere. I'll find the money that the *oyibo* has stashed here, and I'm leaving. I'm leaving first, before you. I'll be the one with the happy life and all the money, and you'll stay here, with your *oyibo* and your son. Suffer this bloody heat and do what you were born to do, cook and clean houses."

Ansara was scared at Ayo's transformation. Before her eyes, he seemed to have changed from a mildly drunk person to a raving lunatic. He continued, "Tell me, you stupid woman, where does your *oyibo* keep the money? It's better for both of us if you just give it to me right now."

"Ayo, I don't know where it is. I really don't." Ansara's voice trembled.

"So you're going to lie to me, huh? You stupid woman, you don't know what I'm capable of."

"Ayo, I can call Martin and ask him where it is. Let me call him and I'll help you find the money." Ansara turned to leave. She could call Martin and ask him to come home as soon as possible. If she went downstairs, she could call the guards in.

Ayo reached over and grabbed Femi. He pulled a gun out of his pocket and pointed it at the boy's head.

"You think you can fool me? You go out of this room, you'll call the police. Hand me the money now, or I'll kill the boy."

"Ayo, please, please don't hurt my child. I don't know

where the money is, but I'll help you find it," Ansara pleaded.

Femi tried to struggle out of Ayo's grip.

"Stay still, you little vermin. Otherwise, I will shoot this bullet right through your head."

The boy squirmed. Ayo's fingers were digging into his flesh. Ayo hit him with the butt of his gun.

Ansara instinctively reached out to her child.

All she heard was a loud bang. Something hit her on her head. She raised her hand to her face. Blood was trickling down her nose. The bullet had caught her right between her eyebrows. She looked up at Ayo and tried to grab her son. She had to protect him, she had to take him away from this monster.

The boy wiggled out of Ayo's grip. He ran to her, but Ansara was on the ground by then. She looked at Ayo. She tried to say something but the words would not come out. She hugged Femi close. It would not be long before the guards came in, they must have heard the gunshot.

Femi whimpered, as loud as he could, the only sounds he could make. She could feel him tug at her. She wanted to hold him close, protect him.

Her eyelids felt heavy and wet. She could feel the blood trickling over them. But she had to make sure her son was not hurt. She forced herself to open her eyes. Femi seemed alright; he was hovering over her.

Behind him, she could see Ayo holding up the gun in disbelief. She heard the front door open. Panic filled Ayo's eyes. He opened the window and jumped onto the terrace.

By the time the guards came running into the room, he had disappeared over the wall.

"Ansara, Ansara, are you alright?" She could hear the guard's voices as her eyes closed and she drifted off.

CHAPTER 31

"No mobile phones in here." The officer in the embassy frowned at Martin and pointed at the sign on the wall.

"Sorry," he muttered. He put it into vibrate mode, but the phone kept ringing. He picked it up and saw five missed calls from his home number. Something must be wrong. Martin got up to leave.

"It's almost our turn. Maybe you should take it afterwards." Tunde gestured at the waiting room packed with people. It wouldn't be smart to miss his turn.

"It seems urgent. I'll only be a minute."

Martin called back his home phone, and one of the guards answered. "Sir, it's Chinua. There was a… a gunshot." Chinua was panting and he could hardly get his words out. "We came in and she was already…shot."

"Chinua, slow down. I can't understand you. What are you talking about?" A knot tightened in his chest.

"Sir, Ansara. She is shot. Madam…is shot."

"What? Ansara? Is she alright?"

"She's breathing, sir. But blood everywhere. I called the ambulance. It's coming."

"I'm on my way. Get her to the hospital quick and call me

if anything changes. I'll be there soon."

Martin ran back to the room. He shouted, "Tunde, we need to leave now."

"But if we leave—" Tunde was beginning to protest, throwing up his arms to show his resignation.

"It's Ansara. She's been shot. We need to go."

"Is she alright?"

"I don't know. We need to get there immediately."

"Yes, of course. My driver will drive fast."

Musa, Tunde's driver, drove like a maniac. "Musa, faster, faster! Cut through that lane!" Tunde urged him into a breakneck speed in one of the most dangerous drives of Martin's life, while he tried desperately to phone the hospital. Martin knew that he would need a special word from someone high up to get the ambulance to his house soonest, if at all. But the lines were busy.

Martin saw police officials by the road. He was certain that if any of them tried to stop them today, he would reach out, grab one of their rifles, and shoot them. But luckily, no one paid them any attention. Musa was breaking many rules. Maybe there was something about the recklessness of his driving that made the policemen assume that either they were lunatics or part of the city's powerful, both of whom would be a hassle to get a bribe from.

But even the rashest driving had its limits in Lagos traffic.

"Sorry, sir, we're stopping," Musa said, apologetic.

"Why?"

"I can't tell. People are stopping their cars and getting out," said Musa, rolling down the window.

Martin looked out. He was still too far from the house to run for it. Traffic had ground to a halt, rows and rows of cars idling, some with shouting drivers. Many were stepping out of their cars, their palms open to the sky.

"Rains!" said Musa, happiness evident in his voice. "Rains, sir. The heat will stop."

Tunde leaned in. "We've to drive, Musa. Can you take another route?"

"No, sir, we are stuck, no way to turn back," he said. "I'm sorry."

Martin saw an okada wiggle its way through. Martin stepped out of the car, ignoring Tunde's calls. "Martin, where you going? No, not an okada!"

The okada, one of the most reckless modes of transport. Martin had been warned, but he didn't care. The okada driver, when he heard the address in the posh part of town, quoted a ridiculous fare. Martin got on anyway and egged the driver on to drive fast, dodging through the traffic while the first overdue raindrops of the season fell fast on him.

As they turned into Rose Villa, Martin noted with a sinking heart that there was no ambulance parked in the driveway.

He raced into the house. "Where is she? Where is the ambulance?"

"She's upstairs, in the library. We called the ambulance, they're on their way," said Ben, running up with Martin.

Martin's heart plummeted when he saw Ansara on the floor.

"Ansara, oh my God!" He leaned over her, holding her hand in his, his back against the bookshelves, in the spot where they had sat together so many times before. Blood was all around them, on the floor, on the carpet. Ansara was bleeding out.

"I'm going to get you out of here. Just hold on, okay? You're going to be alright."

Martin motioned to Chinua, who was standing beside the door. "Chinua, help me lift her up. We need to get her to the hospital quick."

Ansara shook her head. "*Nkem,* no, I don't have time. I'm glad I got to see you."

Martin could feel her hand tighten its grip on his. He leaned over and kissed her lips. "Let me get you out of here." He motioned as if to get up.

"Where's Femi?" Ansara's voice was barely audible. He was standing a little ways away, tears running from his eyes. He moved closer to her.

She grabbed Femi's arm with her free hand. "Femi, my child…" She couldn't get the words out anymore, gasping for air.

Martin could feel her grip loosen and finally give in. With the last shred of life draining away with a shudder, Ansara closed her eyes, her new husband and her son on either side of her.

Martin could not believe what was happening right before him.

"Chinua, quick, help me, let's move her to—"

He shook Ansara's body, willing her to open her eyes again. His own body was shaking violently.

"Ansara, Ansara," he called out, over and over.

After a while, Tunde came in and held him from behind. "Martin, it's no use," he said gently.

Tears flowed from Martin's eyes. He could still feel the warmth and fresh smell of her body, the faint whiff of lavender emerging from her body for the very last time. Martin hugged her close, blood seeping through his wet shirt. And he cried, like only a man who had gained everything and lost everything could cry.

EPILOGUE

"When do stories end?" Femi's voice is loud and clear through the microphone when he takes the stage to give the valedictorian's speech at his high school graduation.

He pauses and looks around like a seasoned speaker, across the crowd that comprises his classmates and their parents. And his own family. His eyes linger for a moment on Martin. Femi sees Martin's mother reach over and squeeze her son's hand. He knows that they are both proud of him, and he in turn, thinks the world of them.

"Stories end when you want them to end, how you want them to end," Femi answers his own question. "Today, we are graduating. It is the finale of our years in school, the end of a story, a story of childhood, friendships, and education. And what a story it has been!"

Tears stream down Martin's face as Femi thanks his classmates, his teachers, and especially his father and his grandmother, who despite not being related to him by birth, took him in and cared for him as well as any child could ever hope for. Martin doesn't need to turn his head to know that his mother beside him is crying for joy too. Femi is the ray of sunshine in her life, a boy who, along with modern medication, lifted her out of the darkness that had shrouded much of her youth and Martin's childhood, and had worsened since her husband's death. She took on Femi's care in the years when Martin himself struggled with grief, making Femi feel welcome and at home in a foreign land in a way that Martin could never have imagined. It was in caring for another, in the selflessness of service, that she found relief from her deepest darkness.

"But this is not just the end of our story, it is also a beginning," Femi continues. "In fact, from now on, our stories become the stories of the world. As adults, no longer constrained or exonerated as children, we take on responsibility for our world. We get to decide, finally," he says, rolling his eyes as his classmates laugh, "who we will be and what we will do."

He is earnest again as he asks his classmates, "What will our story be?" pausing with each word, inviting them to consider their paths ahead. "At every ending and at every beginning, we get to ask ourselves, what next? Wedged between the infinity of the past and the future is a sliver of the present, fleeting in time but unique in its capacity for action. Powered by our memories and fueled by our imagination, it is now that we write our story, the story of our world."

Martin caresses the ring on his left hand, the ring that he has not taken off since the day Ansara put it on his finger in a hot office in Lagos on his wedding day, the day he lost the love of his life. He thought then that his story ended there, with her. And in many ways, it did.

As he looks at Femi now, his curly black hair and dark brown skin glowing under the bright morning sun, his eyes full of hope and optimism, his voice brimming with confidence and cheer, he feels as if Ansara is right there with him. He misses her terribly, today and every single day, but in a way, a story began on that fateful day thirteen years ago, the culmination of which was playing out right before his eyes.

Devastated by the loss of Ansara, Martin adopted Femi and moved to the Netherlands. Resigning from his job at CBX Corp, he went on to work with Blessing and Erika, dedicating his life to the restoration of the earth from the ravages of the industry he had once been part of, and to the protection of the rights of humans often forgotten in the rat race of corporate greed. But what he was most proud of was the life he was able to provide for Femi. With good medical care, a stable home, and a doting grandmother, the little boy flourished. Gaining the use of his voice was just the first step. Femi was growing up to be an eloquent and articulate young man fluent in English, Dutch, and Igbo, and who, undeterred by his mediocre singing talents, could belt out a Femi Kuti song on any occasion without hesitation.

Despite Martin's many efforts, they were never able to trace either Ansara's mother or Ayomide. Endings come in many ways. Some in death, some in escape, and some that require orchestration by our own minds.

"I ask you all to please stand up now," Femi exhorts the crowd, motioning with his hands to rise, "and look under your chairs, where you will find some paper with the lyrics of a song. Please join me in singing along as I dedicate this song, and my story—past, present, and future—to my mother"—and raising his microphone to the sky—"Ansara Okafor.

"Ladies and Gentlemen, 'One People, One World' by Femi Kuti," he hollers as music comes on over the speakers and images from the music video shows up on a large screen behind Femi, his namesake larger than life beside him.

Martin's mind races to the first time he danced to Femi Kuti music during one of their nights out in Lagos. When this song came on, Ansara pulled him to the middle of the dance floor, every part of her body alive and throbbing with the music. She sang with the crowd, her voice loud and clear even when mixed with other voices. She moved closer to him, the gyrating motion of her body egging him to move with the music, and he danced, his body next to hers, his arms around her, their worlds merging, love conquering all divisions and distinctions.

A group of Femi's friends climbs onto the stage, dancing along with him. The crowd joins in from the ground with fervor and passion, people of all skin colors and features, singing and dancing, joining hands as truly One People, One World.

Martin marvels at how different the graduation ceremony

is from what he experienced at that stage of his life. The student body, united in their voice and international in their outlook, lobbied the school management for a new format, moving the event outdoors, keeping the traditional Dutch tradition of signing the diplomas but adding a valedictorian speech, and of course, a party with loud music and dancing.

The girl next to Martin grabs his hand, raising it high and waving it in the air. His mother smiles at him as she does the same from his other side. On cue from Femi, someone releases a flock of doves that flies into the sky, a white cloud rising along with the hopes of these young men and women and their determination to write their own stories, stories of love, unity, care, and peace.

Martin looks up at the bright blue sky speckled with the fluttering white doves and smiles. Somewhere, high above the skies, in a heaven not too far away, he knows Ansara would be smiling too. He feels certain, as he imagines her looking down with joy, that the sky is moving down, just a little closer.

ACKNOWLEDGEMENTS

That this book exists in a published form is a miracle. Without the miracle workers who conspired, cajoled, supported, and guided me in bringing this novel from its first draft to the final version, it would not have existed. For that and more, I am enormously grateful.

Srijith, my forever first reader, who has seen the earliest drafts that ended up in the trash, read more variations of this tale than anyone should ever have to, persevered through my obsessive days of editing and rewriting, kept up the faith and an endless supply of coffee, chocolates, and companionship —even as he tried, usually in vain—to rein in the em dashes.

Nikita, with whom it feels like I co-wrote the book, as I was pregnant with her during the very first draft. She was my inspiration to examine the world we leave behind for the generations to come. In the cold Colchester winter, I labored the last lines just in time to get the draft done before the baby was out. What a ride it was!

Anika, without whom I would not have completed the final drafts of this novel. Every afternoon, as I picked her up from school, she asked me, without fail, about my progress. She had opinions on practically every step of the publishing process.

Her unconditional faith and persistence were instrumental in the completion of the book; together, we made it!

Dr. Sathiavathy and Dr. Ramkumar, the earliest readers of my book and my cheerleaders through not just the publication of this book, but throughout my life. Without the love and support of my parents, I would not have had the courage and confidence to explore new and unconventional paths in life, one of which led to the writing and publication of this book.

Kira Jean discovered and believed in the potential of this book at just the right time. A chance conversation led to a commitment of collaboration, and before I knew it, I was working with Kira and her team. I have loved every minute of this publishing journey, thanks in no small measure to her infectious enthusiasm and quiet strength.

Thalia Suzuma is exactly the editor that I needed for this book. Trusting your first novel to another person is a big step, akin to leaving your child at a daycare for the first time. With Thalia, I felt entirely safe. She guided me through multiple drafts, helping me to elevate the book from its early form to a story that I was finally proud to share with the world.

The Dreamwork Collective team has put in many hours behind the scenes, from copy editing and cover design to printing and publicity and other matters that I am not even aware of, and without their meticulous and hard work, this book would not be.

The Universe deserves mention too, for it was in seeing this book insist on its own existence that I learned how the world really works. What is meant to be will always be. And the only real response to the flow of life is an attitude of gratitude.

Thank you.

ABOUT THE AUTHOR

Surya Ramkumar is a writer based in Dubai, the UAE. Born in Kerala, a beautiful state in the south of India, Surya has lived in nine countries and traveled to many more.

Through writing, Surya brings together various strands of her life–that of a mother, wife, and daughter and that of a technologist, business leader, and sustainability advocate. She is passionate about the power of words to bring about meaningful social change. Her personal mission as a writer is to bring clarity and understanding of a complex world in a way that makes it accessible to more people through clear thinking and engaging storytelling.

The Sky Has Moved Away is her first book-length work of fiction. Her short stories have been included in anthologies (*Silverfish New Writing 7*). Her previous book, *Silent Eloquence* (Spotted Okapi Press, 2020), is a collection of essays chronicling her experiences as she traveled across multiple countries in Asia, Africa, and Europe. You can find more of her writing at: www.suryaramkumar.com.

ABOUT THE PUBLISHER

The Dreamwork Collective is a print and digital publisher sharing diverse voices and powerful stories with the world. Dedicated to the advancement of humanity, we strive to create books that have a positive impact on people and on the planet. Our hope is that our books document this moment in time for future generations to enjoy and learn from, and that we play our part in ushering humanity into a new era of heightened creativity, connection, and compassion.

www.thedreamworkcollective.com
Instagram: thedreamworkcollective

Milton Keynes UK
Ingram Content Group UK Ltd.
UKHW012006131223
434291UK00004B/270